E R E C O T

Grace Tremayne

First printing

Proud to support:

Grace Tremayne supports the work of Harefield Hospital. I have just had my aortic valve replaced at this wonderful unit where everybody cares. I will donate all my royalties from the sale of ERECOT to Harefield, so please enjoy the plot knowing that you are supporting its crucial work.

1 – 8th May 2006, Eurostar heading for Waterloo Station, London

The Eurostar was dead on time as it passed through Vauxhall. Anna Fey grabbed the coat, picked up her rucksack and walked towards the front of the train. She jumped on to the platform as soon as the doors opened at Waterloo and was one of the first to reach passport control. She judged she would be through it in less than a minute. Looking back she saw a long queue forming behind her, with no sign of the woman whose coat she had just taken.

The young passport officer smiled as he returned her passport and waved her through.

'Welcome back to England, Miss Fey.'

She could tell he fancied her because she was used to it and she liked it. Why would any young, heterosexual man not fancy a pretty, twenty-five-year-old with blue eyes and wavy, shoulder-length dark hair, who kept herself in shape? She knew she had good looks so always dressed to show them to their best effect. That's how she got her work as a fashion model. Today she was wearing a figure-hugging white blouse over a bra designed to make the most of breasts that complemented her petite figure. A tight, black leather mini-skirt, black stockings and black leather, high-heeled shoes completed her outfit.

"Enough of that", she thought as she headed for the taxi rank, "it's time for business and the thousand pounds I've been promised".

Not an hour earlier she had seen the woman put a package into the right-hand pocket of the coat she was now wearing. She slipped her hand into the pocket to gain reassurance of its presence. At that moment she felt her arm being grabbed. She turned to see a tall, heavily built, black man dressed in a chauffeur's uniform. Instinctively she tried to pull away, but his grip was too tight.

'Your car is this way, Miss Fey.'

A large, white Mercedes pulled up beside them. He opened the rear door with his free hand, bundled her in and sat beside her. The car pulled away at speed. She tried to break free, struggling for all her worth, but was no match for his strength. She was attempting to scream when he placed a handkerchief over her nose and mouth. She raised her left leg, intending to bring the stiletto heel down hard on his foot, but suddenly lost all her energy. She detected a faint smell of something she did not recognise before she passed out.

2 – 8th May 2006, London

Fey felt dizzy and her head ached as she regained consciousness. Where was she and why had she been abducted? She kept her eyes closed for most of the time, stealing quick peeks through half-open ones as she tried to decide what would happen next. She was sitting on a plain wooden chair, in the middle of a small room with bare floorboards. Immediately above her was a solitary, unshaded bulb hanging by a cord from the ceiling. It cast a dull light over her. There was a wooden door in front of her, with a window to her right. Dark wooden cupboards filled most of the remaining, visible wall space. The pieces of wall she could see had old, peeling wallpaper. Out of the window she saw the newly opened leaves of a plain tree, which told her she was in an upstairs room, probably on the first floor.

'She didn't have it on her?' a man's voice boomed out, with incredulity.

'No, Mr Mancini, she didn't.' The second voice was much more fearful. Its owner sounded unhappy imparting this news.

'Did you check everywhere?'

It was obvious to Fey that he had, and probably enjoyed doing it, because she was naked and tied to the chair. Her carefully selected, expensive clothes lay in an untidy heap on the floor beside her, with the cheap coat on top of them. But why hadn't he found it, because it was in the coat pocket?

'Yes, boss.'

'Then perhaps we'd better ask her?' the first voice replied sarcastically.

Fey felt her face being slapped. 'Wakey, wakey.'

There was no point in pretending to be unconscious because he would only have hit her harder. She groaned and opened her eyes to see a tall, dark haired man looking down at her. He was sharply dressed in a charcoal grey suit, white shirt and black tie, which made him appear even more menacing that his natural looks would have done by themselves. He looked like he kept himself in shape, but his demeanour and body language made him appear threatening rather than attractive. She felt very scared.

She retched, which made him jump back in case she vomited. She didn't, but she did take the opportunity to check where she was. The other man, who must have searched her and put her in this predicament, was the man who had abducted her. If her interrogator frightened *him*, then what was about to happen next was unlikely to be pleasant.

'Where is it, Anna?' His piercing hazel eyes looked straight into hers, enhancing her fear of him.

'It was in the coat pocket. I made no attempt to hide it, so King Kong here must have taken it and done this to me for his own pleasure.'

She hoped this reply might deflect attention towards the chauffeur for at least long enough to allow her to try to understand why the object he wanted was not in the pocket when she had seen the woman put it in there. For a moment it seemed to work as her interrogator turned towards the chauffeur.

'She's lying, boss. I wouldn't steal from you. What use would that thing be to me? I don't know what it is or if it's worth anything. Even if it is, then I still wouldn't know who'd buy it from me.'

The dark haired man considered what he had been told. He nodded before turning his attention back to Fey. She felt his eyes looking right through hers. Why did he keep looking at her in that way? He should have been looking at her legs or breasts, or any part of her body other than her eyes, if she was going to have any hope of manipulating him, like she could most men.

'He's got a point, Anna. Only you and I know the value of the package you agreed to deliver. For you it's the thousand pounds I promised you to get it for me or your life if you fail to live up to your promise.'

Fey knew she was in deep trouble, because she could not distract him with her looks. Could she convince him she didn't have it? That bitch must have just pretended to put it into the coat to shake her off. Her only hope was to plead her case.

'If it wasn't in the coat then I don't have it. Your man has searched me thoroughly as you can see, but you can check for yourself if you like. She must have just pretended to put it in the coat.'

As she spoke Fey opened her legs as far as the bonds would allow, in a last attempt to divert him. His expression changed as a thin smile spread across his face. There was no warmth in it.

'No thanks, sweetheart, you're not my type. I will have to leave it to… King Kong was it you called him? He will help you to remember where it is.' Turning to the chauffeur he added, 'Don't touch her face. Leave that for me if it becomes necessary.' As he moved towards the door he looked back to Fey.

'I don't have it. Please don't hurt me. There wouldn't be any point, because I can't tell you what I don't know. But I could be nice to you, very nice.' Tears began to roll down her cheeks as she spoke.

As he was shutting the door he replied, 'As I said, sweetheart, you're not my type.'

3 – 26th September 1996, Luton

Maisie Jennings had decided to put all her worries to one side so she could celebrate her sixteenth birthday with her friends. Since she had no idea who her father was, had no siblings and her mother spent most of her time in an alcoholic haze, they were all that mattered. They had been the only ones she could turn to as she struggled through school, without parental help or guidance, not knowing what state her mother would be in when she got home or whether there would be anything for her to eat. She had lost count of the times she had found her mother passed out in a drunken stupor and asked for help from Christine's parents. They had always invited her over, given her a warm welcome, a meal and a bed for the night. They even checked that she was alright the next day. She had survived growing up and was now a tough, independent young woman with only herself to please.

She put the final touches to her jet black, back-combed hair before checking herself in the mirror. The dye had done its job well, making it a good match for her long false eyelashes. Both made a striking contrast with her thick white makeup, giving her the Goth-like appearance she was seeking. This was enhanced by an extensive set of body piercings in her ears, nose and navel, each with a metal stud to adorn it.

"These are just the visible ones", she thought as she checked in the mirror. "The right boy is going to love the extra one he'll discover later on." The mere pleasure of the thought tightened the muscles in her abdomen. She applied black lipstick then stood back to admire herself.

She was wearing a deep red, low-cut crop top, which revealed a good deal of her ample cleavage and fifteen centimetres of bare white midriff. She was only one metre, sixty-five tall, so chose shoes with platform soles and fifteen centimetre stiletto heels to enhance her height. She completed her outfit with a black miniskirt that reached just below her bottom. It covered the essentials, provided she bent by no more than ten degrees, after which it remained for her black silk knickers to provide the final rear guard.

Her mother came past just as Maisie was filling her handbag. She took one disapproving look, removing her cigarette for just long enough to comment.

'You ain't goin' out like that. You look like a slut. Wipe that muck off your face sharpish. And find a skirt that's long enough to have half a chance of covering your bum.'

Maisie could feel the anger building inside her. She had been subjected to constant carping from her mother ever since she had started going out on her own. This time she was not just going to let it go.

'I'll do what I freekin' well like; this is me sixteenth birthday and I'm goin' to enjoy meself, so leave me alone, will yer.'

'Don't you speak to me like that. I'm your mother… Bill, tell her.'

Bill Sampson was Maisie's mother's latest boyfriend. She tolerated him because he was a stabilising influence to the point that she could expect some degree of order when she returned from work. He was not her father and didn't try to be. He gave her space but was there if she wanted help or a lift. Secretly she respected and even liked him, but her pride would not let her admit it. She knew he would rather not have got involved. They both knew it would be pointless, but he had to say something just to appease his girlfriend.

'Come on, Maisie, don't talk to your mother that way. She's got your best interest at heart.' He winced as he waited for the backlash.

'Leave it out, Bill; you ain't me father, or at least I don't think you are. Dear mother has never actually got 'round to telling me who he is.'

As she spoke, Maisie grabbed her coat and pushed past both of them. Her mother raised an arm to slap Maisie's face but Bill caught it and swung her into him, allowing Maisie to get by. He knew he had to act quickly to prevent *his* night being ruined. He had something other than beer, cigarettes and darts with the lads in mind for later.

'Leave it, pet. It's the girl's sixteenth birthday. Just let her enjoy it. Anyway, I've got a couple of ideas about what we might do with a night in on our own.'

Maisie half smiled at Bill by way of thanks and was out of the house before her mother could react. She slammed the door, but only half-heartedly, as the relief of getting out unscathed cooled her anger. It was seven-thirty. Darkness had already fallen on a cold autumn evening. The wind was keen, causing Maisie to pull her coat in tightly around her. She regretted not having time to put on the stockings and suspenders she had purchased specifically for the occasion, but told herself it was either cold legs or no evening out.

The Attic Club never got going before eleven, so it was down to The George first, to meet up with her friends. Joe, Christine and Frankie were there when she arrived.

'Happy birthday, Maisie', Christine called

out as Maisie sat down, while Frankie got up to buy her a drink.

'Usual, Maisie?'

'Yes, but can I have a double please, Frankie. It's been a hard day.'

'One double vodka and coke coming up.'

Maisie sipped her drink before announcing, 'I think I might go for it tonight, anyone like to join me?'

Christine was the first to reply. 'Sorry, Maisie, I'd have loved to, but I've got to work tomorrow.'

'How about you boys. Will you keep a birthday girl company?' she asked hopefully.

Joe and Frankie shook their heads.

'I'm up for it, Maisie.'

The London accent came from behind, but was immediately recognisable to Maisie as Mike Chambers. It gave her a start because she had not seen him arrive. They had met two weeks previously when she had been walking home late on a Friday night and made the mistake of taking a short cut through a dark alley. She had found her path blocked by a thug wielding a knife. When she turned to run she found another behind her. She knew she was trapped and feared she was about to be raped. The incident replayed itself in her mind.

'Look at this one, Pete. She looks hot don't

she? Why don't you take your clothes off and cool down, luv?'

'Mind out me way, will yer.' She tried to put as much authority into her voice as she could, but it had no effect.

'Well that ain't nice. I think we need to teach her some manners don't you, Pete?'

He moved to grab her when a voice a little way behind him called out, 'The lady asked you to let her pass, so let her pass, please.'

They all looked in the direction of the voice to see Chambers standing there. He was only one metre, fifty-nine tall, with such a slight build it appeared that it would only take a modest gust of wind to blow him away. He looked insignificant.

'Since you've joined us, short-arse, you can hand over your wallet and if there's enough money in it we might let you watch.'

Chambers opened his jacket as if to take out a wallet, but pulled out a .22 Beretta instead.

'Whatya gonna do with that toy, Shorty?'

'Shoot both of you if you don't leave right now.'

The first thug thought the gun to be fake, so ran at Chambers, wielding his knife. Chambers calmly shot him in the arm holding the knife. Both thugs fled, leaving a trail of blood along the alley. Chambers had escorted

Maisie home, where they had chatted for a while. He told her he had only recently moved into the area and did not know anyone, so she suggested he meet her friends.

He had only seen the group a couple of times, but all the girls were already swooning over him. It was not his body that interested them, but he did have a lot more money and was not averse to spending it on girls who interested him. Frankie had an immediate distrust of him, probably for the same reason that the girls liked him.

Chambers sat down next to Maisie, pulled her towards him and kissed her.

'Happy birthday, Maisie'.

As he let go of her, he handed her a decoratively wrapped present finished with a pink bow. He also gave her a card, but she ignored it, preferring to unwrap her present. After a few seconds of frantic tearing, she opened a box to reveal a gold watch. Maisie gasped, before throwing her arms around Chambers' neck and kissing him.

'Thanks, Mike; this is by far the nicest thing I've been given all day. I got a tenner from Bill, but my mum didn't even bother to give me anything, the mean cow', she blurted, trying to hold back a tear.

'That's really beautiful, Mike. Puts what we

bought her in the shade. Anyway, here you are, Maisie, from Joe, Frankie and me.'

Joe and Frankie added their birthday wishes as Christine handed over a small package and a card. Again Maisie ignored the card and attacked the present.

'What lovely earrings', she exclaimed. She thanked each of them with an embrace and kiss on the cheek. A tear appeared, which she quickly wiped away, but not before Chambers had noticed.

'Tears, Maisie, and we all thought you were really cool?'

'Stop it, will yer. I ain't used to people being nice to me. Now I'll have to go and fix me make up.'

Christine was on her feet in a flash.

'I'll come with you, Maisie. Now you boys are to say nothing about this. We can't have a girl losing her reputation, can we?' before adding, swiftly, 'If you get what I mean.' She took hold of Maisie's arm and led her to the ladies.

4 – 26th September 1996, Luton

'It looks like it's just you and me for the Attic Club tonight, Maisie', Chambers observed as he put a third double vodka and coke in front of her. It was nine-thirty. Her friends had just left. This time he sat much closer to Maisie, who reacted neither positively nor negatively to his approach. He watched her down her drink within five minutes, keeping up with her with his consumption of gin and tonic, which was, in reality, pure tonic.

'It's your birthday, so what would you like to do?' he asked, snuggling up a little closer to her. She did not stop him.

'Let's have something to eat and then go to the Attic Club. It's a bit too early for it now.'

'Suits me, what would you likc?

'Chinese, I think.'

As they left the pub the cold air reminded Maisie of just how much she had had to drink. Chambers could see she was very unsteady.

'Not feeling too well, Maisie?'

'A bit woozy.'

'Have a cigarette and come back to my place. It's just round the corner and I can give you something to sort you out.'

He didn't wait for an answer, half dragging her the short distance to the block of flats where he lived. She found herself sitting on the sofa in his penthouse feeling decidedly unwell as he offered her a glass of fizzing water.

'Drink this, it'll clear your head.'

Maisie did as she was told and passed out just after she finished it.

5 – 27th September 1996, at sea

'Would you like some water?'

Maisie had no idea where the voice came from, but her throat was parched. She grunted something that was taken as a yes, after which her head was raised gently and a glass placed against her lips. A few drops of quenching water slid into her mouth and then down her throat, alleviating the dryness. More drops followed, further easing the dryness and encouraging her to open her eyes. The harsh glare of the light made her close them again almost immediately. The voice, which Maisie decided was female, started again.

'You've had an accident, Maisie. You're in hospital, but don't worry, you're not seriously hurt. Just a little concussion. It will clear quickly. You should rest a little more.'

Maisie needed no further encouragement, drifting off into a fitful sleep.

The next thing she felt was the sheet being lifted off her and a cooling breeze running across her body. It was then she realised she was naked, but didn't have the energy to pull the sheet back to protect her modesty.

'You got rid of all that metal and rubbish from her face, I see. She's cleaned up quite well.'

This voice was definitely male and

although fluent in English, came from somebody whose mother tongue was not English.

'Yes, I did', the female voice responded, 'and I also took the metal out of her clitoris. I didn't think you'd appreciate it.'

'Certainly not. That's disgusting. Why do the parents of these western girls let them do these things to themselves? I'll not go near her until those marks heal... They will heal won't they?'

'Yes sir, they should close off in a month or so and be virtually invisible within six. That includes her face if you will allow a little make up.'

There was some hesitation before the male voice responded again.

'She does have quite a pretty face, so probably. She is a virgin, I trust?'

'Yes sir, and sixteen according to the details sent across with her.'

'Very well then, keep her clean, get her to lose some weight and train her well. If she slims down and those marks heal, I'll use her in a couple of years.'

Maisie heard footsteps leaving and felt the covers being replaced by gentle hands. She knew she was in trouble, but now was not the time to do anything about it.

"Observe and plan", she told herself and

then settled back to sleep.

6 – 18th October 1996, Haranibad, Haranistan

Maisie was dressed in silk knickers, silk trousers and a silk three-quarter length top. A veil covered the lower half of her face. She was wearing nothing else and to make matters worse every garment was diaphanous. She was angry, not only at the clothes but also because she felt very hungry. She had been on a diet that she was told would continue until she had lost ten kilos. To date she had only lost two.

She ripped off the veil.

'I'm not wearing this crap, you can see right through it. I want my clothes and my jewellery, and I want to go home. He cannot keep me here, I'll call the police and you and he'll be arrested. You'll both go down for a long time if you don't let me go… now.'

Maisie's abuse was directed at a tall, slim, fair haired woman in her forties. Even though lines had begun to appear around her eyes and her muscles were not as solid as Maisie's, Maisie could tell she must have been very attractive when she was younger.

'Keep your voice down, Maisie or else you'll be in trouble.'

Maisie was about to scream when the lady slapped her hard across the face. The pain in her jaw stopped the scream. She fell to the floor in tears. Being an intelligent girl she decided that any further attempt to scream was likely to result in another slap, probably harder than the first. She also feared reprisals should she hit back.

'Why did you do that?' she bleated, the tears streaming down her face. 'I think you've broken my jaw.' The women grabbed hold of her face to check.

'Don't be such a baby, it's only a bruise. You might have a black eye for a couple of days, but that's no more than you deserve. To answer your first question, I did it to save your life. If it gets back to the Crown Prince you're being difficult, he'll have you killed.'

'Crown Prince? Who does this prick think he is?'

'Maisie, do you have any idea where you are?'

'No, because you and Crown Prince up-his-arse have kept me prisoner in this hell hole for ever, so how could I know?'

The tears were streaming down Maisie's face as a result of both pain and frustration. The older women took Maisie into her arms and let her cry on her shoulder.

'Have a good cry. Then I'll explain exactly the situation you're in. Trust me, I have first-hand experience of it and I didn't have somebody as understanding as I am to help me.'

Maisie's brain had been attempting to piece together the snippets of information it had been given and her conclusions were not good. It was becoming clear she had been abducted, but that was not the worst part. The woman she was talking to spoke perfect English and almost certainly was English. Had she too been abducted and if yes, was it at Maisie's age? Had she lived for over twenty years in captivity and come to accept it? Was this going to be her fate? She had cried herself out. She felt exhausted, frightened and helpless.

'Rest now, my dear and I'll explain everything to you, tomorrow.'

7 - 19th October 1996, Crown Prince's palace, Haranibad, Haranistan

Maisie was still in bed when the woman, who appeared to be her minder, came into her room. Clean silk knickers, silk trousers, silk three-quarter length top and a veil, all similar to those she had worn the previous day, were laid out ready for her. The lady began.

'My name is Carol Anderson. I was born in Shepherds Bush, West London. I was bought up by my mother in a high rise flat in Hammersmith until I was sixteen. I never knew my father. I was abducted on my way home from the factory where I worked. I was brought here to be a concubine in the harem of King Harani XLVI of Haranistan, which is where we are today. The king liked young white girls, so he had them abducted regularly, usually from England. This gave him variety and fresh girls to replace the older ones of whom he soon tired. He insisted on having virgins. After two years of training in subservience and how to please my master, given by the older concubines, I was introduced to him and became his plaything for a while. He was actually kind and gentle so, although I will always remember that I was being raped repeatedly and I will not forgive him for it, my task was not totally without pleasure. As everybody expected, he tired of me and my summonses became less and less as other, younger girls replaced me.

'Ten years ago the king decided he would improve the lot of women. He declared he would be monogamous and give up his harem. It wasn't really very difficult for him as he had turned sixty and his sexual desires had declined, to say the least. Disposing of a harem containing abducted western girls, which the king could never admit to having taken, was never going to be possible. The older Haranistani concubines were released in a grand public gesture. They had become of no use to him, so he sent them to live together, in relative luxury, in one of his castles. They were offered the chance to be educated and even live as free Haranistanis. Many accepted training, obtained university degrees and now live good lives, although few decided to leave the luxury of the castle for the risks of free living. They weren't granted passports and are not allowed to leave the country.

'Keeping a harem was not then, and still is not, illegal in Haranistan, so Crown Prince Helini, who was young and fit, saw no reason why he shouldn't have the benefits his father had enjoyed. He took over the western concubines, whilst the king turned a blind eye to his activities. I became a senior concubine, taking over the training and trying to help new girls not fall foul of the strict ways here. This is what I will do for you if you're prepared to listen.'

The reality of what had happened to her finally sank into Maisie. She felt downhearted, but also angry. She was not prepared just to give in to her fate but knew that open resistance or a bold escape bid would be likely to get her killed. She would have to bide her time. She decided a policy of listening, understanding, learning and planning was necessary if she was ever to get out of the mess she was in. She told herself she would. All her energy would be focussed on that goal and her planning would start now. Anderson appeared kind and her friendship would be a clear benefit.

'Thank you, Carol, now I know the position I'm in, I promise to listen to you and do as you say.'

'That's a very wise decision, Maisie, so let's get started. You will have a bath before you get dressed, so we can talk while you're bathing.'

Two older concubines led Maisie to the bath.

'Firstly, is there anything you'd like to ask me, Maisie?'

'Will I ever get out of here?'

'No, the Crown Prince can never admit to abducting girls, so you can never go back. Like me, you are going to have to learn to live with your new life.'

'Has any girl ever escaped?'

'No and I strongly advise you not to try. Two girls have tried in the past and he had them both killed. I will talk more to you about them later.'

'What if the Crown Prince doesn't like a girl?'

'That very much depends upon how the girl behaves. Ann and Jane, the two girls who are washing you now, didn't find favour with him, but they didn't make a fuss, so he was kind and let them stay on as servants in the harem.'

'That's kind?'

'Yes. Very much so, my dear. He has had other girls killed if he doesn't like them. You were lucky you passed his initial inspection, although it was a close run thing. He didn't like your studs and thick makeup, and he demanded that you should lose weight. I assured him your piercings would heal and the scars wouldn't show. He even agreed to a little light makeup on your eyebrows and nose to cover any scars.'

'How kind of him.'

'It was. If you'd not been a virgin or had tattoos, he'd have had you killed.'

'He's a real sweetie, isn't he?'

'He has absolute power over your life and you'll do well to remember it. You have got to keep him wanting you. That way you will live in luxury. He will let you have good clothes, watch television and walk in his beautiful gardens. You will be allowed to shop for the best things, providing you do it to please him.'

'How many girls does he shag regularly?'

'Maisie, I implore you to watch your language. The Crown Prince will not tolerate swearing or coarse language. He could have you killed for that alone. You must appear refined at all times if you're going to retain his interest. His attention and good favour has to be earned and maintained. You may not like it, but that's the way life is here. To answer your question, the Crown Prince usually honours up to four girls at any time, with the ones who are going out of favour being seen less and less and the new girls more often, if they please him. I have known girls be rejected after one visit if he doesn't like the way they behave.'

The two girls finished cleaning Maisie, led her out of the bath, dried her and dressed her in the fresh clothes.

'If you stay on the diet I gave you and lose another eight kilos, he will like the way you look, so you're half way there. If you behave correctly, then you will find favour with him. I'm now going to show you what will happen if you don't.'

Anderson took Maisie into a separate room with a large television and video player. She loaded a video and made ready to play it.

'I'm showing you this before you eat, because the contents will probably make you physically sick. I don't do it lightly, but because I need you to understand the fate that befalls any girl who steps out of line, even in a minor way. This is your only warning, because the Crown Prince doesn't give second chances. Watch it right through. If you need it, the toilet is over there.' She gestured to a small door on the other side of the room, hit the play button and stood back.

The film opened on the top of one of the towers of a castle overlooking the sea. There was a mattress in the centre of the floor. In one corner a man was placing large rocks into a canvas bag big enough to fit a person inside. A door to the area opened. Three men came out dragging a girl, using a rope that tied her wrists together. The girl was wearing clothes similar to those worn by Maisie, but hers were dirty and torn. The four men formed a circle around the girl and began passing her from one to the next, with each tearing at her clothing until she had been stripped naked. She shivered with fear and cold as the first man threw her on the mattress and raped her. The other men followed until each had had his way with her. The first rapist then struck her a fierce blow across her face, knocking her unconscious. All of them then bundled her into the sack, tied the cord securely at the top and threw the bag over the battlements. The last shot of the film showed the bag sinking into the sea.

Maisie rushed out to the toilet, vomited and was just caught by Anderson before she fainted.

8 – 28th September 1998, Crown Prince's palace, Haranibad, Haranistan

Two days after her eighteenth birthday Maisie was called to attend the Crown Prince in his bedchamber. The moment had finally arrived. She stood nervously in a large, ornate room trying desperately to remember all the advice Anderson had given her. Anderson stood in front of her, with her two servants beside her. All were veiled and wearing the silk outfits Maisie had now become used to, if not comfortable with. She knew the Crown Prince would see the whole of her body through the clothes; knowledge that brought anticipation and trepidation in equal measure. The other three girls were wearing opaque undergarments so the Crown Prince's eyes would be drawn straight to Maisie, thus ensuring his attention would be held on her. She had been bathed, lightly made up to conceal her facial piercings and perfumed with frankincense. She had lost eight kilos since being taken. This, along with her natural good looks, made her highly attractive. She pondered what her first time might have been like had she not been abducted. Chambers had saved her from being raped two years earlier only to deliver her to be raped by somebody else now.

"It may be more comfortable, and I will not resist, but it's still rape. I can't do anything about it at the moment, but, however long it takes, I will have my revenge on all of them", she told herself, before putting the thought out of her mind in order to concentrate on her plan to survive in the situation she found herself.

Crown Prince Helini of Haranistan entered. All the girls curtsied and bowed their heads. Anderson was the one to speak.

'Sir, here is Maisie, the girl you summoned for tonight. She is ready and at your service.'

He looked her over, then moved directly in front of her. He put his hand under her chin, lifting her head so he looked straight into her eyes. All Maisie's stomach muscles tightened and it took all her concentration not to wet herself on the spot. The prince waved his right hand to Anderson, who took this a sign to remove Maisie's veil.

'You have done well, Carol. You may withdraw.' He spoke fluent English, with only a trace of an accent.

Anderson bowed and left, making Maisie feel even more nervous. Her best support had gone. She was almost on her own. The prince then moved both his hands in an up and down motion, palms upwards, which was the signal for the two servants to remove her top. She raised her arms as they gently lifted the top off her, exposing her breasts to his full gaze. The servants held Maisie's arms aloft to prevent her from covering herself. There was still some resistance left in her, although she was not as foolish as to vocalise it.

"Go on then", she thought, "Have a good look. I will get you for it one day."

He rubbed his thumbs across her nipples, which made then come out. She gasped with pleasure. He carried on for a short while before gesturing up and down again with both hands, but this time palms down. The girls placed both Maisie's hands behind her back and then pulled her trousers to the floor. Instinctively she stepped out of them and stood, motionless with her hands held behind her back where the girls had placed them. He clapped his hands. Both servants bowed and left.

Maisie was entirely alone with him. He advanced towards her, placed his hands on her hips and slowly pulled down her knickers. She stepped out of them and stood there naked in front of him, with her hands by her side, making no attempt to cover herself. She had resigned herself to this being her first time. Not quite how she had planned it, but her day would come. He led her across to the bed indicating she should lie on it. She obeyed, lying on her back with her legs together.

"Be modest at all times." Anderson's voice played over in her head. "He doesn't like girls who are forward."

She felt him spread her legs wide. Closing her eyes she awaited the inevitable. For a moment nothing happened and then he was on top of her. She felt searing pain rising through her abdomen, but refused to cry out even as the pain became more and more intense. Then suddenly it was over.

He wiped a tear from her eye. 'You did well, Maisie. Next time it will not hurt as much.'

She felt an inner satisfaction at not being rejected after one night, but also defiance.

"That's two I owe you", she thought to herself as she lay there waiting to be taken back to her quarters.

9 – 2nd February 2004, Crown Prince's palace, Haranibad, Haranistan

Crown Prince Helini paced around the room, making the wooden floor vibrate. He saw the First Minister waiting nervously for his reaction to what he had just been told. He knew that the incredulity he felt must be showing all over his face. He stopped pacing, turned and looked directly at the First Minister.

'You say my father has no idea of the situation?'

The First Minister fidgeted and looked sheepish as he attempted to frame a response.

'His Most Excellent Majesty, King Harani Anshalari XLVI, long may he reign, has many calls on his time. He has his duty to feed and house his people at all times, to act as our head of government and head of state, and to command our armed forces. Despite his magnificence in these roles he also works tirelessly to establish educational and charitable institutions and has been unrivalled in bringing forward the cause of women. His Excellency is however only human and there are issues he has not brought forward to the head of his magnificent consciousness and the oil situation is perhaps one of them.'

'So he has no idea we're running out of

oil?'

'No, Excellency.'

'How long have we got?'

'Our experts say one year at full capacity and then running down to nothing in the two years after that… unless we make further discoveries.'

'How likely is that?'

'From past experience we will probably discover enough for one more year of partial production.'

With his potential for optimism dashed, Helini felt deflated, but still determined to understand the position Haranistan was in.

'What plans has the government made for alternative incomes when the oil runs out?'

The First Minister looked perplexed. He contemplated how he might respond in a way the Crown Prince would understand, before beginning, slowly.

'Pardon, Excellency, but as I explained, His Most Excellent Majesty, King Harani Anshalari XLVI, long may he reign, is not aware of any problem with the oil supply, so he has not made any plans for alternative sources of income.'

'Yes, yes, First Minister. You told me that, but what plans has the *government* made?'

The First Minister's demeanour changed from one of sheepishness to one of total non-understanding of what he had just been asked.

'But, but, His Most...'

Helini cut in. 'So there are no plans?'

'No, Excellency.'

'Then we had better start making some, hadn't we? I asked you to bring along your most able minister. Is this he?' Helini looked at a man in his thirties, who had been standing back waiting to be introduced into the conversation. The First Minister nodded and gestured towards the waiting man.

'Excellency this is Feisal Mohammed, who is an Assistant Finance Minister.'

Mohammed moved forward, bowed and shook the prince's proffered hand.

'Excellency.'

'What ideas have you got?' Helini enquired.

'We have fish, Excellency. His Most Excellent Majesty, King Harani Anshalari XLVI, long may he reign, has not expressed any opposition to our increasing our fish catch, to reduce the amount we currently import.'

'Good, and how much of our oil revenue could fish replace?'

'About 1%, Excellency.'

'So with this option only 99% of our population will starve?'

The prince let the impact of his words sink

in before continuing.

'What else do you have?'

'Excellency, His Most Excellent Majesty, King Harani Anshalari XLVI, long may he reign, has disapproved of what might have been our best options, so we cannot pursue them.'

'Enough. While it is only the three of us, you may just refer to my father as 'the king' as we have established beyond doubt that you wish him to reign for a long time. You may also address me as sir and we can then proceed at a greater pace.'

This outburst relieved his frustration, allowing him to be more rational. He addressed Mohammed directly.

'Young man, we are facing a serious crisis here. Tell me, what options there are and I will try to persuade my father to drop his resistance to them. Given me the best first.'

'Tourism, sir. Tourism is by far the best, sir. Yes, it is definitely the best. We would need to build it up over the years, but it might even get us to self-sufficiency within five years if we pull out all the stops.'

'Pull out all the stops?'

'Yes sir, but this would mean preparing the country's infrastructure for tourism by building hotels, enlarging the airport and constructing a shipping terminal to tap into the lucrative cruise market. Tourists will expect luxury in addition to seeing the traditional lifestyle of the Haranistani people so much loved, espoused and supported by our king.'

Helini pondered on what he had been told. He knew Mohammed was right, but also knew that the government, from the First Minister down, would not have the ability to drive it through.

'You're right, Feisal, but we will need to keep this separate from the business of government led by the king. First Minister, you will ensure the government adopts a policy of expanding our fishing industry, with all the changes it entails. This will of course include expanding our port to cater for modern fishing vessels.'

'Sir, might that include supply ships up to a size of, say 100,000 tonnes, to allow for the modern trend for larger ships?' Mohammed enquired, with a slight smile he hoped the Crown Prince would pick up but the First Minister would not. Helini was about to castigate Mohammed for his stupidity, but then reflected on the smile that had accompanied it. It was then when he tuned in to Mohammed's coded language.

'Precisely, Feisal… First Minister, I wish to have Feisal attached to my personal staff, so you will arrange for him to be reassigned to me. Now please set to it. Feisal and I will continue, but you will have lots to do getting fishing established as government priority.

'Of course, sir'. The First Minister replied, feeling relieved at not being party to the further plans he could hear hatching before him.

10 – 6th February 2004, Crown Prince's palace, Haranibad, Haranistan

Helini was in a good mood as he received Mohammed for their first one-on-one session.

'Feisal, we appear to be getting somewhere with the tourism idea. My concern is to understand what we could persuade tourists to come to see in Haranistan. What do you have in mind?'

'Top of the list, sir, would have to be opening the chambers of the tomb of King Harani Anshalari XVI and its magnificent gold statue of the RECOT, to public view. The problem is, though, that the king has specifically forbidden it.'

'What in all this kingdom is the RECOT?'

'Pardon, sir; the Red-Eyed Cyclops of Thebes.'

'Oh that. Would tourists actually pay to see that?'

'Most certainly, sir, but the king fears thieves might attempt to steal the ERECOT, that's the eye of the cyclops, sir. It's very valuable. It's an ancient masterpiece made from carved ivory inset with a very valuable, pigeon blood ruby. In fact, the king is so concerned to deter thieves, he has put around a story that the true eye was stolen and what is in the RECOT is a lower quality replacement.

'Now we're getting somewhere. We have a legend, a statue, a story of daring theft and fake artefacts. We could add a bit about the true eye being recovered by our excellent secret service and we would have a very good tourist attraction. We could add in visits to the excavations under Cyclops Square to improve the package.'

'But sir.'

'But, what, Feisal?'

'The king will never allow it, sir.'

'Not while he's alive he won't, but we can make plans for it. Setting up something like this will take time. Have plans drawn up for turning the tomb into a visitor attraction.'

'At once, sir'.

Mohammed bowed and began stepping back as if to leave to set about his task.

'Just a minute, Feisal, that's not going to keep the population alive while we await either the king's change of heart, or his death, neither of which would appear to be imminent. What other ideas do you have?'

Mohammed coughed and looked sheepish.

'Sir... I hardly dare mention it...'

'These are desperate times, Feisal. If you have any ideas, *any*, then let me have them.'

'Since the king has put it out that the ruby

was stolen, although in truth it was not, we could announce to the world it had been recovered, as you said yourself, by our excellent secret service, and then make a block-busting movie about it. That might bring in as much as $10 million.'

'Nice idea. How long would that keep the country going? Not long term, but enough to make a start and I like your thinking, Feisal. Any more ideas like that?'

'Well, sir, the ERECOT does have one more weapon in its arsenal. It is alleged to have hieroglyphics that lead to a very great treasure for anybody who can decipher them.'

'Do we have men who can decipher them?' Helini asked, not realising he had interrupted Mohammed in his development of a completely different plan.

11 – 13th February 2004, Crown Prince's palace, Haranibad, Haranistan

Helini had been looking forward to his regular meeting with Mohammed. He respected him for his intellect and had come to like him as an individual. He greeted him warmly.

'Hello, Feisal, what new ideas do you have for me?'

'Good morning, Excellency. I think I have something that might please you.'

'Yes?'

'Gambling would bring rich tourists who would need hotel accommodation, food and of course a casino, which our government would run. The winnings would not be taxed, but we would make a good income from running the casino itself. Alternatively, we could franchise commercial casinos and tax their income.'

'I like it Feisal, anything else.'

'Sir, we could run major events, related to gambling, at the casino, to bring in extra tourists. Poker obviously, but also an international Contract Bridge competition perhaps, which would attract some famous players if the prize money was large enough. We might even get Omar Sharif.'

'Good, yes, I like that one too. Please continue.'

'How about trying to get a Formula One Grand Prix, sir? We could use the streets of Haranibad, in a similar way the Monaco Grand Prix use Monte Carlo. If we were able to run professional sport as well then we could run competitions for the most popular, like soccer, cricket, baseball, American football… in fact the list is quite long.'

'I like all of these ideas, Feisal. How many of them are specifically forbidden by my father's edicts?'

Mohammed's head dropped.

'All of them are, I'm afraid, sir. The king will not allow gambling or competitions for prize money. No professional sports are allowed either. If we ran the bridge competition it would have to be for honour alone, which is not really practical.'

'Feisal, you're reading from a file; does it contain all your ideas?

'Yes, sir.'

'And are there many more?'

'Another sixteen, sir.'

'Do you have anything in your file that the king has not forbidden?'

'Yes, sir, there are two, but neither is amongst the more profitable of my ideas.'

'Go on Feisal, astound me.'

'By special edict of the king, the ban on

professional competition does not extend to skills and sports considered to be part of the Haranistani way of life, for example camel racing and ploughing.'

'They don't have a big international appeal do they, Feisal?' Helini knew Mohammed and his team had racked their brains for anything, but this appeared to be scrapping the bottom of the barrel.

'How about music, sir? The king approves of music and we already have national competitions with small prizes being awarded. Perhaps we could extend this to an international competition?'

Helini's eyes looked upward in desperation.

'And the other idea, Feisal?

Mohammed took a deep breath. He was about to play his last card without knowing how the Crown Prince would take it.

'How about issuing commemorative stamps and coins, sir? Other post offices appear to do well by releasing commemorative issues, rising to quite high face values, up to ten times a year. Collectors seem to have an appetite for them even though there is always enough supply to meet demand so they're very unlikely ever to increase in value. I don't think they realise they are being exploited by mints and post offices around the world, so we should cash in before they do.'

Helini hesitated, deep in thought, for at least a minute, while Mohammed, fearing his idea was not liked, waited, dutifully, for his response.

'I like that, Feisal, because it gives me another idea. Is there anything else before we finish?'

Helini noticed how Mohammed looked concerned about saying something.

'You can speak freely, Feisal, what's on your mind?'

'Thank you, sir. Might it be possible for you to persuade the king to look favourably upon at least some of the less radical ideas we're putting forward. It's not like we're recommending state run prostitution.'

Helini stopped and his demeanour changed.

'Now *there's* an idea, Feisal. I assume that one isn't in the file.'

He stayed silent for a few seconds as he savoured the idea, which had amused him. He came out of his reverie to respond to Mohammed's request.

'I'll see what I can do with the king. That'll be all for now, but I want you to do some research into Haranistani history for me before we next meet.'

12 – 8th Oct 2004, Crown Prince's palace, Haranibad, Haranistan

Helini read the notes that Mohammed had sent him.

Haranistan is one of two countries that makes up the island of Herenath, situated in the Red Sea. The Herendits mountain chain separates Haranistan, on the Arabian side, from Ensharla, on the African side. They provide a natural border, with the only land routes between them being where the mountains meet the coast. It requires experienced climbers to get across by any other route.

At the height of their powers, the Greeks invaded the Arabian side, up to the Herendits, enslaving the local people. It ran the area as a colony until Haranistan established its freedom in AD205. The State of Haranistan was established by Harani Anshalari, following his defeat of the Greek forces. Haranistanis finally broke free from the yoke of the invader at the battle of Haranibad. The battle lasted for three days and two nights, throughout which time the slaves fought bravely although outnumbered and having inferior weapons. On the third day, under the heat of the midday sun, when it looked like they would be defeated, the gods sent the Red-Eyed Cyclops of Thebes to help them. The Cyclops killed the Greek's champion, Philophodes, in single combat.

This so demoralised the Greeks that they fled in fear back to their ships and across the sea, never more to attack the Haranistani people. Harani Anshalari was declared Sultan Harani I of Haranistan, a newly independent and free country.

The Cyclops of Thebes was feted as a national hero, given his own palace in the capital Haranibad and made a citizen of Haranistan. The Order of the Cyclops of Thebes, which still exists today, was established in his honour. However, although nobody realised it at the time, he had been mortally wounded in the battle. He retired to a nearby cave, where he slowly passed away. Sultan Harani visited him every day, but neither he, nor any of his physicians, could save the Cyclops. With his last words the Cyclops declared:

'I will forever be a citizen of this beloved country of Haranistan, whose people have made me welcome. I will rise again to fight any enemy that threatens its lands, but I will never leave Haranistan nor will I fight in support of any campaign to invade another country.'

He was buried at Cyclops Square in the Centre of Haranibad. A thirty metre statue of him, with his final words written on its base, towers above the square. He retains an important place in Haranistani culture. The National Flag has at its centre a golden Cyclops, with a red eye.

The Greeks only conquered the Arabian side, because they assumed there to be nothing of value beyond it. The mountains were impenetrable, so they did not bother to venture on to Ensharla, which was the local name meaning, 'Unknown land'. Harani I is believed to have come from there. His family name, Anshalari, is a corruption of 'Ensharli', which means 'one from the unknown land'.

There was constant conflict between Haranistan and Ensharla. Generations of Haranistanis fought against Ensharla and its allies on the African mainland, bringing back slaves, gold and jewels. Haranistan sought only to improve the lives of the Ensharli peoples by making Ensharla part of its own territory. It intended that Haranistani nationals would assist Ensharlis in running plantations. Although they fought bravely in this cause and had some successes, there were constant revolts by disruptive elements, which prevented them obtaining effective control.

Sultan Harani XIV realised he could ensure the safety of Haranistan by using direct reprisal raids on Africa, so abandoned attempts to control Ensharla and sealed the coastal land borders to prevent counter-attacks. It remained that way until the Period of Darkness, between 1916 and 1919, caused by the Great War in Europe, when King Harani XLIII was exiled and factional fighting meant there was no effective government in Haranistan. The victorious powers of the Great War reinstated His Excellency Harani XLIII as King of Haranistan. The king declared that Haranistan would exist peacefully with the independent state of Ensharla. This peace is guaranteed in a little known clause of the Treaty of Versailles.

The nation of Haranistan has thrived under the Anshalari dynasty. It has become very wealthy, initially through the abundance of jewels mined from the Herendits and later through the discovery and exploitation of its oil reserves. The Anshalari dynasty survives to the present day, with every ruler adopting the name Harani. The present ruler is His Excellency King Harani XLVI, long may he reign.

In AD602, following the death of His Excellency Sultan Harani XVI, his son declared that henceforth Haranistan would be a kingdom. He would be known as His Excellency King Harani XVII. He built a grand tomb for his father, which is in a secret location to protect it from robbers. Such is its magnificence that it took two years to complete. The tomb is protected by a solid gold, life-sized statue of the Cyclops. The eye of the statue is made from a pigeon-blood ruby encased in ivory. Its location is still known only to the Haranistani royal family.

Despite all these precautions, the eye was stolen in 1918, during the Period of Darkness. In 1920 the thief was captured by His Majesty's secret service and brought back to Haranistan from his hideout in South America. Having been found guilty after a fair trial in the Court of Haranistan, the thief was executed, by beheading, at the order of the king. The eye of the Cyclops was never recovered. The present eye is a replica made by the Haranistani Crown Jewellers.

Helini's train of thought was interrupted by his valet announcing the arrival of Mohammed, together with another man whose business card read 'Ibrahim Mohammed'.

'Good morning, Feisal. I have just been reading the notes you sent me. Can I confirm that they have been taken from the official Haranistan government records?'

'Indeed they have, sir.'

'So the world believes the eye of the Cyclops to be a copy?'

'Yes, sir. Why, is that not the case?' Mohammed knew that it was not, because he had told the prince so himself, but did not see it as his place to remind a Crown Prince of the facts.

'No, Feisal. It was a story put about my father to deter thieves, by making them think that it wasn't there to steal.'

'Ingenious, sir. A fine idea of the king.'

'Indeed, Feisal. And an opportunity for us, but let's leave that for another time. Is this our Postmaster General?' Helini was looking at a fresh-faced man in his mid-twenties.

Mohammed smiled one of those smiles Helini had come to know and respect. It meant what he was about to say had a very fine subtext, which the words alone would not convey. He had first encountered it when Mohammed had suggested that the new docks, intended for supply ships supporting the fishing industry, should cater for vessels as large as 100,000 tonnes. At the time he thought Mohammed did not know what he was talking about, because the largest supply ships were less than 10,000 tonnes currently and highly unlikely to grow to more than 15,000 tonnes. He then realised that Mohammed was planning for large cruise ships, which could be up to 100,000 tonnes, but did not wish to convey his message to the First Minister, who was present at the conversation. Mohammed's coded recommendation had made the docks capable of supporting a highly lucrative cruise industry. Helini had signed off the plans for them only the previous week.

'It is with much regret, sir that the Postmaster General, who has served the king for over thirty years, is now in failing health and is unable to attend here today. He extends his most profound apologies and hopes to be well enough to fulfil his duties for the king next week, but recognises that Your Excellency is working to a very strict timetable and would not be able to postpone your meeting until he is fit. He has therefore asked me to introduce to you his newly appointed deputy, Ibrahim Mohammed, in whom he has complete faith, to act on his behalf. Mr Mohammed carries his full authority and he requests his deputy be at your disposal in all matters for the foreseeable future, while he attends to the requirements of His Excellency King Harani XLVI, long may he reign. He trusts such an arrangement will meet with Your Excellency's approval.'

The man stepped forward and bowed.

'I am at your service, Excellency'.

The Crown Prince took a long look at him before responding.

'Yes, this arrangement does meet with my approval, thank you, Feisal. Now please tell me whether my eyes deceive me. This man looks similar to you and he bears the same name. I think this is not a coincidence?'

'You are of course right, Excellency. Ibrahim is my younger brother.'

'That's good, Feisal. I imagine you had a hand in this arrangement.' Feisal Mohammed realised there was no need to answer, so he smiled and bowed, allowing Helini to continue.

'I expect you to help Ibrahim to understand the nature and confidentiality of the work we are undertaking.'

'Of course, Excellency.'

'So, to business. The king has approved a set of stamps to commemorate the 1800th anniversary of the birth of Haranistan as a free country and nation. I have some ideas as to what they might be for our Post Office to work up. We should issue five sets next year. They should be on the dates of the uprising, the arrival of the Cyclops, the declaration of the state of Haranistan, the appointment of Harani I as Sultan and the death of the Cyclops… those should be edged in black.'

Ibrahim Mohammed looked distinctly nervous. He blanched, turned towards his brother and was about to speak when Feisal spoke instead.

'Of course, sir. That would mean the third set, the declaration of the state of Haranistan, would be issued on 4th June, our National Day, so working back from then, the uprising, which we know was in the spring, on 1st April and the arrival of the Cyclops on 3rd April. Looking forward, the appointment of Harani I on 11th June and the death of the Cyclops on 30th June. Is that satisfactory, sir?'

'Perfect, thank you, Feisal. It will leave us time for issues at New Year and on the King's birthday beforehand and some more sets in the second half of the year. Perhaps you could put some thoughts into those issues, Ibrahim?'

Ibrahim Mohammed nodded and bowed but did not speak, so Feisal continued.

'Would you like to issue a commemorative coin on each date as well, sir? Perhaps starting with a one Haranistani Crown, followed by a five, ten, twenty, and finally a fifty crown. We could then have, say, 100 sets of specially minted, gold coins, all numbered, to sell to special customers or use as presents for Royal Visits?'

'Splendid idea, Feisal. Please ensure I am asked to write a foreword to the blurb accompanying those stamps and coins. I will also vet the final text. That will be all for now'.

Both men bowed and left.

Ibrahim turned to Feisal.

'Where did you find all those dates? They're not on our website or in the documents in our National Library. Even our National Historian could not provide the exact dates. They have been lost in the passage of time. But His Excellency knew them. How?'

'Because I told him what they were.'

'But how do *you* know them?'

'Because I made them up. But there is nobody to prove me wrong, is there? The whole nation is going to know them soon. This is ancient history in the making, my dear brother.'

13 – 28th November 2004, Cheeton House, Devon

Sir Henry Chase MP, great grandson of Sir Archibald Chase, was catching up on his mail when the contents of one letter caught his eye.

'I see the old thief has finally popped his clogs.'

He addressed the remark to his wife, as they both sat in the drawing room of their Devonshire country home on a cold winter morning.

'Who, darling?'

'Brian Farquhar, the apprentice who survived the collapse of the rocks that killed great grandpapa. You know, the one who was supposed to have the ERECOT.'

'ERECOT, dear?'

'The Eye of the Red-Eyed Cyclops of Thebes. I've told you about it several times.'

'Oh, that… him. There's nothing in the obituaries columns.'

'Don't be silly, dear. He was a little nobody, living out his life in a care home in Essex. I doubt he even made it into the Harlow Times.'

As Chase picked his way through the contents of a package he had received in the previous day's post he came across a newspaper cutting entitled, 'Harlow's oldest resident dies'. It read, 'Brian Farquhar, aged 105 and believed to be Harlow's oldest resident, died peacefully on 23th November at the Eventide Nursing home.'

'Oh… Apparently it did. His age was newsworthy, although nothing else about him was.'

'Who's the letter from, dear?'

'It's a private detective I've had do a bit of digging.'

'You seem to be taking a lot of interest in this little nobody, dear, is there an angle in it for us.'

'It's great gramps' reputation I'm concerned about. His expedition perished in Haranistan, trying to find the tomb of King Harani XVI with its treasure, which included the RECOT. This little nobody survived and was believed to have got its eye, but he claimed he was too traumatised to talk about it. If he had it, then it should be returned to Haranistan with as much publicity as possible. We're trying to do business with the Haranistanis. I'll be leading a delegation there the summer after next. Think what a triumph it would be if I could announce the return of the eye to its rightful place. It would be great for British trade and my career. I might even get a cabinet post out of it.'

'Then we must make sure you find it, dear. But doesn't the trail go cold with the death of this Farquhar chappie?'

'Hopefully not. My detective tells me he's got a great nephew who inherits everything he had, which I doubt amounts to a hill of beans. That's with the exception of the eye of course, if he had it. My man says his will includes a letter to an Alfred Farquhar, who visited him occasionally, but he's not as yet obtained a copy of it. I've told him to keep an eye on this chap.'

'An eye for an eye, dear? Talking of which, it's time we got ready to go to church.'

14 – 29th November 2004, Tenterden, Kent

Mary Stainsby rolled over and snuggled up to Charles Mancini. He could feel her warm body against his bare chest.

'Charlie', she began as she playfully pulled on one of his chest hairs.

'Again?' he asked, a little surprised and desperately worrying if he could recover so quickly.

'Well, maybe, in a little while, but can I ask you something first?'

'What is it, darling?' he asked, feeling relieved at getting a little time to recover before their next wild session. He had known her for three months, which had been a period of adventurous love-making he had most enjoyed, even if it had left him feeling very tired at times.

'I need to tell you a story first.'

'A story? This is a side of you I haven't encountered before.'

Detecting mockery in his tone, she pulled out the chest hair she had been playing with.

'Ouch, that hurt. Tell on, Scheherazade, I'm all ears.'

'Eh?'

'Never mind, please just tell me your story, Mary.'

She breathed in deeply.

'When I was a little girl my Nanny Liz used to tell me stories about her father.'

Mancini was about to interrupt with a sarcastic comment, but thought better of it. He wanted a partner he could talk to as well as enjoy for her other charms.

'He was Sir Archibald Chase. You know, the famous archaeologist who led an expedition to discover the secret tomb of King Harani XVI of Haranistan. He and her mother were never married but he visited her when he could. She was the result of one of those visits.'

Charles could not resist his own humour. Before he could stop himself he quipped, 'I trust you're more careful than your great grandmother.'

She took hold of another of his chest hairs, rolled it around her finger and pulled gently.

'Yes. Now shut up and listen or this one comes out as well.'

'I'll behave.'

'He used to tell her stories about the expedition and the legend of the Red-eyed Cyclops of Thebes. He called it the RECOT, although I never knew why.'

Charles looked at her, surprised by her lack of understanding.

'It's an acronym, Mary'

His explanation was met with a blank look.

'You know…An acronym. Where the first letters of each word are used to spell another. It makes it quicker to write or say and easier to remember.'

'Oh. Anyway, this RECOT was supposed to be nearly twice the size of a man and made of solid gold. It had a red eye made from a very valuable gem. A pigeon blood ruby, I think she said. I've no idea what the other one was made of.'

'Mary, a Cyclops is a fanciful creature from legend that only has one eye, right in the middle of its forehead.'

'Yuk, that's weird.'

'Never mind, you've got me interested now.'

'Anyway, Sir Archibald was killed in a rock fall shortly after Nanny was born. She said he'd found the eye just before he died. She cried every time she told me the story, but kept coming back to this eye, which she called the ERECOT.'

She stopped for a few seconds, appearing to be in deep thought.

'Oh, I get it now, Eye of the Red-Eyed Cyclops of Thebes; very good. Anyway, the whole party of archaeologists was killed, except for their apprentice, Brian Farquhar. She claimed he knew what happened to the ERECOT, but wouldn't say. Something about being too traumatised to talk about it, whatever that meant.'

'When was this?'

'Sir Archibald was killed in 1917.'

'So Brian Farquhar must be long dead by now? Surely?'

'Funnily enough, no. He lived until he was 105. He died last week. He was rumoured to have a safety deposit box.'

'How do you know this, Mary?'

'My friend works for the Providence Bank in London, where the box is.'

'Do you know what's going to happen to it?'

'I can try to find out.'

She rubbed her head against his chest then kissed it.

'It might cost me a good lunch for my friend and a bung as well, because she'd lose her job if she was caught giving away customer secrets. I'm skint at the moment. Can you cover it? The rumour is the box contains the ERECOT with that pigeon-blood ruby.'

'You know I can't resist you in this mood, Mary. Okay I'll fund a nice lunch and a bung of a ton, but it better be worth it. Now about that other matter…'

15 – 2nd December 2004, Threadneedle St., London

Alfie Farquhar arrived at the London offices of the Providence Bank with a letter of introduction from his late great-uncle, Brian. He asked to be sent to the Office of Deposits. His level of anticipation rose as he realised he was coming to the end of a complex adventure that had started two weeks earlier, when he had received a letter from Derek Peebles, of Bates, Barker and Peebles, Solicitors at Law in Harlow. The letter asked him to collect a package deposited by Brian Farquhar. It explained that the instructions from his great-uncle had been very clear. The law firm was to hand a package to Alfie, upon adequate proof of his identity, as soon as possible after his death. The package was not to be posted, but instead had to be handed over in person at their offices. Alfie was not a wealthy man and lived a long way from Harlow, so he had picked up the package straight after his uncle's funeral. It contained two letters, one addressed to Alfie and the other to the Office of Deposits at Providence Bank.

His letter read:

Dear Alfie

I have been holding a secret that has plagued me ever since the fateful expedition in 1917 when I just escaped with my life from a rock fall that killed Sir Archibald Chase and his entire party, except me. It has had such a profound effect on my life that I have chosen never to speak of it. Many believed I had blanked out the whole incident, but regrettably that could not be further from the truth. I remember the incident very clearly and I am still haunted by it.

The accepted explanation at the time was that the rock fall was caused by slippage after abnormally high rainfall, but I know this not to be the case. It was triggered by a booby trap which must have been prepared by the ancients who constructed the chambers within those caves. When Professor Chase picked up an object that interested him it triggered the rock fall. The trap was meant to kill and neither he, nor anybody close to him, had any chance to get away.

Just before the first rock hit him he threw the object to me and unknown to anybody else I have kept it ever since. I have tried to understand what it is and why so many people have died because of it. Legend says it is cursed and I can understand why. It has brought nothing but misery to me, so it is with some concern that I write this letter informing you of its existence. Because I believe it to be of great value, I am allowing you the choice of what you do about it and the knowledge of its existence.

Effectively, you have three options and the one you take must be your free choice:

> ***Option 1 – Do nothing***
>
> *You could choose to leave the object in the bank and either pass these options on to a legatee of your choice or to nobody at all. This is probably your wisest choice, although, knowing you as I do, I do not expect you to take it.*
>
> ***Option 2 – Pass the object on to an expert organisation***
>
> *You could give the object, plus all the information I have left you, to either the British Museum or to the School of Archaeology at Empire College. The latter perhaps has the greater claim to the object since it was its professor who found it and gave his life for it. This is a riskier option in general terms but should be safe for you, making it your next wisest option.*
>
> ***Option 3 – Use it as you wish***
>
> *The object is in a safe deposit box, the contents of which I have bequeathed to you. You can therefore do with it as you wish. All options,*

including selling it, trying to determine its purpose or even destroying it, are open to you. In my view this is your least wise choice and I do not recommend it, but as I have said, it is your choice not mine. If you decide to claim the contents of the box then you will need the combination, which is 4-5-8-5-4-1-5.
As you know, I have never been a religious man, so I will just wish you all the best and trust to fate to guide your choice.

Yours
(Great) Uncle Brian

'Mr Farquhar, may I see your proof of identity, please?'

The voice belonged to a dapper man in his sixties, dressed in a long black jacket and pin striped trousers. Alfie thought he had probably been working for the bank his whole life and worn the same style of dress all the time. Although seeing many changes, he would have been the model of consistency, doing things the way they had always been done and quietly disapproving of any change. "That's his problem", Alfie concluded as he handed over his passport. After careful examination, Mr Pinstripe returned it.

'Thank you, Mr Farquhar, that's all in

order. Would you follow me, please?'

Alfie knew then he had rejected what his uncle considered to be his wisest option. He also knew deep down that his uncle expected he would. But what would he do next? He followed Mr Pinstripe to a bank of boxes, each with a keypad beside it. Mr Pinstripe placed an electronic key into an adjacent socket and entered a number. He left the key in place.

'Mr Farquhar, you will be given two minutes and three chances to enter the correct code. If you do not know the code then please tell me now, because once you hit the first key, you will be committed to the process and if you fail to enter the correct combination the bank is required to retain the contents until another claimant arrives. This stipulation is part of the instructions left by Mr Brian Farquhar. Do you understand?'

'Yes, I do, thank you', Alfie responded firmly.

'Please sign this document confirming your understanding.'

Alfie quickly read through the document before signing it. Mr Pinstripe then undertook a well prepared exit routine beginning with a short explanation.

'Thank you, Mr Farquhar, I shall now withdraw the key and leave you alone in the room. You will have two minutes to open the deposit box and then as long as you wish to examine it. Please ring the bell when you are ready to leave.'

He removed the key with a flourish and left, closing the door behind him.

Alfie entered the number from the letter. A red light came on together with the message, "Incorrect PIN, you have 2 attempts remaining."

He was stunned. He was sure he had entered the PIN correctly. He concluded he had no choice but to try again, so re-entered the number. He keyed 4-5-8-5-4-1-5 very carefully ensuring that each number had entered correctly. This time a green light came on and a message read, "Pin confirmed, please withdraw the box from the rack to open it." He did as instructed.

On opening the box he found a letter, £1000 in cash and a small object in the shape of an eyeball. Thinking what a useful bonus the cash was and wondering why his great-uncle had not mentioned it in his previous letter, he pocketed it before turning his attention to the object.

It was about five centimetres in diameter, white, with what appeared to be a red jewel set into it making it resemble an eye, but with a red centre instead of a black one with a coloured iris that a true likeness of an eye would have had. On the opposite side from the jewel were hieroglyphics etched in black on the white surface. The white looked like ivory. Being no expert, Alfie could not tell if the red was a valuable jewel or a cheap alternative.

He opened the letter:

Dear Alfie

It comes as no surprise to me that you have ignored my advice and I admire you for it, but I urge you now not to ignore my pleas for you to be careful. The object of which I spoke in my previous letter, which you are probably holding now, is believed to be the Eye of the Red-Eyed Cyclops of Thebes or the ERECOT as we came to call it. You know of the Red-Eyed Cyclops of Thebes, the RECOT, because we spoke of it many times when we met, although I deliberately pretended to be unaware of anything after the rock fall.

Before I begin my story about the ERECOT, I must first disappoint you about the money you have no doubt just slipped into your pocket. It is yours, but you will need to pay the bank's deposit charge from it, the amount of which will depend on how long the box has been with the bank before you open it. I have ensured there will be sufficient to pay the charge with some left over. You could use it to aid your investigations, although, I would rather you gave the ERECOT, if indeed that is what it truly is, to Empire

College and then forgot all about it.

Returning to the story of the fateful expedition. We were searching for the burial chamber of King Harani XVI, which was supposed to be guarded by the RECOT. We had local guides who thought they knew where it was, but most would not help us because of the legend which held that anyone who looked into the Eye of the Cyclops would be cursed. They would either die immediately or suffer a long, miserable life. A few younger ones were prepared to take us, for a fee many times the norm for guiding foreigners. One of them told us how a thief called Saleem had found the burial chamber, with the RECOT guarding it. He could not carry off the RECOT, because it was too heavy, being over three metres high and made of solid gold. Instead he stole its eye, which is supposed to contain a pigeon blood ruby of great value.

What happened to Saleem or the ERECOT was not known, so you can imagine our excitement when the light from the Professor's torch picked up a red glow from one of the walls. He went across to find this object wedged in a crack in the wall, with the skeleton of a man beneath it. The guides immediately decided the object was the eye and the skeleton was that of Saleem. They were arguing about whether or not they should leave the cave when Professor Chase prised the object from the wall, causing the chamber to start collapsing. The professor threw the object to me just before the rock fall hit him. I was standing right by the entrance, so I just had time to catch it before diving out of the chamber, striking my head on a rock as I did so. I now believe the object to be the ERECOT.

It was in my pocket when one of the outside team found me and took me to hospital. They decided I had not sustained any serious injury, but I used concussion as my excuse for having no memory of the incident. I was a poor student at the time and believed I had something of great value, which I could sell when all the fuss died down. Of course the expedition was cancelled and I was sent home. I deposited the ERECOT with the bank and said nothing.

When I returned home, I learned that my older brother, your great-uncle Henry, had been killed in action in France. I signed up to fight with noble thoughts of avenging his death. During the Great War, my platoon was ordered to advance on the German lines on the Somme. I was the only one to survive the attack. The same thing happened on a second advance, after which the war soon ended.

On my return home I was told my father had died of a heart attack and six months later my mother was diagnosed with cancer. She died in agony ten years later. My childhood sweetheart, Gracie, to whom I got engaged before I left for the war, ran off to America with another man. As you know, I have never married and that is because I could never find a girl to replace her. Sixty years, to the day, after my mother died, I was diagnosed with the same form of cancer she had. All my muscles are wasting away and I'm in a wheelchair now, so am choosing to write this letter to you while I still can.

Yours, with my very best wishes for a long and happy life,
(Great) Uncle Brian.

Alfie folded the letter, put it in his pocket together with the ERECOT and rang the bell. Mr Pinstripe arrived in no time.

'I have emptied the box and should like to settle up with the bank please?' Alfie declared. Mr Pinstripe straightened his back before responding.

'Certainly sir, I can finish up here. You are aware there will be a storage charge to be paid first aren't you, sir?'

Alfie nodded.

'Thank you, Mr Farquhar, here is the bill, which includes VAT.' Lowering his voice he added, 'It comes to £617.18p, sir. I will take you to the cashier to settle up.' Alfie refused to wince, deciding he was still nearly £400 better off, so this had been a good trip.

As he left the bank heading for the Underground, Alfie had already decided what he intended to do with the ERECOT. He looked across the road to see a man in his twenties, wearing a hoodie and jeans, looking across at him. He was convinced he had seen the same man before he went into the bank. This, combined with the fact that he was carrying so much cash, made him feel uneasy. He became even more uneasy when he saw the man again in the carriage behind him on the Northern line. It was time to take precautions. He went into the nearest post office, banked £350 and despatched the ERECOT, by registered post, to his brother's jewellery shop in Hatton Garden.

16 – 4th December 2004, Hatton Garden, London

Joseph Hinds picked up the strange object on Freddie Farquhar's desk and instinctively reached for his eye loupe to examine it. Holding the eye loupe between his left cheek and eyebrow he examined the object closely under his bright inspection light.

'What's this, Freddie?'

He was not expecting an answer, because he was about to check it out with the normal thoroughness of any jeweller considering something he might buy.

'You're the master jeweller, Joseph, you tell me.'

'The first thing I can tell you is that it's not a ruby, or even a garnet, but I'm not sure what it is. Could be glass, but it's very old so it might not be. The white casing looks like ivory; in fact, I'm sure it's ivory. There's writing of some sort on it as well. Not valuable, but an interesting curio.'

Hinds put his loupe back in his pocket and returned the object to Farquhar, who put it into a cotton bag before placing it in his safe.

'Is somebody trying to flog it to you?'

'Joseph, so many questions and I haven't even had my first cup of coffee. Firstly, I think your analysis is spot on, so we're talking about something with little value based on what it's made of, but might have significant, historical interest.'

'So it's not for us, then?' Hinds concluded, not letting Farquhar finish.

'Yes and no, Joseph. This was sent to me by my little brother, Alfie, who is hoping it's valuable. He thinks the stone is a ruby and he wants me to make it into a ring for his girlfriend Alice so he can propose to her. Alfie doesn't have a lot of money, so I'm intending to let him think he's right, make him a ruby ring and say it's my engagement present to him.'

'But a ruby of that size would cost tens of thousands, Freddie; you couldn't afford it.'

'Indeed it would and as you say, Joseph, I can't afford it, so I need your help in a little subterfuge, please.'

'Carry on', Joseph replied, intrigued.

'I intend to tell him it is of poor quality with many flaws that cannot be polished to produce a large solitaire ring, but we could break it up and produce a ring with a small central ruby surrounded by a cluster of seven tiny ones. I can afford to do that for him and I even have the rubies in stock. I need you to tell him all this, because as my top gem specialist he'll believe you. Will you do it for me, please,

Joseph?'

Joseph smiled, warmed by the generosity of his long time employer, but he was concerned. He shrugged his shoulders before replying. 'But Freddie, I have my reputation to think of. If it gets out I've declared a piece of glass, or whatever else it is, to be a ruby, then it will be in tatters.'

'Then don't say it, Joseph. Just say the piece will not make a good solitaire ring because it would break during polishing, but we can make a ring with a small central jewel and a cluster surrounding it. That's true isn't it? I don't expect Alfie to ask about the ivory casing, but if he does then I'll tell him we had to destroy it to get the ruby out. You don't have to be part of that lie.'

'Freddie, you're a sly dog. Now I know why you're the salesman and I'm the jewellery maker. Okay, so be it. What will you do with this thing?'

'It's an interesting curio, so I'm going to keep it. Alfie hasn't told me how he came to possess it, so it's a good plan in case his ownership claims prove to be tenuous. One day I might have the time to get it out of him and investigate what it really is, but for now my brother has a very sweet girl to woo. Oh, and just one other thing. Have you got some small pieces of ivory you could put some marks on and I can give back to Alfie as the broken iris, please?'

'Freddie, today you want everything. It's as well that I'm in a good mood at the moment.'

'I know I'm going to regret asking, Joseph, but why is that?'

'Because I'm expecting a big Christmas bonus from you, isn't it?'

'Now who's being a sly dog? You don't even celebrate Christmas.'

'No, I don't, but you do, Freddie and I'm sure you'll want to be full of Christmas spirit.'

17 – 10th December 2004, Tottenham, London

Alfie Farquhar was awakened by banging and crashing outside Alice's house. Before he could work out what was happening the bedroom door burst open. Three large policemen entered his room.

'Police. Put your hands on your head', one yelled pointing a Taser at him. He sat up in bed and stayed still.

'Put your hands on your head where I can see them. Do it now', the same policeman demanded. Alfie obeyed. One pulled the duvet off of him, leaving him shivering in his underpants.

'Stay there', he commanded, totally unnecessarily as it happened because Alfie was frozen to the bed in fear. A plain-clothes officer walked in.

'He's clean, guv.'

'Okay, get him dressed and down the station, then get a forensic unit up here.'

Alfie plucked up enough courage to ask a question.

'What's going on? Where's Alice?'

'She's outside, where you pushed her.' One of the policemen responded. The plain-clothes officer interrupted sharply.

'That's enough, Hanson. Let's hear what this man has to say down at the station, under caution and with a solicitor present.'

Turning to Alfie, he continued, in a much calmer voice, 'Alfred Alan Farquhar, I am arresting you on suspicious of the murder of Alice Mary Adams. You do...'

Alfie did not hear any more as he felt faint, wetted himself and passed out.

18 – 10th December 2004, Tottenham, London

Alfie sat in the interview room dressed in a forensic cover-all suit. The duty solicitor was sitting beside him with Inspector George Peters and a detective sergeant sitting opposite them. Peters turned on the tape, recorded the names of all present and started the interview.

'Alfie, please tell me in your own words what happened last night.'

Farquhar was still stunned and shaking but made a brave effort.

'It was going to be the start of our lives together. I took Alice out to dinner at the Golden Slipper. You know, the Chinese on the Seven Sisters Road. She was wondering why I'd taken her to such a posh place. I could see the anticipation in her face as we talked. She looked beautiful. I proposed to her over coffee and she accepted me. I gave her the ring. I was so happy. She put it on and said she loved it. It was a bit tight, so I said I'd take it back to Freddie to have it altered. She said I could, but she wanted to wear it all night. We went back to her parent's house. They're on holiday in Mallorca, so she said I could stay the night. We made love for the first time.'

He stopped, as tears welled up inside

him.

He wiped his eyes then blurted out, 'I wouldn't kill Alice. I loved her. We were going to get married. My brother made the ring 'special. Central ruby with a cluster of seven smaller rubies round it, it had. She loved it and she loved me. We were going to spend the rest of our lives together and now she's dead.'

He put his head in his hands and dissolved into tears. The duty solicitor broke in.

'Inspector, you can see that Mr Farquhar's in no condition to answer your questions. Can we please suspend this interview and let him recover.'

'Very well. Interview suspended at 08:15.' Peters turned off the tape.

'For now we'll let him pull himself together and see where we go from here. I'll have the doctor look at him again.'

Peters left the interview room with his sergeant, heading for the area being fitted out as an incident room. His sergeant was the first to speak. He knew Inspector Peters to be a fair and thorough policeman, who listened to what his team said.

'I'm not sure we've got the right guy, guv. Farquhar's got no criminal record and he seems genuinely upset. If he did kill her would he make love to her first? Then why wouldn't he have run away and pretended he'd never been there rather than just stay in the house and go back to sleep. It was as if he didn't even know she was dead until we told him. And there's something else. Alice wasn't wearing a ring and we didn't find one anywhere else. Could this have been a robbery that went badly wrong?'

'I wondered the same thing, Steve. There are a few things we need to check out. Firstly, was anything else of value taken? Will you look into that, please? Secondly does that ring really exist? Farquhar said it was tight, so there might still be a mark on her finger. I'll ask the pathologist and also check whether she'd had sex before she was killed. Will you enquire about a ring at the Golden Slipper, please? Somebody might remember him giving her one. His brother's coming in today; I'll see if he mentions it before I do. He's supposed to have made it, so with any luck he might have kept some record of it.'

19 – 10th December 2004, Leyton, London

Lenny Clark was ringing the doorbell at the back of Arnie Sparrow's Jeweller Shop sharp at nine. His big frame filled the doorway so, without needing to look at the camera, Arnie thought he knew who it was. He checked the other cameras to make sure Lenny had not been followed and that nobody else was watching him. Deciding he could not be too careful, he then checked the door camera just to confirm it was Lenny before he opened the door.

'Lenny, you're bright and early this morning. What have you got for me?' he asked cheerfully.

Clark was not in the mood for pleasantries. 'It's that bird's ring you asked for, plus two other rings, a brooch, three necklaces and two watches. That should be worth a goodly sum and don't forget you promised me ten ton for the ring.'

Sparrow took a good look at the haul.

'There's not much else of value here. One of the watches is quite nice. I'll give you the thousand I promised you for the ring, plus another hundred for the rest.'

'Eleven ton for the lot. That's daylight robbery.'

'Now come on, Lenny. You know we

don't use language like that around here. We don't want to offend anybody now, do we?

'Make it fifteen ton and you've got a deal.

Sparrow, could sense the desperation in Lenny's voice.

'Eleven hundred is my offer Lenny, take it or leave it."

"How about thirteen ton? Meet me 'alf way.'

'Eleven hundred Lenny, or I'll just take the ring for ten as I promised. And I've not got all day.'

'Make it twelve ton and I'll be on me way.'

'Lenny, it's not worth it.' Sparrow hesitated in the pretence of thinking everything through, even though he already knew what he was going to say next. He had Lenny thinking what he wanted him to.

'I'll give you eleven, fifty because you're a regular, but I'm cutting my own throat at that.'

Clark grumbled a bit more before accepting the offer, as Sparrow knew he would. He took the cash and left without even a farewell. Arnie scooped up all the jewellery and took it into the counter in the front.

'Have you got that ring for me, Arnie?'

The voice came from behind and made Sparrow jump. He turned to the source to find a small, dark-haired man dressed in a suit and tie. He could see the tell-tale signs of a shoulder holster beneath the man's jacket. Although it was only holding a point two-two Beretta, the gun was still clearly visible under the buttoned jacket.

'Mike Chambers. I might have guessed. You gave me a real start, creeping up on an old man like that. Yes, I've got it. It's a very nice piece and it looks new.'

"We both know it's new, Arnie, but what I want to know is how old are the rubies in it and do they come from the same source?'

Sparrow examined the ring carefully before giving his opinion. 'The little ones are a close match for the big one, but definitely not from the same stone. Mind you, anyone who broke up a big stone, like you think might have happened, would try to keep it to a few large stones. They wouldn't break a big stone to get eighth carat ones. Huge waste that would be. They'd just use ones from stock.'

'Did the big one come from a pigeon blood ruby, Arnie?'

'Again, that's difficult to say, Mike. Pigeon Blood is not a definitive term used in the trade see. The ruby's good quality, though.'

'Stop beating about the bush, Arnie. I don't have all day to discuss the finer points of rubies with you. I'm a patient man, but I'm getting bored waiting for an answer. Has that stone come from the ERECOT?'

Chambers cracked his knuckles as he spoke. This along with his tone made Sparrow very nervous.

'I can't be sure, Mike, but I don't think so. You should get a second opinion, though.' As he spoke he passed the ring to Chambers, who put it in his pocket.

'Don't worry, Arnie, we will.' Chambers turned to leave.

'We did say two thousand, Mike and I would like cash. You see, Mr Mancini, fine gentleman though he is, doesn't have an account with me.' Chambers handed over an envelope.

'100% profit, Arnie, that's not bad for a morning's work.'

Sparrow could see the twenty pound notes in the envelope and gave it a quick flick as he took it to ensure there was no paper inside. He would feel uncomfortable counting the money in front of Chambers, because he had no wish to appear distrusting. With the thickness of the envelope, he knew it to be about right. Neither of the Mancini brothers was known to short-change anybody, so it was better not to risk offending them.

'I have my expenses, Mike. Have you any

idea of the rates and insurance I've got to pay on this place? And then there's the consultancy I've just given you. Not that Mr Mancini isn't welcome to my cooperation of course, but I do have costs.'

Chambers gave a thin smile.

'Of course, Arnie. I'll be sure to explain that to Mr Mancini.'

20 – 10th December 2004, Tottenham, London

'Mr Frederick Farquhar is here to see you, Inspector.' The desk sergeant's voice boomed down the telephone, making Inspector Peters wonder why he bothered to use it, because he could hear his voice echoing down the corridor.

'Thank you, Sergeant, please bring him along straight away.'

Freddie Farquhar looked worried.

'This is terrible. Who would want to kill Alice? She was such a sweet girl. And how is Alfie? He must be distraught. His solicitor said you think he might have killed her. Well, I can tell you, he didn't. He loved her. He was going to propose to her yesterday. He was so excited when I told him the ring was finished and he could collect it. Can I see him, please?' He had blurted this out within seconds of entering Peters' office.

Peters was pleased with what he had heard, because he now knew there was an engagement ring, as Alfie had claimed. This, coupled with the statement he had already received from his sergeant that items of money and jewellery were missing, confirmed his suspicion that Alfie Farquhar was not the murderer. He now had to move fast, before any trail went cold. Firstly, he had to calm Freddie Farquhar, so he could get as much information out of him as possible.

'Please sit down, Mr Farquhar. Cup of tea, or would you prefer coffee?'

'Tea, please, milk and two sugars.' Freddie replied, automatically, as he sat down.

'The doctor is with Alfie now. Just making sure he's alright. We'll then get him dressed and you can see him. Did you bring some clothes for him, as we asked?'

'Yes, here they are.' Freddie handed a small holdall to Peters, who passed it on to the desk sergeant.

'Thank you. Now may I ask you a couple of questions, please?'

'Sure, fire away. Anything I can do to help.'

Farquhar had relaxed and was now seated on the other side of the desk, listening attentively.

'You said you gave Alfie a ring you had just finished.' Peters asked and then paused.

'Yes, it was a ruby engagement ring we made for him. I run a jewellery business, so this was my engagement present to them. It had a central, one-carat ruby with a cluster of seven, one-eighth carat rubies around it. I designed it myself, because I wanted them to have something original, but now she'll never wear it.' Farquhar's voice choked up but he managed to suppress his urge to cry.

'No, I'm afraid she won't, but that ring could help us track down her killer. Would you recognise it again if you saw it?'

'Yes, of course. But I can do much better, Inspector. I can provide you with the design drawings for it. And a photograph, if it will help. Our mark is also engraved inside the ring, so I could pretty much prove whether any ring you come up with is or isn't the one I made. I can also provide you with a receipt for the central stone, which came from a batch I bought from one of my regular suppliers. He provides individual descriptions and pictures of each significant stone he provides.'

Peters could hardly believe his luck. With this much information he would be able to positively identify the ring, should it appear on the black market.

'Thank you, Mr Farquhar, you've been most useful. I will arrange for you to see Alfie and then he can go home with you. I'll get one of our cars to take you and perhaps we can pick up the paperwork on the ring at the same time?'

Peters took Freddie to Alfie. He was on his way back to his office when the desk sergeant called to him.

'Guv, Dr Edwards called to say she's completed the post mortem on…' he hesitated, remembering who was with the Inspector, but recovered quickly, 'our latest case, and will fax across her report. She suggested you might drop by to talk over some of her findings'.

21 – 10th December 2004, Tottenham, London

Visiting Dr Fiona Edwards was always a pleasant experience for George Peters. Not only was she a very good pathologist, she was also pretty and had a bubbly personality. The two of them got on very well. He held out his arms as she approached.

'Fi, lovely to see you.' His greeting was accompanied by a hug and a kiss on the cheek.

'And you, George. But I'm sure you only want me for my bodies, or yours in this case.'

'Yes, Alice Adams. Found by a milkman at five a.m. this morning on the pavement outside her house. Did she fall out of the window as we surmised?'

'No George, she did not. Although her killer wanted you to think she did. He compressed her windpipe as if he was going to strangle her but appeared to stop, probably when she passed out. He may have thought she was already dead. He then dragged her out into the street and smashed the back of her head on the pavement to make it look like she'd fallen out of the window. It was the blow to the head that killed her. That blow couldn't have been caused by a fall and there were no other injuries to suggest a fall.'

'Fi, you said, "*he* dragged her outside".'

'Yes, the bruises left by the strangling action were made by a very large hand and the angle suggests by an assailant over two metres tall, which indicates a man to me. I also said "dragged outside" because we found traces of wool, almost certainly from a carpet, in her heels. And there were tiny amounts of sand, probably from the pavement. I've given the samples to the forensic team, with my money on there being a match with the hall carpet and the sand between the paving stones.'

'Were there any other injuries?'

'Yes, her left ring finger was broken, just underneath where her ring was. The ring must have been tight, because it left a significant indentation in the skin, which was still visible inside all the bruising from the break.'

'Could the break have been caused by the killer trying to remove the ring, which would have been difficult if it was tight? By the way, last night was the first time she'd worn it.'

'Quite possibly. The bruising was caused ante-mortem, so my guess is he tried to pull the ring off her finger with his right hand while he held her throat with his left to prevent her from screaming.'

'So he strangled her with one hand? Well worked out, Fi, but why do I suspect you've got more to tell me? You said the build suggested a man, but you've got proof it was a man haven't you?'

'Yes, George. You're really in luck this time. He may have been a big bugger, but she fought like mad and managed to nick him. There was sufficient skin and blood under one of her fingernails to take a DNA sample, which we sent off for matching. I got a fax just before you arrived, saying they've got one. You were copied of course, but I assume you haven't been told yet. Your murderer is Leonard Albert Clark.'

'Fi, I love you. Lenny Clark, eh? I'm not really surprised because he's known to be vicious and not averse to injuring victims to get what he wants. With this, we can put him away for good. I'm going to make some calls and then I think I owe you lunch. You can even choose the sandwich shop.'

'Wow, George, you really do intend to spoil me don't you?'

'Fi, that's only the half of it, I'm going to buy you a coffee as well.'

22 – 12th December 2004, Tenterden, Kent

'So this is the ring I've paid so much to get, is it?' Charles Mancini held it up to the light with his left hand. 'Don't look much. It ain't a big pigeon-blood like you told me, Mike, but is it at least a genuine ruby?'

Mike Chambers was feeling nervous. It was not he who had told Charles about Alfie Farquhar's inheritance, the supposed ERECOT held in a safety deposit box, which had set in train the disastrous events of which Charles was not yet fully aware, but he had agreed to obtain the ring allegedly made from the ruby it was believed to contain. It was his pickpocket who had followed Alfie into the Post Office and stolen his recorded delivery receipt to obtain the address of where it had been sent. He who had organised the bugging of Freddie Farquhar's shop to learn of his intention to make the ring and he who had arranged to have it stolen. He knew he was caught up in the mess that Lenny Clark had created, so placating Charles was an urgent requirement.

'Oh, yes, Charles, it's genuine alright. A nice one at that. A ring like that would probably fetch five grand in Burlington Arcade.'

'But I've already paid two and a half grand plus your fees and we ain't selling it in

Burlington Arcade, are we? I must remember to lease a shop there next time something like this comes up, mustn't I? What's it worth on the black market?'

'Normally I'd say about half that, but we have a couple of problems with this particular piece.'

'Problems, what problems? I pay you to fix problems, Mike.'

'Yes, Charles, I know you do and I've fixed the main problem already.'

'Main problem? You're talking in riddles, man. What problems do we have and what have you done about them?'

Chambers could detect frustration and annoyance it Mancini's voice.

'The main problem was Lenny Clark. He killed the girl when he stole the ring, so it's as hot as hell at the moment. I've fixed Lenny already and the police won't find him, so there's nothing to trace anything back to us.'

'Good. But I'm left with a hot ring I can't get rid of and it's cost me lots. Is there any good news?'

'There might be, Charles. We know Farquhar's ERECOT wasn't genuine, so the real one's still out there somewhere.'

'Do we know where it is?'

'No, but there is somebody who claims to

know.'

'I'm sure there are lots of chancers out there who *claim* to know where the genuine ERECOT is and any one of them would be happy to take my money to tell me. Why should we believe this one?'

'Because he's published photographs of it.'

'What? He put it on eBay or something?'

'Not eBay, exactly, but there's a secret website where you can buy all sorts of things that are not generally available, if you get my drift. It's part of the Dark Web. Users jokingly referred to it as Fence-Bay. Stolen art, famous jewellery and any sort of weapon you could wish for. It's come up there, with some very convincing evidence of authenticity. And that's not all.'

'Are you having me on, Mike, 'cos I'm not in the mood?'

'No, straight up, Charles. The seller claims there are hieroglyphics on the ivory casing which tell the secret location of all the treasure of King Harani XVI, which, for safety, was buried separately from his tomb.'

'Suppose he knows how to interpret these hieroglyphics as well, does he?'

'Yes, he claims to. Before you ask, he explains why he's not gone to the location itself. It's because it's not easily accessible and he doesn't have the resources to act alone. He's offering to sell the eye for fifty-thousand dollars, which he claims to be the black market value of the ruby, plus he'll act as guide and consultant to get the buyer to the treasure. For that he wants another fifty-thousand in advance, plus 5% of the treasure payable when found.'

'What's this unique evidence of authenticity, he's claiming?'

'Hear me out on this, Charles. Haranistan recently issued sets of stamps and coins to celebrate 1800 years since its declaration of independence from the Greeks. In addition to those on sale worldwide there were 100 special sets created with solid gold coins and special bank notes as well as the other stamps and coins. Each set was sold in gold-leafed albums with accompanying notes written by Crown Prince Helini, no less. Most were reserved for presents for state visits and the like, so they're not generally available, but there are rumours of a few getting into private collections. The special notes also tell the story of the burial of Harani XVI, including the making of the gold statue of the Cyclops containing the ERECOT, and the legend of the hieroglyphics on the ivory case. Don't forget that those notes were only circulated with the hundred special sets. The accompanying albums went into detail about the size and construction of the eye, although, for security, it masked out the hieroglyphics. None of this was in the general release, so the information's not widely known. The photos of the eye this guy is selling have rulers included and the dimensions are correct. Of course it could all be a big hoax with the seller having seen those notes, but if it's a forgery it's got to be one with a pigeon blood ruby and those things don't come in Christmas crackers. And he's offering to stay with the buyer to collect his share of the treasure. Why do that if it's a con. He must be expecting to find something?'

'Still sounds a bit fishy to me, Mike. Do a bit more digging and if you're convinced he's kosher then arrange a viewing. By the way, how did *you* get hold of all this stuff?'

'I have my ways, Charles and, as you said, that's what you pay me for.'

23 – 12th December 2004, Cheeton House, Devon

The phone rang in Chase's Office. He hit the hands-free button and barked, 'Chase'.

'Sir Henry?'

Chase instantly recognised the voice of his private detective. He picked up the receiver and spoke much more softly into it.

'Just a minute.' Turning to his secretary, he added, 'Julie, would you like to take a ten minute break? And would you collect the post while you're about it, please?'

'Off course, sir. Shall I get you some coffee as well?'

'Please.'

Speaking back into the phone he asked, 'Do you have any news?'

'Yes, sir, but it's all a bit weird really.'

'How so?'

'From what I can gather, Alfie Farquhar picked up a package from a deposit box in London then sent something, registered post, to his brother's jewellery shop in Hatton Garden.'

'The ERECOT?'

'It could well have been, because the next thing I hear is Alfie has proposed to his girlfriend, Alice Adams, in a restaurant on the Seven Sisters Road. He comes up with a big ruby engagement ring. My source told me it was really nice and would probably have cost five thousand from a respectable jeweller. There's no way Alfie Farquhar has that sort of money, so putting two and two together, I reckon he'd had his brother make the ring from the ERECOT.'

'So that's it. The ERECOT's been destroyed. Damn.'

'It seemed that way, sir, but strange things have happened since.'

'What strange things?'

'Farquhar's fiancée, Alice Adams, was murdered the same night and her ring was stolen. The police think they know who did it. Guy called Lenny Clark. Bit of a nasty piece of work with gangland connections, but now he's gone missing.'

'Stay with this. See if you can find out if it was the ERECOT that was used for the ring, or if not, then what's happened to it. I'll send you a cheque to cover your costs to date.'

'Thank you, sir, will do.'

24 – 20th December 2004, Haranibad

Mohammed felt honoured to be sitting next to the Crown Prince in the prince's personal box at the recently completed King Harani XLVI National Stadium, just outside Haranibad. The stadium was part of a complex he had suggested for holding major indoor and outdoor events. Today's inaugural event was the first of an annual, international camel racing competition for the King Harani XLVI Cup. The stadium, capable of holding 120,000 people, was about one percent full as the king made a speech prior to cutting a ribbon, which would open the stadium and start the events of the day.

'This National Stadium complex was an excellent idea, Feisal. The king looks very happy to be opening it.'

'Thank you, sir, but how did you persuade him to build such a large stadium when all we can hold is events like camel racing, which don't attract large audiences? Even if we could attract foreign visitors, I thought the king would not allow tourist visas?'

'It took some doing, I can tell you, Feisal. I told him camel racing needed a large arena to make racing viable. Funnily enough, about the size of an international football pitch with a running track around it. So I recommended he surround it with stands to view the event from all angles. Of course, anything built in Haranistan has to be big, to keep up with, and preferably beat, the Emiratis' buildings. This magnificent stadium is the result. Just look how happy my father is. He's got guests from the Saudi Royal family and most of the Emirates. Now cast your eyes over the crowd, such as it is. Do you see many Haranistanis?'

'I can't be sure, sir, but going by the dress, my guess is they are Saudis and Emiratis.'

'Precisely, Feisal, and how did they get into Haranistan?'

'On tourist visas, sir?'

'Right again, Feisal.'

'Sir, how did you persuade the king to accept the concept of tourist visas?'

'I played on his desire to have an event like this, which would allow him to show off Haranistani talents and assured him a Haranistani competitor would win.'

'Sir, how could you possibly assure him a Haranistani winner when there are eight countries competing?'

'Come on, Feisal, you've worked with me long enough now. You know how I do these things. You tell me.'

Mohammed hesitated. He had indeed worked with the Crown Prince for some time, so knew he was expected to work it out. He also had the comfort of knowing he would not be castigated if he did not. The Crown Prince liked him and respected him for his intellect. His brain demanded, "Come on Feisal, use the intellect which has gained his respect." Then it came to him.

'Of course. The king disapproves of competitions for money. He thinks the glory of winning is the only reward a competitor needs, so there's no prize money. The winner gets the honour and the cup for one year, but that's all.'

'Good. Now go on, Feisal'.

'So nobody could afford to travel here to compete unless they were sponsored. This is an invitation event, with travel and accommodation funded by Haranistan. The king is not looking for profit, only kudos for himself… Sorry, begging His Majesty's pardon, for Haranistan. I'm guessing that you offered to organise the event to take pressure off the king, who is very busy. As any loyal subject should.'

Mohammed watched the prince, who nodded, then continued.

'You will have chosen competitors from abroad who would make *suitable* opponents for our fine Haranistani camel racers and ensure an exciting competition.'

'Feisal, I couldn't have put it better

myself.'

'If I'm not mistaken, isn't this the day of the world famous Egyptian Camel racing festival, which has prizes intended to attract the best camel racers?'

'Really, Feisal? I hadn't realised. That's such a pity, but this was the only date available from the king's very busy diary.'

'What a shame, sir. It must have tested the loyalty of the Haranistani camel racers, but I see they've all come out to support our beloved king. Just as I would expect… How did you manage that, sir?'

'Simple, really. I cancelled all travel permits for this week, offered them all a one thousand Crown loyalty bonuses and a secret five thousand Crown prize for the winner. They only get the loyalty bonus if an Haranistani wins. That way they will also work as a team to prevent any of our guests winning.'

'Of course, sir. Wise precautions, which will ensure a successful opening day for our fine national stadium complex. And we have the Concert of Haranistani Music in the indoor arena tonight, probably with a similar level of attendance as this event, to add to this most successful day. You must be very pleased, sir.'

'Feisal, this is you and me talking, in private. We could put the words you've just used about the success of today's events into our national press. In fact please make sure we do and you can credit them to me. Now tell me what you really think.'

'Really think, sir? The total, unvarnished truth I would always deny saying, or just something allowing a modicum of scepticism?'

'Unvarnished, job-losing truth, if it were even uttered outside this box, Feisal.'

Mohammed took a deep breath, trying to convince himself the Crown Prince really meant what he said. No matter, it had to be said anyway.

'Well sir, this is a success. We have built a magnificent stadium complex, which we can barely afford, of which Haranistan can be proud. And the king is delighted. That makes today a success. But this stadium is only one percent full and I doubt if many who attended today paid for their tickets. So we are making a huge loss. We cannot afford for this complex to be a white elephant. Haranistan needs it to make money, lots of foreign currency to replace the oil revenue we are shortly to lose. We have to fill it with tourists paying good dollars, euros and the like to see events of international importance. The soccer world cup, cricket tournaments and boxing title fights in this stadium. We also need world renowned artists in the indoor arena. We still have a mountain to climb to get the king to agree to tourist visas being the norm. Then we have to build hotels, expand our airport and significantly improve our infrastructure to make it all possible. How do we do it with time running out?'

'Well put, Feisal. You have set out the problems with great clarity. All we need to do now is get similar clarity with our solutions. That's my job, but your help will be vital. I have ideas, although I will not reveal all of them to you at the moment. We have made a start by getting the king to provide the legislation to permit tourist visas and, it will be announced tomorrow, he has also approved the building of a new luxury hotel in Haranibad. The building and land rental will provide income and Haranistani jobs now and when our plans succeed, income for the future.'

"That's excellent news sir. You have made a fine start."

'Quite so, Feisal. Now to our other plan. The one only you and I know of.'

'You mean portfolio 35-05-07-25-39-21, sir?'

'Do I, Feisal? I'm sure I do. I'm all for a codename, but why 35-05-07-25-39-21?'

'It's the location of the new town, sir. And congratulations on remembering the number accurately after being told it only once.'

'Put it down to my military training, Feisal. Now, have our technicians made it yet? Are we ready for the next phase?'

'Yes, sir.'

'That's good, now we have a job for your brother.'

'But, sir, I think we need to work more to refine the plan. It's too risky at the moment. Can we have more time, please? We need a month to get everything ready.'

'We don't have the luxury of so much time, Feisal. You can have a week. Do what you can with that.'

'Yes, sir, thank you.'

Mohammed's face portrayed his concern, but he knew he had no choice.

25 – 3rd January 2005, South Bank, London

The swarthy, dark-skinned young man sat on a bench facing a bookstall under Waterloo Bridge. He was wearing boots, heavy jeans, a hooded, fur-lined anorak, gloves and a scarf wrapped around the lower half of his face. Although it was bright and sunny, he was still cold from the biting easterly wind blowing up the Thames. He had been there for two minutes although it felt much longer. It was now precisely 12:30, the time he had agreed to meet his contact. He shivered and looked up as Mike Chambers sat down on the bench next to him.

'It's cold enough to freeze the balls off a brass monkey', Chambers said in a casual, friendly way.

'And the eye out of a cyclops', came the reply in an accent that made it clear the mother tongue of the man Chambers was addressing was not English. Chambers rose and started walking east along the river. The other man joined him.

'Have you got the money?'

'Not here. Mr Mancini doesn't do business in public. Come with me.'

'I'm not going anywhere. I don't know. I'm not stupid.'

'Of course you're not. We'll go to your

hotel if you like. Which one is it, I'll have Mr Mancini meet us there.'

'It's the Tower Hotel; by the bridge.'

'That's a bit of a way, let's take a cab.'

Without waiting for a response, Chambers hailed a cab, which pulled up beside them. He opened the door, just as two men, one European and the other oriental, came from behind to bundle the young man in.

26 – 3rd January 2005, Docklands, London

The young man tried to understand where he was before anybody realised he was awake. He was sitting tied to a hard chair in the middle of a large, enclosed, shed-like building. He could smell oil and hear the footsteps of several different men.

"I'm alright", he told himself, "I have information they need."

'Is he awake yet?' Charles Mancini asked. Chambers could see he was getting impatient.

The oriental heavy responded, 'He's coming round, boss.'

Charles Mancini was pacing around behind the chair. His heavy frame made his steps highly audible and echo around the building.

'So this is the eye he claims comes from the Cyclops. This is just a piece of red glass, in white ivory, with a few black marks on it. He must think I'm stupid. I've a good mind to kill him here and now. He's wasting my time, Mike.'

'Let's not be hasty, Charles. Let's hear what the lad's got to say for himself, shall we?'

The young man knew he had to think quickly, but did not know with whom he was dealing. He had only dealt with Chambers, who had said he was acting on behalf of a reputable businessman. He looked up at the tall, heavy-set man holding the fake eye he had brought with him. If this man was considered reputable in England he certainly would not have been back home.

He struggled to bring to mind the right words in English. 'You did not expect me to bring the real eye with me, did you? How did I know if I could trust you? I now know I can not.'

His voice was faltering, but defiant. The European man, who was one of the two who bundled him into the taxi, hit him across the face.

'Show some respect when you address Mr Mancini.'

'Alright, Bill, I'll see if I can regain this young man's trust.' Mancini interjected.

Chambers did not like his tone. He knew Charles was running out of patience, so things could turn ugly if he did not react quickly.

'I've got the real eye somewhere very safe, but what I have brought you is valuable because it contains an exact copy of the hieroglyphics. With it I can take you to the treasure. All you have to do is to pay me the fifty thousand dollars you promised and we can start straight away. You'll get the real eye after we've found the treasure and you've paid me my cut of it.'

'You're hardly in a position to bargain. I would say you're too tied up with other things at the moment. Like that chair you're sitting in, for example.'

'You will not be able to find the location without me. I am the only one who can translate the code for you.' He was fully awake now. He spoke slowly and deliberately to ensure Charles Mancini would understand his heavy accent.

While they had been talking, Mancini had passed the fake eye to Chambers, who had examined it carefully before passing it to Chin, Mancini's other heavy. Chin looked at it and nodded back to both of them.

'Don't be so sure of that.' Mancini retorted, his voice betraying the satisfaction he felt.

'I'm going to kill you. You can be part of the next M25 service station.'

Mancini pulled a thirty-eight Smith & Wesson from his jacket with his left hand.

'Charles, let's not be hasty. He could still be useful. We don't need to kill him.' Chambers begged, but to no avail. He had barely finished speaking when Mancini's muffled revolver put a bullet in the back of the young man's head.

27 – 10th January 2005, Sidcup

Charles Mancini felt nervous as Chin drove him to his older brother's mansion in Sidcup. William had been head of the Mancini family since their father died eight years earlier. He had let Charles have his head on a number of projects, some of which had been successful. He had made one major error that had cost the family a lot of money, but William had forgiven him. He had said, 'Charles, we are all allowed to make *one* mistake and you're family so it's alright, even though it's a big one.' The accent on the word "one" had made it clear a second error would not be tolerated. He knew of other employees, who were not family, disappearing after a second mistake, never to be seen again. William knew everything that happened within the organisation, so what did he want?

'Drink, Charles', William offered a large measure of twenty-five year old, single malt whisky in a fine Waterford glass.

'Thanks, Will.'

'Par devant les domestiques, Charles', William replied in a thick Cockney accent, while looking at Chin.

'Sorry, William.'

'What's this about an ERECOT thing, Charles? I understand a girl's been murdered and two men have been used to support the base of the new M25 service station. What is it and what are we going to gain from it?'

Charles pondered how best to answer that question, cleared his throat, swallowed then began, nervously.

The Red-eyed Cyclops of Thebes, the RECOT, is a large gold statue, guarding the tomb of King Harani XVI of Haranistan, who died in 620 AD. The eye of the RECOT, the ERECOT, was made from a large, pigeon-blood ruby set in a sphere of ivory to give the appearance of an eyeball. There are black marks on the ivory, which tell the location of a vast amount of Harani's treasure that was not buried with the king for fear it would be looted if his tomb was ever found.'

'So there's a Cyclops guarding some of Harani's treasure, with an eye telling where the rest is. All sounds a bit fanciful to me, Charles. Why do you believe it?'

'There was an expedition in 1917, led by Sir Archibald Chase, a leading archaeologist of the time. He found a chamber, but a rock fall killed him and his entire party except one, a Brian Farquhar, who was a student helping out and learning his trade. Rumour was that the expedition had found the eye. It was in an antechamber of the tomb, and Farquhar had it.

He was knocked out by the fall and claimed he couldn't remember any of the incident, but he was lying. When he died, in December last year, he admitted he did have the ERECOT. He told the story in a letter to his great nephew, which he had deposited with his solicitors. He willed the ERECOT to his great nephew.'

'You know this, how, Charles?'

'I have my contacts, William. I've seen a copy of the letter. We traced the ERECOT to a jeweller in Hatton Garden, who was supposed to have made a ring from the stone. I had the ring stolen, but it didn't have a large pigeon-blood ruby; just an ordinary one. Nice, but not what I was looking for. I was going to put the whole thing down to experience when we spotted someone on Fence-Bay offering to sell the ERECOT. There was plenty of evidence, including pictures, to suggest he had it. I arranged to meet him, but all he brought was a fake with some writing on it. He said only he could translate it and lead us to the treasure. Claimed he had the original somewhere safe. Said he'd not gone for it alone, because he didn't have the money to fund an expedition. Cocky little sod thought he'd be safe because of what he knew, but Chin here said the writing was just Chinese characters, which he could get translated. He'd outlived his usefulness at that point, if you get my drift?'

'Where's this fake now?'

'I have it here, William.'

William took the eye, looked it over and then turned to Chin.

'What does this say, Chin?'

'It's a series of Chinese numbers, sir. A friend in Chinatown translated them for me.' Chin reached into his pocket for a piece of paper.

'The numbers are: 313, 761, 221, 613, 13 and 25.'

'Thank you, Chin, I'll take that bit of paper. Why don't you pop down to the kitchen for a bite of lunch? We'll call when we need you again.'

Chin bowed and left.

'Well, Charles, I can't even use these for the lottery, so you'd better be able to find the treasure with them.'

'I'm working on it, Will.'

'See that you do, Charles. There's been too much agro on this one not to get a big pay out.'

28 – 17th June 2005, Prince's palace, Haranibad, Haranistan

Helini welcomed Mohammed for another of what had become regular meetings, but this time the atmosphere was tense. Both men were worried about their plan.

'Feisal, do we have any news of Ibrahim?'

'No, sir it's now been five months since we've heard anything. I'm very concerned.'

'What's happened? … Exactly.'

'As you suggested we used our Chief of Police to start the process. He's a very well informed man, sir, especially on the subject of international crime. He put the eye on Fence-Bay and had an offer of a meeting with a Mr Smith, in London. That was back in January.'

'Fence-Bay, Feisal?'

'It's just an underworld joke, sir. It's a secret web site. Part of the Dark Web, where stolen property is offered to those in the know.'

'Thank you, Feisal, now I understand. But I interrupted, please continue.'

'Of course, sir. We didn't know whom we were dealing with, so chose an open location. The South Bank on the Thames in London. We had two of our men watching. Ibrahim met Mr Smith at the appointed place, a bench on the river bank. After a couple of minutes they started walking along the bank but we lost them in the crowds. Ibrahim never returned to his hotel. We thought that he might be laying low before trying to get back to us. Our friends in the Sen Shun Triad paid the bill and collected his belongings in case anybody came looking for the real eye, which Ibrahim intended to tell them he had, but nobody did. They have tried their contacts and followed up on several leads. They even leaned rather heavily on a few suspects, but nothing came of it. They've returned his possessions and admitted they have no more leads.'

'So we've heard nothing of Ibrahim since. Do we have anything left to go on?'

'Nothing relating to Ibrahim sir, no, but there was an interesting development. Again, it was our friends in the Sen Shun Triad who reported it. It was their men who were watching Ibrahim. They felt really guilty about losing him.'

'Was it about the eye?'

'Yes, sir. A Chinese restaurateur who belongs to the triad was asked to translate some Chinese characters. They were given to him on paper, but were the same as the ones from our fake eye. He told them they were Chinese numbers, so they've worked that bit out.'

'Do we know who's asking the questions?'

'Yes, sir, that's one thing we do know. It's Charles Mancini. He's number two in the Mancini syndicate. He used a guy called Mike Chambers. The Chief has used Chambers before, so he was able to get it from him without making him suspicious.'

Helini stayed silent deep in thought, then appeared to reach a conclusion.

'We have no choice but to make contact again, but prepare yourself for the worst. Don't worry about Chambers, I should like to entertain the person asking the questions. Get the Chief of Police to arrange that.'

'Of course, sir. When did you have in mind?'

'I don't have any formal engagements after the middle of July, so let's spend a couple of weeks on my yacht. Please have my jet ready for a flight to Monte Carlo then. Invite the Chief and his friend with the cutting sense of humour to join us.'

'Now it's my turn to be confused, sir.'

'Don't worry, Feisal, the Chief will know who I mean.'

29 – 21st July 2005, Crown Prince Helini's Yacht, North Sea

Helini poured a large measure of cognac and offered it to Mohammed, who looked very pale.

'No, thank you, sir. I don't drink.'

'This is medicine, Feisal and you need it. Now take it and drink it.'

Mohammed knew this was not a command and he could still decline if he wished. The Crown Prince was acting as a friend who cared for him. He took the glass and drank it down. It did not make him feel a lot better, but at least he knew he was not going to faint.

'I'm sorry sir, I have never seen anything like that before. It was brutal; horrible… barbaric.'

'Yes, Feisal, it was all those things, but it was also justice and you had to witness it. Even though we've not recovered your brother's body and I doubt we ever will, we know from our sources that this man killed him and stole the package he was carrying on our behalf. We punished him for both crimes and now we have to move forward. We have started down the path of teaching these criminals that they cannot behave towards us in the way they did without reprisals. But we have only just started the process, there is more to do. A lot more. Are you ready to carry on or would you like a break first?'

Mohammed breathed deeply, trying to think of a way to respond that made it clear he was committing freely, rather than accepting an order.

'All causes shall give way: I am in blood, stepp'd in so far that, should I wade no more, returning were as tedious as go o'er.'

'So you are familiar with Macbeth, Feisal. I'm very impressed. Obviously my father's education policies are working. My reply is "A little water clears us of this deed" and to be sure we cast the rest of him into plenty of it.'

'Sir, I plead you not to risk misfortune by naming the Scottish Play after what has just happened and also what we are planning to do.'

'You're right, Feisal, now is not the time to tempt fate. Please permit me one final quote. "If it were done when 'tis done, then 'twere well it were done quickly." Are you ready? Shall I call in our Chief of Police?'

'Yes, sir. Let's do it before I have time to ponder on the consequences.'

'Very wise, Feisal, we must move to the next phase of our plan, fiscal punishment of the Mancini family.'

'Sir, do you mean our sting?'

'Precisely, Feisal. Before this I had merely planned to sell a few fakes, at high prices, by dangling the carrot of the discovery of the lost treasure of King Harani XVI, but now I want much more. I want to break the Mancini finances before we take our final steps. Is everything in hand?'

'Yes, sir. The first eye has been made and the others will be produced over the next month. I suggest the advertisement on the Internet be released in a week's time to coincide with William Mancini receiving the package.'

'Good thinking, Feisal. Now are we ready for the Chief of Police?'

'Yes, sir.'

30 – 21st July 2005, Crown Prince Helini's Yacht, North Sea

'Chief, please ensure the results of our justice are sent to his next of kin. They should be sent from within the UK in order to distance us from this.

'Of course, Excellency.'

'And now to the next stage of the plan. Give it a week for our parcel to arrive and then post our response.'

'Yes, Excellency.'

The Chief of Police bowed and made to leave, but Helini held up his hand.

'Wait, there is another matter.'

Helini put Wagner on his music system, setting it to play throughout the yacht. He turned the volume down in his suite such that they could speak and be heard inside, but not outside.

'We have reached a position where decisive action must be taken to prepare Haranistan for the time when it does not have its oil revenue. Feisal has come up with excellent solutions which we cannot delay putting in place. We must set up a tourism industry, casinos and major sporting events. We have made a start by building an impressive national stadium complex and, thanks to Feisal's ingenuity, a port capable of taking large cruise liners. We have to finish the job without delay.'

He waited for a moment to let his words sink in. Mohammed was the first to react.

'Sir, does this mean that the king has agreed to our plans. This is excellent news.'

'Indeed, Feisal, it would be excellent news if it were true, but I regret it is not. I learned before I left Monte Carlo that, despite all my warning and protestations, my father has refused to agree with these plans.'

'Then, sir, surely we have an insurmountable problem?'

'A problem, yes, Feisal, but we cannot allow it to be insurmountable. For the good of Haranistan we must overcome it.'

'But how, sir?'

Helini looked to his Chief of Police, who spoke slowly, quietly and firmly.

'By deposing the king and putting Crown Prince Helini in his place. There is no other way.'

Mohammed was horrified. He was not expecting such drastic action and it frightened him.

'This is treason. We could all be executed for this. We cannot do it.'

'Feisal, we can and we must, but there is work to be done to put everything in place. This is why what we have said here today must remain between the three of us until we are ready. The Chief will arrange for our armed forces to be deployed to support the coup when required. Your job is to plan the new government. You will be my new First Minister. You must decide who will continue and who will be retired.'

'Me, sir? Why me? There must be other more capable men?'

'No, Feisal. If there were then they would be in this meeting and you would not. The Chief trusts you and I know you are the right man. You must do this for your country. You do not have a choice.'

Mohammed hesitated. He knew he would never leave the yacht alive if he refused. He realised he could do it. His ideas were the ones needing to be implemented to save Haranistan. He had concerns, so now was the time to express them.

'Sir, when you said retired, you did mean *retired* and nothing worse?'

'Yes, Feisal. I want a bloodless coup. You have seen today how I deal with those who wrong me, wrong you and wrong Haranistan. I will deliver criminals to justice, but I will not permit butchery. How else would the people trust me?

'Then, sir, I shall do my duty.'

31 – 21st July 2005, Crown Prince Helini's Yacht, North Sea

She moved across to embrace him.

'Wagner on the yacht's system? So he's finally decided to do it?'

'Yes, and he wants me to be his First Minister, his head of government.'

'Then head of government is what you shall be, Feisal, my love.'

'On the other matter, have you got it?'

'Yes, it's all taken care of, but how will you deceive the prince?'

'He has ordered more than one, so I can keep moving them around until we can get a copy. My concern is if we cannot make a good copy, will you be able to deceive *her*?'

'I'll find a way, leave her to me.'

'Now I know why I love you.'

'It's a good job you do, with this secret I have on you. I think it's time for my first payment.'

She moved out of the shadows to kiss him.

'Here? Now? On his yacht?'

'He's busy right now, with something new I've prepared for him, so we'll be alright if we're quiet.'

32 – 27th July 2005, Sidcup

Although he was making every effort not to show it, Mike Chambers felt nervous as William Mancini came into the room. He had no idea why he had been called so suddenly.

'Siddown, Mike, make yourself comfortable, there's coffee on the table. Drink?'

'It's a bit early for a drink, but I'll take a coffee, thanks. Can I pour you one?'

'Sensible man. Yes, I'll have a coffee with you. I won't drink either.'

Chambers passed him a black coffee without sugar. He had known William Mancini long enough not to need to ask how he took it.

'What's on your mind, William?'

'I'll come straight to the point, Mike. I'm worried about Charles. Ever since he's taken up with this tart.' Mancini hesitated. 'Mary something, he's become obsessed with this ERECOT thing. You know anything about it?'

'Yes, William, Charles did tell me a little about it. It's supposed to show the location of a secret hoard of treasure from Harani XVI of Haranistan, which wasn't buried in his tomb. He got hold of a copy from a guy who said he had the original. Claimed the hieroglyphics on the copy were a faithful reproduction and he knew how to interpret them, but all we got was a set of

Chinese numbers.'

'Spot on, Mike, and by then he'd disposed of the guy. I wasn't happy about that I can tell you. It's not our way now. All that violence is behind us. It's so passé, Mike. The Mancini family runs proper businesses now. We pay our taxes and support our community. The odd, slightly less than legal, deal, I can accept, but not this.'

'I agree, William. I did try to stop him, but I'd hardly got the words out of my mouth before the poor guy had a bullet in the back of his head.'

'I'm sure you did, Mike, but you don't get any marks just for trying. You actually have to succeed, but I'll let that pass for now. We've got to deal with the situation the family finds itself in. Is Charles getting anywhere with it?'

'He's got Chin working with his contacts in Chinatown but he's playing his cards close to his chest, so I don't know what progress he's made. I'm looking into the Haranistani legends for clues.'

'I didn't have you pegged as a culture buff, Mike. Have you found anything?'

'The Haranistanis have recently released further information about the RECOT on their website, including an inscription on its base. It's allegedly a quote from the Cyclops, stating, in

Greek, "To receive the rewards of life we must use our own resources and learn from the work of our enemies". There were rumours this was the work of a hacker, but it was confirmed as genuine when Haranistan issued its first sets of commemorative postage stamps and coins. Both a coin and a stamp included this quote.'

'Greek, philately and numismatics, Mike? Is there no end to your talents?'

'I've still got to solve the clues, William. I've a customer who works at the Haranistani embassy, who's been a little too free with his gambling. He owes you quite a bit of money. I'm sure he'd love to help us. I'm off to see him as soon as we've finished.'

'Before you go, have you seen Charles recently? He's not answering my calls. That Mary floozy says she doesn't know where he is.'

'Sorry, William, he's not been in touch with me either. Last time I heard from him was a week ago, when he was off to see one of Chin's contacts. Chin's gone off radar as well.'

'Don't let me keep you then, Mike'.

33 – 24th July 2005, Sidcup

An hour later Mancini picked up the house phone.

'Yes?'

'Boss, we've got a package downstairs. Delivered from Scotland. It's says it's private and only to be opened by you. I'm suspicious about it. What would you like me to do?'

'I'm not expecting anything. How big is it?'

''Bout eighteen inches by twelve by twelve, boss.'

'Have you x-rayed it?'

'Yes, that's what's worrying me. It's faint, but I don't like the look of it.'

'Explosives?'

'No, that's not what's worrying me. The dog's not bothered with it. I'm pretty sure it's not drugs or explosives.

'I'll come down.'

Mancini removed the outer wrapping to reveal a large cool box typical of the type used to carry picnics or keep bottles cool. He lifted the lid carefully. When nothing happened he took a look inside and vomited instantly.

'This is war.' He declared once he had recovered. 'Call a meeting of the council for this afternoon.'

34 – 28th July 2005, Sidcup

William Mancini was both sad and angry, but was intent on not allowing his emotions to cloud his judgement or drive his actions. He was determined to act in a cool, rational way to ensure maximum chance of success.

'Mike, we cannot allow this to go unpunished. I don't care if Charles did kill some chancer over this damned ERECOT; nobody kills a Mancini and lives. What do you know?'

Chambers picked up on Mancini's approach. He decided to present just the facts, as he knew them, without giving condolences or showing emotion.

'The contact Charles made through Fence-Bay has come back to us. Before I tell you what he said, I must warn you, William, we're being provoked so we must act very carefully.'

William Mancini took a deep breath before responding.

'Alright, Mike, I'm warned. Tell me what he says.'

Chambers read from a printed note.

'By now you will have realised that you cannot kill one of our agents without reprisal. Your brother was found guilty of theft and murder. He has been punished for both crimes in a time-honoured way. You have the evidence to confirm this. The matter is now closed and we are prepared to resume our dealings with you. As a gesture of good faith we are prepared to sell the genuine ERECOT to you and explain how you can decipher the hieroglyphics. Because of your previous bad faith, the price has gone up to $100,000 for the eye and another $100,000 for the translation. We will waive our right to any part of whatever you find. If you want to do business in good faith this time then place an advance of $50,000 in a Swiss bank account, the number of which we will send you on agreement. Should you decide to deal with us and then break our agreement again, William Mancini and all members of his family will suffer the same fate as his brother.'

'Cheeky, bastard. There's no chance of him getting fifty grand up front. Not in dollars, sterling, euros, or even yen.'

'Absolutely not, William. I would not expect you to pay anything yet, but let's keep him interested.'

'What's your thinking, Mike?'

'To start with, we'll make him sweat on our answer for a week, while we try to find out who he is and where that location is, using other means at our disposal.'

'Go on.'

'I've had a chat with my friend at the

Haranistani Embassy. He reckons he's worked it out. He'll give us the location, plus his explanation of how he got to it, in exchange for clearing his debt.'

'How much does he owe me?'

'Two grand, rising at a hundred a month.'

'Is he genuine, or just trying anything to get you off his back?'

'Not easy to tell. He's scared, no doubt about it.'

'Tell him I'll stop the clock on the interest for a year while we investigate. If it's genuine he gets off his debt and gets a grand for his trouble, but if we find nothing then the full debt, plus suspended interest, will become payable immediately. If he doesn't go for it, he gets six months to pay off everything, including accrued interest. That should tell us if he thinks he's got it right.'

'Nice one, William. I'll get to it.'

35 – 7th August 2005, Oslo

Inspector Sven Ffolkes was working away quietly when the phone rang. He recognised the voice of Commander Magnussen immediately. 'Sven, I've had a call from the Lofoten Islands. They've had a body washed ashore and need our help. I know you were brought up there, so your local knowledge will be an advantage. Can you free yourself up, please?'

Ffolkes had been a police officer long enough to know this was neither an invitation nor a request, but Magnussen had very good manners, preferring invitations to orders.

'Of course, sir. Are there any more details?'

'Not many. I know it's the body of a man with his head and left hand missing, but that's all. My secretary's booked you on a flight to Leknes this afternoon. I'll get him to bike the tickets over along with a situation report from the local officer in charge, Sergeant Carlson.'

Ffolkes read through the details on the flight up. The body was of a man in his thirties. It had been in the water for some time, which made identification difficult, but there were some things to go on. The victim's head and left hand had been sliced off cleanly with a very sharp implement, probably a sword. In each case the removal had been effected by a single blow. He was dressed in a Savile Row suit, hand-made leather shoes from a top London retailer and a Jermyn Street shirt.

"Our victim had expensive tastes and shopped extensively in London. So well off, but was he British?" Ffolkes mused. There was nothing to identify him. His pockets were empty apart from a small piece of ivory, no more than a chip, with a small black mark on it.

Ffolkes met Carlson at the airport. They knew each other well. Ffolkes had worked for Carlson during his early career, before he moved to Oslo. Ben Carlson was the sergeant in charge of the criminal investigation team at the time. He might have progressed further had he not needed to stay on the Lofoten Islands to look after his sick mother. Normally he could deal with bodies washed up on the shore, but not those with a head and hand missing in a way that ruled out a boating accident or shark attack. He was out of his depth with murder, which was so rare he had never had to deal with one.

'Inspector Ffolkes, we've made some progress since the last report we sent through. The seashore where we found the body is a busy place, so it would have been found very soon after it was either placed there or washed ashore; certainly within twenty-four hours. A fisherman digging for bait came upon it. He was out early, so we suspect the body had drifted in overnight with the tide. It had started to decay, so must have been in the water for at least a week. It can't have been left on the beach or placed in the sea from this coastline because, even if it had been put in the water with a strong ebb tide, it would've come back onshore within 48 hours. We must conclude it was dumped from far out at sea with the intention of it never being found.'

'Ben, please call me Sven. We have known each other too long for formality. Now, do we have any idea from where?'

'Thanks, Sven. We've been in touch with our coastguard and the Oceanography Department of Oslo University, but neither's come back yet. They really need the post-mortem to give them an idea of how long the body's been in the water. That was under way when I left to pick you up, so we should have something very soon.'

'What about identity?'

'It was too decomposed to get fingerprints, so it's probably down to the DNA. There's a tattoo, "ACAB" in gothic script, on his left forearm. Might give us something. We've sent pictures of it, together with DNA results, to police forces of countries surrounding the North Sea and also to Interpol, because we suspect this body isn't Norwegian. Again, let's hope there's something when we get back.'

Ffolkes hesitated, wondering how his host would take the next question, but it had to be asked.

'The small piece of ivory found in his pocket, how did you know it was ivory? Was it sent for analysis?

'No, Sven. We don't have analysis capabilities here, so I took my best guess. It looked like ivory, so that's how we recorded it. I have a modern ivory chess set that's begun to discolour in a similar way, so I made the assumption it was ivory. Why, do you think it's important?'

Carlson looked sheepish, wondering whether he had been unprofessional. 'We still have it in the evidence room, so I can get it checked. We'll have to send it to Oslo, though.'

'It could be nothing, but I'd like it checked out, please. It's a little out of the ordinary, so can you ask forensics to take some photographs for me. Can they confirm it really is ivory and if yes, how old they think it is? Of course, if they've any idea what it came from, even better? I'd also like to know how those black marks were made.'

'Of course. I'll get somebody on to it.'

As the two men came into the incident room a young detective approached Carlson.

'We've identified the tattoo, Sarge. It's found on a lot of cons and ex-cons who've served time in British prisons. It stands for "All Coppers Are Bastards", although one prison chaplain claimed it meant "Always Carry a Bible". I admire his faith, but I'd go for the former explanation, myself. We've been in touch with Scotland Yard, who tell us they do have a missing person with that tattoo, so we might be on to something.'

Carlson turned to Ffolkes.

'That's interesting. If it's their body, it looks like bad luck for us him being washed up on our shores.'

Ffolkes' experience made him concerned.

'I don't want to rush to conclusions, but these things are normally either rivalry within a crime syndicate or between syndicates. This could escalate pretty quickly unless something happens soon, so we'd better get Scotland Yard involved immediately. Who's your contact there?'

'It's an Inspector George Peters.'

'Well, well, well... I know George Peters. He's a good man. I worked with him when I was on an exchange with the Cornwall and Islands police a while back. He'd moved down from London and was a sergeant then. He must have moved back. That's a piece of luck.'

36 – 8th August 2005, Leknes, Lofoten Islands

Ffolkes and Carlson arrived at the mortuary to find the post mortem well under way. Dr Johannsen looked up to acknowledge them.

'Good morning, gentlemen, please don't be offended if I carry on. You can ask me questions while I'm working if you wish.'

Carlson only knew the pathologist from social gatherings and his post mortem reports on the occasional drownings he had to deal with, but his greeting sounded friendly enough.

'Thanks Bjorn; works for us. Can you start with when he died and how long the body's been in the water?'

'There's evidence of sea scavenger activity, so my best guess is, in the water for one to two weeks, but it might be a bit longer.'

'Cause of death?'

'Being decapitated I would think. I reckon the hand was cut off while the victim was still alive, followed by decapitation, again while he was still alive. Both the hand and the head have been removed by single cuts from a large sharp blade. A sword probably. Whoever did this knew what they were doing, because it's difficult to cut either off with a single blow.'

'Professional execution, perhaps?'

'Looks that way to me. I've seen post mortem reports of executions in Saudi Arabia having pictures pretty similar to those of our body.'

'We're a pretty long way from the Arabian Gulf so, what would you say; travelling executioner or travelling body?'

'Travelling executioner's more likely. I can see no evidence of this body having been in a hot climate recently. The clothes are Western style, more suited to Northern European conditions.' As he spoke, Johannsen emptied the contents of the stomach into a dish.

'Hello, what's this? Some small white pieces with black marks on them. It looks like they're broken pieces coming from the same thing. They must have been painful to swallow, so I doubt he did so voluntarily.' Johannsen examined the oesophagus to check his guess.

'Thought so. Lots of scratches and some swelling in the throat. I don't think they liked him very much, judging by his treatment before they killed him.'

'Could the fragments be ivory?' Ffolkes asked.

'Sorry, I'm no expert in that area, but they could be. I'll separate then out, photograph them and send them to the lab for you.'

'Any idea what it was before it was broken?'

'From these pieces I'd say something spherical, or at least having part of a sphere in its construction. The lab should be able to give you more information on that.'

'Anything else of interest at the moment?'

'Only that his last meal, apart from these broken bits, was some time ago. There's only water in the stomach. You'll get all the details in my report.'

'Thanks, Bjorn, we will leave you to it.'

37 – 8th August 2005, Heathrow Airport

Inspector George Peters came towards Ffolkes, his right arm outstretched and a broad smile on his face.

Ffolkes opened the conversation as Peters drove them to Walthamstow police station. 'George, it's good to see you again. Here's a little something from Norway I know you'll appreciate.' Ffolkes said as he passed him a packet of Norwegian smoked salmon. 'I wasn't sure whether you'd like Stockfish. It's an acquired taste even though it's our local delicacy.'

'Thank you, Sven. I'm sure you're right. It's been a long time since Cornwall, so we've much to catch up on, but perhaps we can leave that until this evening. There's a lot of business to attend to right now. I've arranged for you to stay with me in Walthamstow rather than use one of the very expensive and impersonal hotels London is known for.'

'That's really very kind of you, George, but I don't want to put you to all that trouble.'

'It's no trouble. Jane's taken the children down to her parent's house in Cornwall for the summer holidays so we'll have the place to ourselves.'

'Well, if you're sure, that'll be really nice,

thank you.'

'So to business and firstly a surprise for you. Your body. Our body? I really don't know whose body it is, but it's not who we thought it was, despite the tattoo.'

'Really, who did you think it was?'

'Nasty criminal called Lenny Clark. He's our prime suspect for a robbery and murder last December. He stole a ring from a girl, killing her in the process. He's a big bugger, six foot, seven, sorry two metres to you, but she fought hard. Scratched him and got his DNA under her fingernails. He went missing the day after and hasn't been seen since. Seemed likely it was him, but the DNA didn't match.'

'Might he have fled abroad?'

'We thought so at first, but all the stuff he would have needed; passport, driving licence, money and lots of clothes, was still in his flat. There was no evidence from the crime scene there, so it's likely he didn't return home after the murder. He's either lying low with somebody he trusts and has been for eight months without a whisper, or he's dead.'

'George, I sense you think that even though he's not our body, this Lenny Clark is somehow relevant to the killing. They have a tattoo in common, but is there something else?'

'You're right, Sven, I do. But it's only a

copper's nose. The tattoo is fairly common in prisons, but also in the British-based crime syndicates in London. It's a sort of response to the Chinese-based triads with their dragon tattoos. And an insult to us policemen as well.'

'So my problem is I have an unidentified body and yours is you're missing a suspect. They have a tattoo in common, but otherwise there's no evidence to link the two cases. Despite that, at least at the moment, we both think they're linked?'

'So you think there's a link as well, Sven?'

'Yes George, I do. The same tattoo appearing in murder cases around the same time is unlikely to be a coincidence. I'm sure there's a link somewhere, but the question is, what is that link? I've been given a fair degree of freedom on this one. Since I've been flown over here, at vast expense to the Norwegian taxpayer, would you be happy for us to work together on it?'

'Nothing would give me greater pleasure, Sven. There's coffee in the incident room and I've called the team together for a briefing in fifteen minutes.'

38 – 8th August 2005, Walthamstow

Peters sat down in his lounge with Ffolkes for a nightcap following their evening meal at a local pub.

'George, I've been thinking about this murder Lenny Clark committed. He stole a ring alleged to have been made from something looking like a red eye, which Alfie Farquhar inherited from his great-uncle. Did you follow up on that?'

'No, Sven. We knew who our murderer was, so just intended to arrest him and tidy the whole thing up. We would have asked Clark about it, but as yet we haven't located him. Why, what's your thinking on this?'

'It could be nothing, but you did say there was other stuff Clark didn't steal.'

'Yes, but we put that down to his being disturbed by his victim.'

'That's reasonable. Has the ring, or anything else he stole, been traced?'

'Not a thing. It's a total blind alley.'

'Isn't that a bit unusual for a simple burglary. Could there be more to it?'

'I'd wondered that, but not just because the stolen items haven't turned up. With Alice Adams having been murdered in the process, no fence would want to touch them, so that's not unusual. It's because burglary wasn't Lenny's normal activity. He's more of a crime syndicate villain.'

'Do you think he might have been paid to steal the ring?'

'Could well have been. Are you thinking perhaps it was somebody in the same syndicate, with the same tattoo? Maybe our body?'

'It's a lot of leaps, but could be. I'm over here now and not totally clear on what to do until we've identified our body. Would you mind if I followed up with Alfie and Freddie Farquhar?'

'Sounds like a good idea, Sven. I'll get one of my team to act as liaison for you.'

39 – 9th August 2005, Tottenham

Alfie Farquhar sat nervously on the edge of the single chair in his bedsit. He seemed to be staring into empty space. Constable Sheila Conroy was the first to speak.

'Alfie, firstly I am pleased to confirm what we told you previously, which is that we no longer believe you to have been involved in the death of Alice Adams. Please accept our condolences on your loss and our apologies for the way you were treated when we arrested you. We hope you will forgive us and accept this visit is part of our investigation to gather evidence about Alice's murder.'

Alfie nodded. A thin smile of recognition appeared momentarily before a lifeless stare returned. Although it had been eight months since his fiancée's death, he had not worked, slept properly or gone out. Conroy registered his understanding.

'This is Inspector Ffolkes from the Oslo Police Force. He's visiting us in relation to a case that might be related to Alice's murder. He would like to ask you some questions, is that alright?'

A life and eagerness came to Alfie's face. He spoke with purpose for the first time since the police had arrived.

'Yes, anything I can do to help find out why somebody wanted to kill my darling Alice. Anything.'

'Thank you, Alfie. It appears the key to Alice's murder is her ring, so can we start with that, please?'

Alfie appeared cross and saddened at the same time.

'It's that damned eye. Uncle Brian warned me it was cursed. He said he'd been condemned to live a long and painful life while all those he loved died around him. Now I'm cursed. I will suffer the same fate.'

Alfie began sobbing as he took an envelope containing the letters from Brian Farquhar. He passed them to Ffolkes. Ffolkes read the letters quickly, passing them to Conroy when he had finished.

'May we keep these for evidence, please, Alfie?' Ffolkes asked.

'You might as well, I'll remember what he said for ever.'

'Thank you, Alfie. Please tell me why you think the eye was responsible for Alice's death?'

Again Alfie became highly animated.

'Freddie made her ring from the ruby in it. It was a really big one, but he said it was of poor quality so he'd have to break it up to make gems suitable for a ring. He did. He made a lovely job of it. That ring was beautiful. It was right for my beautiful Alice. She deserved something as good as that. Now all I'm left with are the curse and these pieces of broken ivory from the eye. I thought I might find somebody who could use them to lift the curse.'

Alfie passed a matchbox to Ffolkes. It contained some broken pieces of curved, white material with black marks, suggesting they were from a round object, but Ffolkes' face portrayed surprise. Conroy noticed it, although Alfie did not.

'Alfie, I should like to talk to your brother, where might I find him, please?'

'He'll be at his shop as always. I'll get the number for you.'

40 – 9th August 2005, Hatton Garden London

Thirty minutes later Ffolkes and Conroy were in Farquhar's Finest Jewellery shop in Hatton Garden, meeting with Freddie and his jewellery maker, Joseph Hinds. Freddie appeared nervous as he addressed them.

'How can I help you, lady and gentleman?'

'Firstly, Freddie, I should tell you we are investigating the theft of Alice Adams' ring which resulted in her murder. Nothing else. We're here to seek your help on that alone.' Conroy's words were intended to reassure Freddie, should it transpire he had no right to be holding the eye. Freddie picked the sub-text clearly, which allowed him to respond in a more relaxed way.

'Thank you, Constable, please ask away.'

It was Ffolkes who began. 'You told Alfie you made Alice's ring from the eye, but you didn't did you? Those pieces were plastic, not ivory.'

'You are right of course, Inspector. They came from the cap of a deodorant stick. A necessary deception, I'm afraid.'

'Please go on.'

'The eye was made from glass, encased in ivory. I couldn't make Alice a ring from it, but I didn't want to disappoint Alfie.'

Joseph broke in. 'Worthless glass and nothing but a curio. I made Alice's ring from Freddie's stock of rubies. It was my best work. Freddie was too kind to tell Alfie, so he just gave him the beautiful ring out of his own pocket. It's just like Freddie, he's too generous for his own good.' His intervention showed his love and respect for the man who had been his employer for nearly forty years.

'Do you still have the eye, Freddie?'

Freddie took it from his safe and passed it to Ffolkes.

'Alfie thinks it's cursed. I've seen nothing to persuade me he's wrong.'

'May we take it as evidence, please?'

'It belongs to Alfie, but I can't think he'd object. Just give me a police receipt for it and you've welcome. It's brought nothing but grief to my family. Let's hope it will help you find Alice's killer, but somehow I doubt it. I'm happy to be rid of it.'

41 – 10th August 2005, Empire College, London

Professor Arnold Roberts led Ffolkes to his study on the first floor of a Victorian building in London that housed the Empire College School of Archaeology. Having settled him into one of two armchairs by the fireplace and placed a cup of coffee on a small table beside him, he examined Ffolkes' card very carefully.

While he drank his coffee, Ffolkes checked out his host and then his surroundings. Roberts was a tall, fair-haired man in his thirties. His study was large by London standards so he had to be important to the college. The award of the chair of Archaeology to one of his age was testament to its regard for his work, with the size and position of his study supporting this conclusion.

'Inspector Sven Ffolkes of the Oslo Police Force. You are a long way from home, Inspector, so what brings you to me?'

Despite his deep analysis of his surroundings, Ffolkes had remained alert and responded immediately to the professor's question.

'Please will you tell me about the Eye of the Red-eyed Cyclops of Thebes?'

Roberts held his hands together in a

steeple formation with the tips of his fingers supporting his chin. After a few seconds he responded in a way that was no surprise to Ffolkes and acted to confirm his initial assessment of Roberts based on his observation of the professor's study.

'The Eye of the Red-eyed Cyclops of Thebes, or the ERECOT as we call it for short, is a very big subject of which little is known, much is speculated and even more exists as legend. It's taken me ten years to learn what I know about it today and I strongly suspect there is more that I don't know about it than I do. Can you be a little more specific, please, Inspector?'

Still hoping to draw Roberts out with his next question, Ffolkes also wanted to assure him his interest was serious and he was listening to every word.

'Perhaps we can start with the facts. What is generally regarded as known about the ERECOT?'

'Certainly, Inspector, that's a good place to start. I'll tell you what is at least widely believed to be known, although I wouldn't swear to all of it being true in a court of law. The RECOT is a spectacular statue, cast in gold, made to guard the tomb of King Harani XVI of Haranistan, who died in 620 AD. Its eye contains a large, pigeon-blood ruby, which reflects light with an intense red glow. It is intended to deter thieves from proceeding further into the chamber where the sarcophagus is located. The ruby is set in a sphere of ivory to give the appearance of an eyeball. The RECOT is said to have been placed directly in front of and facing the entrance to the burial chamber, so its eye would pick up the light when the door to the antechamber was opened. It would also reflect the light from lanterns, or latterly, torches. I say, "Said to" because nobody outside of the royal family of Haranistan has been allowed to see it, so our information is mainly from official Haranistani sources.'

Roberts took his hands from under his chin and suddenly looked much less assured. He looked down, covered his face with his hands and appeared to be wrestling with his conscience. Ffolkes knew better than to speak, leaving Roberts to come to whatever decision he deemed appropriate. Eventually Roberts spoke.

'Inspector Ffolkes, I have been asked by the Norwegian Ambassador, who is a personal friend of my father's, and also happens to be my godfather, to give you all the help I can, as it might help you catch a murderer. I am happy to do just that, but it means giving you information which, if attributed, could cause great embarrassment to a friend. Please treat what I'm about to tell you as a rumour going about the bazaars, literally in this case, and do not reveal the true source.' He looked to Ffolkes for assurance, who nodded.

Roberts continued, 'I talked about the RECOT with Crown Prince Helini, many times. We became good friends when he studied here. It was when I was doing my doctorate. He couldn't say much because his father expressly commanded him to tell only what official Haranistani sources state, which is that the RECOT sits, undisturbed, in front of the tomb of Harani XVI, with its eye still discouraging visitors with a menacing red glow. However, one night, when he was extremely drunk, he told me the original ERECOT had been stolen and the present one is a copy. This information must never be attributed to the Crown Prince, so please assure me you will be discreet. Needless to say, but I would deny ever saying the Crown Prince told me what he did.'

Ffolkes knew the value of diplomatic relations, for indeed he had used such forces to provide him with this contact. He did not need to be asked twice to keep the source of his information safe, immediately giving Roberts the assurance he sought. A grateful professor continued.

'The purpose of the RECOT was to scare a

simple people into believing the body and treasures of their late king were protected by a statue with supernatural powers. Those powers are claimed, by Haranistani legend, to derive from the legendary Red-eyed Cyclops of Thebes himself. He was, and still is, a hero to the Haranistanis. He has become part of Haranistani nationalism and appears on its flag.'

Roberts paused, expecting Ffolkes to comment.

'Can we talk a little more about the statue of the RECOT please? Has anybody outside of the Harani Royal Family ever seen it?'

Roberts considered the question carefully, before answering.

'It's easy to see drawings and descriptions of it, because the Haranistani Royal Family has released them to learned archaeological journals and to Encyclopaedia Britannica, but I am unaware of any outsider ever having seen it, or even taking photographs of it. I cannot be absolutely sure even if the royal family still knows where it is. During the First World War, King Harani XLIII, the present king's great-uncle, was so in fear of his life that he fled the country for a secret location, thought to be in the United States. There followed a period of instability, between 1916 and 1919, which became known as the "Period of Darkness".

During this period, in 1917, Sir Archibald Chase, an eminent archaeologist who was a predecessor of mine as Professor of Archaeology here at Empire College, got permission to lead an expedition to look for the tomb. The expedition went into caves in the Marretsy Mountains to the north of the country, but it ended in disaster.'

'Please go on', Ffolkes urged as Roberts appeared to be about to finish.

'Sir Archibald was killed in a rock fall along with nearly all of his party. Only one, a student called Brian Farquhar, got out alive. He was knocked unconscious, but otherwise had only cuts and bruises. He was so traumatised about the events he never spoke of them. He left his studies and went into the British Army, where he fought at the Somme. Amazingly he survived that as well, returning home intending to marry his childhood sweetheart, only to find she had emigrated to the United States with another man.'

'That's rotten luck after he had survived so much.'

'I agree, and it's that, plus the fate of Sir Archibald's search party, which has given credence to the legend of the RECOT, or more specifically the ERECOT, being cursed. The legend says anybody who touches the ERECOT will be afflicted by the curse. They will either die within twelve months or, even worse, live a long life of misery with all their friends and loved ones dying around them. As a scientist I would rather believe these were accidents or the result of poor safety provisions, rather than a curse, but it does make for a good way of discouraging anybody to even look for the RECOT, let alone attempt to steal it or any part of it.'

'Do we know whether Sir Archibald found the RECOT?'

'Nobody knows for certain, because Brian Farquhar never spoke about it. There were rumours circulating among the workers at the base camp that Sir Archibald's team had found an outer entrance and was going into it on the day of the accident. I've never been able to track down anything definitive, but stories from several sources, mainly descendants of those workers, are consistent on that point. I've also visited the site of the rock fall, but the Haranistani government will not allow it to be excavated. Having said that, I did see a lot of work going on around there, so I suspect they're investigating it themselves.'

'Is there anything else you think might help my investigation, Professor Roberts?' Roberts thought for a full minute, then took a deep breath.

'We are definitely in unproven territory

now, but I will tell you anyway. There has built up a legend saying the ERECOT holds a secret code giving the location of great treasure, although exactly what the treasure is nobody knows. Also, how anyone is supposed to find it when the ERECOT is cursed I'm not sure, but that's the nature of legends for you.'

'Would you allow me to make your research a bit more complex, please, professor?' Ffolkes asked as he revealed the eye Freddie Farquhar had given him. The professor gasped, then took it from Ffolkes. He examined it closely before making a comment.

'This is not the eye from the legend, but I suspect you already know that. It is made of polished obsidian, encased in ivory. The means by which the two pieces of ivory are joined, a hand-carved screwing mechanism, suggest it's very old. The hieroglyphics don't look like anything I've seen on other Haranistani artefacts. Most interesting. I'd really like to show this to one of my colleagues, Dr Simon Blake. He's off today, but maybe on his return, tomorrow?'

'Most certainly professor, I will contact him then.'

42 – 11th August 2005, Scotland Yard, London

Peters opened the meeting with his team and Ffolkes.

'DNA matching has identified our body as that of Charles Mancini, younger brother of William Mancini, the leader of one of the nastiest crime syndicates in London. The syndicate has recently started up some legitimate businesses, but it's still into drugs and protection with a bit of prostitution on the side. I say this for Inspector Ffolkes' benefit, because I'm sure you're all well aware of that.

'Charles was washed up on a beach in the Lofoten Islands, which is why my good friend from the Oslo Police Force is with us. We are lucky to have him, because I know from first-hand experience how fine a detective he is. It seems our Charles was in the water for one to two weeks before he was found. Prior to that he lost his head and left hand.'

He turned to his sergeant.

'Bill, can you get on to where we last saw Charles Mancini and what he was up to. This is a messy killing, which might be the result of syndicate rivalry. As soon as we tell William, I'm sure all hell will break loose as he tries to take his revenge. And he won't worry about proof beyond reasonable doubt.'

'Will do, guv.'

'So how did Charles get there? To explain, I will pass you over to Inspector Ffolkes… Sven?'

'Thank you, Inspector Peters. Our local coastguard and the Oceanography Department of Oslo University agree, Charles Mancini could not have been dumped on the beach, or dropped into the sea close by, because he would have floated in on the tide within forty-eight hours. He must have been dropped into the deep North Sea, well away from the coast but closer to Norway than the UK, in the last week of July.

'The post mortem concluded he was killed by decapitation. The left hand was severed while he was still alive. Both the severing of the hand and the head were made by single blows from a sharp object, probably a sword. To use just a single blow requires significant skill and experience to achieve the accuracy required.'

Ffolkes paused to allow this information to be digested by the team before he continued.

'We did some checks on the shipping in the area, particularly those passing closer to the Norwegian side. We came up with eight tankers, five cruise liners and twenty-eight cargo ships. There were also five warships from the British, Danish and Norwegian Navies, but we think we can discount them. Of course this is only the shipping required to provide us with sailing plans. Smaller craft are not required to file a plan and most don't. We'll check with our navies and the coastguard to see if we have any information on those.'

Ffolkes looked back to Peters, who picked up.

'So we need more information on what Charles was up to and of whom he fell foul. Is this a family feud gone messy or are we talking about a rival syndicate? The form of killing is brutal, so are there any clues we can glean from it? Sheila, would you investigate please? Inspector Ffolkes has brought pictures of the injuries if you need them.'

'Guv'.

'Inspector Ffolkes and I are going to visit William Mancini. Not that I'm relishing the prospect. We will liaise with Kent Constabulary. If there are no questions, then let's get to it.'

Peters had barely put down the phone from his call to Superintendent Graham Gibson of Kent Constabulary, when it rang.

'Inspector Peters, this is Superintendent Alan Forest of Anti-corruption Unit AC7. Please drop everything you're doing and come to see me on the tenth floor in Scotland Yard. Don't tell anybody where you're going and don't bring anybody with you. Do not answer "sir", is that clear?'

'Yes, of course. Thanks for telling me.'

Ffolkes could see Peter's face go white.

'Is everything alright, George?'

'Yes, fine thanks, Sven, but I have to nip out for a bit. Ask any of my team for help if you need anything.'

'Of course, but it's not a problem. I've got to see Dr Simon Blake at Empire College. I'm going to get his opinion on the eye we recovered from Freddie Farquhar.'

'If you are going to see Blake would you ask him about this as well, please? Let me know what he thinks and also what you think as well. Keep it just between us and Blake until we've talked.'

On his way to Empire College, Ffolkes took out a hand-written letter from the package Peters had given him.

Dear Inspector Peters

Although I cannot tell you how, I know that your enquiries into at least one murder in London have led you to investigate the history and legends behind the ERECOT, believed to have been stolen from a statue reported to exist in Haranistan. I enclose an artefact that I hope will be of assistance to you. I can only describe it as a fake ERECOT.

Despite being a fake, it contains a genuine ruby, which makes it of considerable value. When you have completed your investigations would you please ensure it is donated to the family of Alice Adams, who have been some of the many victims of the power of the Eye of the Red-Eyed Cyclops of Thebes?

Please do not try to find me, because you will be wasting precious time and all your enquiries will come to dead ends. I cannot help you further, but wish you every success with your hunt for justice for the innocent victims of the ERECOT.

Concerned citizen

43 – 11th August 2005, Scotland Yard, London

Superintendent Forest was in his office with the door open when Peters arrived.

'Come in, Inspector Peters. George isn't it?'

'Yes sir.' Peters responded, feeling reassured by the warmth of the greeting.

'I apologise for the cloak and dagger stuff, George, but you were about to barge in on a rather delicate investigation. Can you tell me why you called Superintendent Gibson?'

'Of course, sir. We have the body of Charles Mancini, or at least most of it. He's the brother of William Mancini, the crime syndicate leader. Both live in Kent, so I was just going to advise Superintendent Gibson I was on his patch and see if he had any information that might help me.'

'Yes, I know about the Mancini brothers and you were right to make contact, but things are a bit tricky at the moment. We probably have the rest of your body. Are you missing a head and left hand?'

'Yes, sir.'

'Is that all?'

'Yes, sir.'

'Well, that's one good thing. There's a problem though. We're investigating

Superintendent Gibson for corruption relating to the Mancini gang. William Mancini received the head and left hand via a courier just over a week ago. He reported it to Gibson, who should be investigating the murder, but we think Mancini's told Gibson to leave it to him, which is probably why you haven't heard about it. I've arranged for the investigation to be transferred to you, since you have a valid interest and Gibson is overloaded anyway. Gibson knows, so you will both get a directive from AC Gordon confirming it. It's probably already in your inbox.'

'I understand, sir.'

'Good. As soon as you can, make an appointment to see Gibson and get all the details. He doesn't suspect anything of my investigation and I want to keep it that way. You can tell none of your team about this meeting. Not even our Norwegian colleague. I know you've got a lot of respect for him, which by all reports is justified, but I really don't want to air our dirty linen in public. Just say it was AC Gordon's secretary who called. Got that?'

'Yes, sir.'

'Fine, and good luck with the investigation.'

44 – 12th August 2005, Empire College, London

'Inspector Ffolkes, back so soon?'

Roberts' opening comment was confirmed to be friendly by the warm smile and firm handshake he gave Ffolkes before leading him to his study.

'And how may I help you this time?'

As the two men entered the study a third man stood up to greet them.

'I know you're going to see Simon Blake about your ERECOT, so we can go down to his lab when we're ready, but you also said on the phone that you were looking for more information about Haranistan. That's why I've asked Dr Max Fleet to join us. Max is our expert on Middle Eastern affairs.'

'Thank you, Professor, and thank you, Dr Fleet, for coming to help me as well. I will get straight to the point. Our investigations are all starting to revolve around Haranistan, so I need to understand more about the country to help piece things together. I have already obtained all the information I can from official Haranistan sources, but this appears to be very limited. I also suspect it has been written in a way intended to put Haranistan, and specifically its kings, in a good light, even if this is at the expense of historical accuracy. I was looking for a more independent view, which I'm sure I will get from you. I would like to be more specific, but regret that at the moment, I don't even know what I don't know.'

Roberts spoke first.

'In my view, Inspector Ffolkes, it's a wise man who admits to not knowing, especially when others might think he ought to know. I think Max will be able to lead you in the right direction, so over to you, Max.'

Fleet gave a wry smile, then began.

'I'm not surprised you're confused by Haranistan, Inspector Ffolkes. It's quite an enigma and definitely a product of its history and location. Haranistan is one of two countries comprising the island of Herenath, in the middle of the Red Sea. The Herendits, a chain of mountains, separates Haranistan from its neighbour, Ensharla, providing a natural border between the two countries, with the only land routes between them being where the mountains meet the coast. The mountains are impassable to all except experienced mountaineers. They've only ever been crossed once. That was in 1984, by a team led by an experienced American Mountaineer. In their heyday, the Greeks conquered the island and ran it until it established its freedom under Harani I in

AD205. I think Arnold has already explained that bit to you?'

'Yes he did, thank you'.

'The location of Herenath, in the middle of the Red Sea, means its culture has been influenced by both Arabia and Africa. Haranistan is closer to the Arabian side and picked up more of its influence. The descendants of Harani I, the Anshalari family, may have kept his name, but not his liberating ways. They started to collect wealth and became kings and absolute rulers of the country. They raided the African mainland for gold and slaves. It was the slaves who built the tomb of Harani XVI. Legend has it that the slaves were killed after the work was completed to ensure they did not reveal where it was. Latterly the wealth of Haranistan has come from its oil, which is on the western side of the vast Arabian oil fields. It's lucky there, because it is right on the edge of those fields. There is none in Ensharla, or to be precise, none has yet been discovered there.'

Fleet stopped for a moment, then added, 'Is this the information that you're looking for?'

'Certainly. The early history is very useful. How have things changed since then?'

'At the core, not a lot. Slavery was abolished some time back but the kings are still absolute monarchs and very rich as a result of the oil. The present monarch, King Harani Anshalari XLVI, is a traditionalist in most things, although he is seeking to improve the lot of women. He has abandoned his harem and settled for a single wife, although polygamy is still legal. He permits the education of girls in Haranistani schools and sponsors the education of bright students in Universities abroad. He also sponsors chairs in Oil Technology, at Imperial College, and Music, at Sussex. He will allow foreigners to live in Haranistan, providing they have work, particularly in the oil fields, but there is no tourism industry. Many, including his son Crown Prince Helini, regard this ban on tourism as a wasted opportunity.'

'What of religion and the law?'

'There is no state supported religion so Haranistanis are free to follow any religion or no religion as they wish. Consumption of alcohol and the smoking of tobacco and opium are legal, although the use of hard drugs like cocaine is not. The laws are again a mixture of Arabic and African seasoned with a Western influence. Capital punishment still exists for crimes like murder and trafficking of banned drugs, but public floggings and the removal of hands for stealing, although still on the statute books, were discontinued a long time ago. Since there is no state sponsored religion, the only legally recognised form of marriage is a contract witnessed by a state registered official and adultery is no longer a crime.'

'How about taxation?'

'Because the state owns the oil industry, it can fund most of government from oil revenues. There is income tax for higher earners. Luxury goods including yachts, private aircraft, cars over 1,000 cc engine capacity, alcohol and tobacco are taxed, but the average Haranistani worker pays little or no tax.'

Ffolkes pondered what he had heard and then realised an apparent inconsistency.

'Max, you said the Greeks conquered the Island of Herenath and then Anshalari took it from them to establish the Kingdom of Haranistan, but how and when did Herenath become split into two with the establishment of Ensharla?'

'An excellent question, Sven. You have exposed some lax terminology, which has become prevalent amongst scholars of the region. The Greeks only conquered the Arabian side up to the Herendits, because they assumed there to be nothing of value beyond it. The mountains were impenetrable, so they didn't bother to venture beyond them to Ensharla, which was the local name meaning, 'Unknown land'. In fact, we believe Harani I came from there and his family name of Anshalari is a corruption of 'Ensharli', which means 'one from the unknown land'. Later generations of his family raided Ensharla and the African mainland, bringing back slaves, gold and jewels. They tried to make Ensharla become Haranistani territory, with the intent that Haranistani nationals would run plantations using African slaves. They had some success, but there were constant slave revolts, which prevented them from obtaining effective control. It's a pity they didn't learn the lessons from their own history. They were having more success with direct raids on Africa, so abandoned attempts to control Ensharla and sealed the coastal land borders to prevent counter-attacks. It remained that way until the Great War, when Harani XLIII fled. This set up a power vacuum, which resulted in factional fighting and no effective government in Haranistan. The victorious powers of the Great War allowed Harani XLIII to return as King of Haranistan provided he agreed to exist peacefully with the independent state of Ensharla. This peace is guaranteed by the victorious powers in the Treaty of Versailles.'

45 – 12th August 2005, Empire College, London

Roberts took Ffolkes to Simon Blake's laboratory in the basement. This was a much different environment from Robert's office, designed for handling old objects and fragile documents in a clean environment. They were greeted by a small, round-faced man wearing a white lab-coat over an open-necked blue shirt, brown trousers and sandals.

'Inspector Ffolkes, I believe you have an interesting object for me. Professor Roberts tells me it's a copy of the ERECOT. I should like to make some three dimensional images of it if I may. I can then blow them up to extract as much information as possible. Will that be acceptable?'

'Of course, Dr Blake.'

Ffolkes handed him the eye he had obtained from Freddie Farquhar. Blake donned white cotton gloves before taking it. He examined it close up with a magnifying glass.

'Hmm. It's very old. Hand carved ivory, if I'm not mistaken. There are black markings on it. Looks like they were scratched into the ivory, then filled with a marking material. Could be animal charcoal bound with spirit gum. I don't recognise these hieroglyphics. Don't think they're Haranistani or a related language, so I'll need to work on that. Very interesting.'

He tested the screw mechanism, finding it to open easily, allowing him to remove the central red sphere.

'A nice piece of work. It's probably over a thousand years old and yet it opens smooth as silk. Amazing craftsmanship and something that belongs to a bygone era, I fear.'

Looking at the red piece inside, he observed, 'This looks like a piece of polished obsidian. Must have taken ages to do that. Even by ancient standards this piece would have taken a long time to make, yet the materials are cheap. Very interesting. Now let's take those 3D images, starting with the two pieces of the case and the glass separately and then the whole assembled piece.'

Blake put the glass into his scanner unit, input some data and set the machine in motion.

'This will take some time. Shall we have a coffee while we wait?'

'Most certainly, but before you take you gloves off, would you like to have a look at this?' Ffolkes produced the second ERECOT that had been sent to Peters.

'Two ERECOTs?' Blake observed, showing fake surprise. 'This *was* a cyclops, you know.' He sniggered at his own joke then examined the second eye in the same way he had the first.

'A much more modern piece. Machine-turned ivory and a polished ruby. Very nice. The ruby is much smaller than the polished obsidian of the other eye. I'm no jeweller, but I'm sure this is genuine and I reckon a ruby even of this size will be valuable. The hieroglyphics are completely different from the first eye. Could be Chinese, but I'm not sure. I'll take images of this one as well and get back to you as soon as I have anything to tell you.'

46 – 12th August 2005, Sidcup

William Mancini looked at Peters' card.

'Inspector G. P. Peters, Murder Squad, how may I help you?'

'Firstly, Mr Mancini, may I express my condolences on the loss of your brother.'

'Thank you, Inspector, but I'm sure you didn't come all this way just for that. I've already had a visit from Superintendent Gibson, who's investigating my brother's death.'

'Superintendent Gibson sends his regards, Mr Mancini. He has been asked to concentrate on other cases, so your brother's case has been transferred to me.'

'Has it indeed now, Inspector Peters. Have you apprehended his killer?'

'Not as yet, Mr Mancini, but we have located his body, which we hope to be able to release to you soon, so you can arrange a funeral.'

'Thank you again, Inspector. Is that all, because I have told Superintendent Gibson everything I know and I do have things to be getting on with.'

'Of course, Mr Mancini. If I can ask a couple of questions first. Your brother's body was found on a beach in Norway and we suspect it was thrown from a ship out in the North Sea, probably between two and four weeks ago. Were you aware of any plans your brother had which might have included a journey like that by ship? A cruise perhaps?'

'No, Inspector. I'm not aware of any business that would have taken Charles to sea in the direction of Norway. Also, as far as I know, he wasn't planning a holiday, but Charles was his own man, dealing with his end of the business largely independently of me, so I wouldn't necessarily know, especially if it was just a holiday. You could ask Mary, she might have planned something with him, but if that was the case then I'd expect her to have been with him.'

'Mary, sir?'

'His new girlfriend, Mary Stainsby.'

'Where might I find Mary Stainsby, please Mr Mancini?'

'You're in luck there, Inspector. She's been staying with us since we heard of Charles' death. She's taken it very badly. My daughter, Helen, has been looking after her.'

Mancini spoke on his house phone.

'She can see you in five minutes. Chin will come to collect you. Will that be all?'

'Just one final question, please? What part of your business did Charles run?'

'He looked after nightclubs and casinos.'

'Did that include collecting outstanding debts?'

'Of course, that's a vital part of the business.'

Chin arrived. He took Peters to see Mary Stainsby, who was having tea with Helen Mancini in a small dining room. Peters could see that she had been crying quite recently. She did not get up as Helen greeted him.

'Good afternoon, Inspector, will you have a cup of tea with us? Mary has agreed to see you, although the doctor has said she should rest. Please be gentle with her.'

'I understand, and yes please, tea would be very welcome.'

After Peters had greeted Mary and taken tea from Helen, he began his questions.

'Mary, can you please tell me when you last saw Charles?'

'It was Thursday, three weeks back. He was working in his office and said he had to go out for a bit, but he never returned.'

Peters checked his diary.

'That was 21st July. Would that be correct?'

'Yes, that would be right. I'd told him to be careful because of the bombings on the 7th.'

'Did he say where he was going?'

'No, but then again he never did, so that wasn't unusual. I was expecting him back for supper. Sometimes he gets delayed, but he always phones through to let cook know, so she can delay our meal. He never called so I was getting worried by eight, because supper was set for seven.'

'What did you do?'

'I asked around, but nobody knew anything, so I called William. He was out for the evening. Chin said he'd not be back till the morning, so to call then. I was getting really worried when William called next morning to check if he was back. I asked if I should call the police, but William said no, he would deal with it. He told me a week later that Charles was dead. He'd been murdered.'

Peters tried to be as gentle as he could with his next question.

'Do you know of anybody who might have wanted to harm Charles?'

Mary's faced changed as she appeared to go into a daze. She said nothing, but looked at Helen and then Chin. Peters could detect no response from either and was about to speak again when Mary spoke.

'Not somebody, Inspector…Something. It's that damned eye, ERECOT or whatever it's called. I should never have told him about it. It's cursed, that thing is.'

She was about to say more, but Helen

hugged her to prevent her from continuing.

'There, there, Mary. You mustn't distress yourself.' Turning to Peters she continued, 'She has this fixation about the ERECOT, but it's just a piece of jewellery, which is supposed to have come from some tomb in the Middle East. Chin, can you explain, because you know the details better than I do.'

Chin bowed, then began.

'Inspector, the Eye of the Red-eyed Cyclops of Thebes, the ERECOT, comes from the golden statue of the Cyclops that guards a king's tomb. It was supposed to have been recovered by Brian Farquhar, a member of an archaeological team undertaking a dig in 1917, and willed to his great nephew. Farquhar died recently, so Mr Charles was trying to purchase it for Miss Stainsby. She is a descendent of Sir Archibald Chase, who was the leader of the expedition. He was killed in a rock fall when the eye was found. Charles thought Miss Stainsby might like it as a keepsake, but the great nephew didn't want to sell it, so Mr Charles stopped trying to obtain it. That was the end of the matter, so there's no reason for him to have been cursed, but Miss Stainsby blames herself, because she told him about it.'

Mary tried to speak, but Helen spoke first.

'That's right, isn't it dear? You must stop

blaming yourself.' She hugged Mary, who started to cry.

'Inspector, you can see how upset she is. Can we stop now, please, so I can take her to lie down?'

Peters agreed, allowing the two of them to leave and Chin to show him out.

47 – 13th August 2005, Sidcup

Mike Chambers was feeling much happier visiting William Mancini at his home because, this time, he had some good news. William could tell this from the smile on Chambers' face. He began the conversation.

'Mike, has your boy at the Haranistani Embassy come up with the goods?'

'Yes, William, you can read me like a true poker player, can't you? He's given me a location and an explanation of how he solved it. Would you like me to talk you through it?'

'Are you convinced by it, Mike?

'It all makes logical sense.'

'That's not what I asked, Mike. Is it the right location?'

'It's in Haranistan and close by some old gemstone mines. This makes it a logical place to hide a hoard of gems.'

'That's still not an answer, Mike. Do you have misgivings?'

Chambers could detect annoyance in William's voice. He knew his answers had been equivocal and they had to be.

'I can't be sure, William. How could I be? All I can say is there's nothing to tell me it's not right. It's definitely worth following up.'

'What value are we putting on this?'

'Again difficult to say. We're talking top grade gems, mainly rubies and sapphires, plus some diamonds and lots of gold. If they could afford to place a three metre solid gold statue of the Cyclops just to guard the valuables *inside* the tomb and what was hidden is purported to be up to ten times as much, we could be talking anywhere between five and fifty million pounds. Let's be conservative and say ten million.'

'Alright, Mike, I'm interested. You're my ideas man. How do I manage to get a team to search for a hoard of gemstones and gold, in a foreign country, without arousing suspicion?'

'I'm glad you asked. I put it to our man at the embassy to see if he had any ideas. I even gave him a few winning bets to loosen his tongue. He's come up with something.'

'Which is?'

'The Haranistanis are thinking of reopening their gemstone mines. They've had surveys done. Reckon they can find more gem-bearing rocks using the latest technology. It makes exploration viable again, when it wasn't by just leaving things to chance. They're going to need Western technology to make it all viable.'

'But you know we don't have mining in our portfolio, Mike, so how does this help us?'

Chambers smiled, this time knowing he had the right answer.

'Infrastructure, William… Infrastructure is the key. They need a road built into the site and accommodation for their mineworkers. They're planning a whole new town there.'

'Now, you're talking, Mike. We've got those skills in spades… Literally.'

'Precisely, and we can look for the site while we're about it. Our man says we can negotiate a contract whereby we purchase the land and sell it back to the Haranistani government for an agreed price at the end of the deal. What we discover is then legally ours. There's another little bonus you might not want to tell everybody about. If we buy land in Haranistan then sell it back at a profit, we get a good source of clean money, which we've funded from our other, less reputable, businesses.'

'I like it, Mike. Let's set up a meeting with the Haranistanis.'

48 – 14th August 2005, Cheeton House, Devon

Chase recognised the number on his office phone.

'Julie, I'll take this one in the bedroom.'

He picked up the bedroom phone. 'It's been a long time. I'd almost given up on you.'

'Yes, sir, things went quiet for a while, but there has been movement recently. I've learned that Farquhar did not use the ERECOT to make Alice Adams' engagement ring, because it didn't contain a ruby.'

'What?' Chase shrieked down the phone, almost deafening his private detective. 'What the hell was it and come to that, how do you know?'

'Easy, boss, easy. Let's take things one at a time. The ERECOT was very old, but contained red obsidian in a hand-fashioned screw case made of ivory. Farquhar kept it as a curio, but handed it over to the police when they started investigating. They've taken it to Professor Roberts at Empire College.'

'That's handy. I know Roberts.'

'That's not all, though. The police received another eye from an anonymous source. This one's modern and an obvious fake, but it contains a genuine ruby.'

'That's strange. Who gives away a valuable

artefact, even if it is a fake?'

'The message with it asked that when the police had finished with it they should give it to the family of Alice Adams. Somebody with a guilty conscience perhaps? The police have taken that one to Empire College as well. There's one more thing. The ivory on both examples has black hieroglyphics on it.'

'Thank you. I'll talk to Professor Roberts. Please keep your ear to the ground for anything else.'

49 – 14th August 2005, Scotland Yard, London

Superintendent Forest was in his office with another man when Peters arrived. He beckoned Peters.

'Come in, Inspector Peters, this is getting to be a habit, but I'm really glad you called. This is Inspector Ian Gordon from the Serious Crime Squad. He'll explain the situation. Ian; George Peters. For reasons that will become obvious, nothing that's said here today may be revealed to anybody else without my prior authority.'

Gordon was the first to speak. 'I understand you're investigating the murder of Charles Mancini and also the disappearance of Lenny Clark, who was a known associate of the Mancini syndicate. I know the Super's already told you of our anti-corruption investigations, but that's only part of the story. We've been investigating the Mancini syndicate for some time and our investigations have reached a delicate stage. We know William Mancini was spooked when you took over the investigation of his brother's murder and we don't want to worry him further. We want you to continue your investigation, but I don't expect you to make much progress.'

Peters frowned, but Gordon continued

before he could speak.

'Please don't be offended. This is not a criticism of your ability. It's rather more the facts of the case. We know, but I cannot tell you how, that Charles Mancini was abducted, probably by a Triad gang, on or about 21st July and his head and hand were delivered to his brother a week later. The rest of him was not seen again until it was washed up on a Norwegian beach on 7th August. How long did the pathologist say he'd been in the water?'

Peters responded slowly, analysing the information he had just been given as he spoke.

'One to two weeks, which fits the timescale. It doesn't narrow the window of death any more, though. He died between 21st and 26th of July, with the body being thrown into the North Sea no earlier than 24th July. I'm saying 26th because it was the date that the courier company said it despatched the package from Aberdeen.'

'Seems right to me, George. Did the post-mortem give you any idea where he was kept before he was killed?'

Peters was unsure why Gordon was asking his questions, but decided to cooperate rather than antagonise anybody when he was the one seeking information.

'There was nothing on the clothes to indicate a specific type of location like a warehouse or ship's hold, so by negative inference probably in some form of normal accommodation.'

'Thanks, George. I asked in case there might be evidence of a location typically used by Triads, which there isn't. Also, the method of killing doesn't fit with them, so maybe Charles was handed over to somebody else.'

Superintendent Forest offered his analysis.

'Somebody who took him to the middle of the North Sea, killed him and bought his head and left hand back to Aberdeen. However, there is no evidence of his having been on an oil platform, which is an obvious possibility for the North Sea. He might have been, or he might have been taken by ship to somewhere with no witnesses when his body was dumped. Either way it's quite possible he was alive and well when he left the UK, although I'm sure he didn't leave voluntarily. Maybe your Norwegian friend still owns this one?'

'Are you asking me to drop my investigation, gentlemen?' Peters asked, desperately trying to hide his annoyance. This time it was Gordon who responded.

'No, George. No, far from it. I want you to carry on as if you hadn't been given this piece of information, but you might not want to spend too much time on Charles' last movements.

William Mancini must think you're doing everything you can, but not that you know anything you shouldn't about what Charles was getting up to.'

'I get that, of course, but what I need is to find a reason why Charles was killed. He must have done something crime syndicate related for his head to be sent to William. That has to be both a notification of retribution and a warning, unless you can think of another logical explanation?'

'No, George, I agree with you; hundred percent.'

'Can your team give me any ideas on what he did? I think he killed Lenny Clark, but I can't see that upsetting many people. Clark was a member of the Mancini syndicate, so if anybody was annoyed it would be William. Would William kill his own brother for disposing of low life like Clark? And if he did, would he go through the charade of sending Charles' head and hand to himself to put us off the scent? And there's another thing. Why cut off his left hand? That sounds like the punishment of a thief. Did Mancini steal something and if so, what?'

'That I don't know, George, but I will try to find out, because it'll be of use to my investigations as well. Will you leave it to me please, to ensure William Mancini is not alerted to our investigations? I'll tell you if I find anything, but only through this route.'

Forest interrupted. 'George, is there anything else you need, because I'm keen to keep the path clear for Ian's team. I'd also like to get our Norwegian friend repatriated, because I don't want him stumbling into anything he shouldn't through a lack of understanding. To be clear, you can tell him nothing of what you've heard today. It would be much better if he operated back in Norway with you feeding him only what it is safe for him to know.'

'I understand, sir. Inspector Ffolkes is a fine detective and thorough to boot. Probably too thorough for these circumstances, so it makes sense. I would like to know what happened to Clark, so we can give some closure on the murder of Alice Adams. Did the Mancinis kill him and if yes, why, and where's the body? Can you help with that, Ian?'

'We think he's dead. Probably killed by Charles Mancini or Mike Chambers, one of his more vicious henchmen. If he is, then the usual method of disposal is in concrete at one of their construction sites, but we can't follow that line for fear of compromising our investigation. We might be able to do something at the end of our operation, if we're successful, but not now. I'm sorry, but it's just too risky, especially solely to give closure on a case you have already solved and there is nobody to bring to trial.'

Peters was frustrated, but knew Ian Gordon was right. He would just have to wait and send Ffolkes home.

50 – 15th August 2005, Empire College, London

Roberts met Chase in the lobby of the Empire College building. He took him to his office.

'Henry, how lovely to see you. You should have told me you were coming. I'd have arranged lunch, but I'm busy today. Anyway what brings you to see me, as if I couldn't guess?'

'No problem with lunch, Arnold. This is just a fleeting visit to ask you about the ERECOT, or should I say ERECOTs? Have you got them?'

'No, Henry, but I have the next best thing.' Roberts moved to his computer. He brought up images of each.

'Here's the first. Very old with a beautifully hand-carved ivory case. It's got to be many hundreds of years old, yet it still works perfectly. Inside is obsidian. That's a form of ancient glass. But the best bit is that it has hieroglyphics on the case. None of us had any idea the ERECOT had writing on it.'

'What does it mean, Arnold?'

'We don't know, Henry. It's always been rumoured that only a fraction of Harani XVI's treasure was buried with him and the rest was hidden at a different location for fear of grave robbers. Nobody knows if this is true, and if it is then where that location is. According to the legends surrounding this burial, the secret was recorded somewhere in the grave, so the king could get to his treasure. But nobody knows what form it took, so maybe it's these hieroglyphics.'

'Can you decipher them, Arnold?'

'I can't. I've asked one of my experts to try, but so far he hasn't succeeded. All he can say is he thinks they're of African origin, which if true would put paid to our theory. I'll keep you informed of progress if you like.'

'Yes, please. What about the other eye?'

'That's really strange. It's smaller than the original is claimed to be and clearly modern. It's got a machine-turned ivory case and a genuine ruby, so it's worth a bit yet it was sent anonymously to the police.'

'Does it have hieroglyphics as well?'

'Yes, but they're modern Chinese numbers. The Arabic equivalents are: 313, 761, 221, 613, 13 and 25.'

'Do you know what they mean?'

'That's the sixty-four thousand dollar question, Henry. We haven't got a clue at the moment, but we are working on that as well.'

'So you have seen two ERECOTs and

neither of them had a pigeon-blood ruby, yet all the Haranistani government literature talks of the true eye having this ruby. Do we have two fakes, one ancient and one modern?'

'You tell me, Henry. Your guess is as good as mine. I think it's got the police stumped as well.'

51 – 10th October 2005, Haranistani Embassy, London

A secretary led William Mancini and the Head Salesman of the Mancini Construction Company into a large conference room situated at the top floor of the Haranistani Embassy building. It was precisely ten o'clock, the agreed time of the meeting. Mohammed was already in there looking out at the view over Regent's Park. His team were seated around the table. He opened the proceedings.

'Welcome gentlemen, I trust you had a pleasant journey. It is indeed a fine day, so let us hope it is one upon which we can make a fine deal. We have selected the Mancini Construction Company as our preferred supplier with whom we will contract for the building of the new town of Harani XLVI, in the Northern Region of Haranistan. This is dependent only on our being able to resolve all the issues each side has with the draft contract, which has been prepared by our team following input from yourselves. Mr Mancini can I ask you to set out any outstanding issues you have with this draft, please?'

'Thank you, Mr Mohammed. To save time we have prepared a document containing all our issues, which I have just passed around. I will read them out to you:

1. Land purchase and valuation: we would like to understand the basis of your valuation of 79,000,000 Haranistani crowns for the 5,000 hectare development site and check whether it includes the 25Km access road, estimated at 250 hectares.
2. Payment mechanisms: we are required to purchase the land up-front and sell the completed buildings and land back to the Haranistani government at a fixed price per unit, plus a final payment of 10% on completion of the last building, to re-purchase the remaining land. The total price is 350,000,000 Haranistani crowns. This would mean 35,000,000 Haranistani crowns would be retained until the end of contract. We request that this figure be amortised into the price of each building, with all the remaining land being included with the payment for the last building.
3. Use of a Haranistani workforce: we will need to bring in extensive

skills and expertise from the UK and other outside countries and are concerned that this clause might impede our ability to do this. Please would you clarify this requirement to state that it only applies to construction workers?

4. Force Majeure: we are pleased to commit to delivering to the timescale given in the contract, but require a Force Majeure clause to prevent us from being penalised for events beyond our control. As an example, wet weather is well known for impeding construction work.

5. Inflation: the period of this contract is 26 months, during which time we run the risk of inflation with a fixed price. Can you please include an indexation clause allowing us to increase prices by the level of inflation one and two years into the contract?

Mohammed gave his initial response after which followed suggestions and counter suggestions with each side taking time out to discuss them. It was nearly five o'clock before

Mohammed was able to conclude the discussions.

'Gentlemen, it has been a long, hard, but eventually very productive, day. I should like to thank Mr Mancini and his colleague for the constructive approach they have taken. I shall now read out the changes to the draft contract, which we have agreed today:

1. The agreed price for the 5,000 Hectare site for the new town of Harani XLVI will be 75,000,000 Haranistani crowns, payable in two instalments of 30,000,000 crowns on contact signature and 40,000,000 three months later. The remaining 5,000,000 crowns will be withheld by the Mancini Construction Company as payment for the construction of the road, which is to be completed within those three months. Should completion not be within three months then, following a grace period of two weeks, the second payment will increase by 100,000 crowns per week or part week of delay. The Haranistani government will retain title to the

land upon which the road is built, but the Mancini Company will be entitled to any minerals and mineral-bearing rock that is excavated in the process of building the road.

2. The Haranistani government will purchase buildings and the land they stand on at the revised pricing which we have agreed. There will be a final payment of 1,000,000 crowns for the purchase of all remaining land after all buildings have been completed. During the time of construction the Mancini Company will grant access across its land to Haranistani government officials for the purposes of inspection of works.

3. The Mancini Company may increase all outstanding charges after the first year anniversary of contract by the rate of inflation, subject to a limit of 5%.

4. The Mancini Company will purchase construction labour from the Haranistani government to a minimum of 30% of the contract value, less 75,000,000 crowns,

which represents the purchase of the land.

5. There will be a Force Majeure clause, which in deference to the requirement that the supplier must take complete responsibility for its delivery, shall only apply to adverse weather conditions preventing construction work taking place. It will apply on a day-for-day basis to the grace period for all buildings in the process of construction on days of inclement weather that reasonably prevent construction work taking place. This is the only provision allowed under Force Majeure, with all other events deemed to be under the control of the Mancini Company.

6. As an additional service, the Haranistani government will make available mining assessment of spoils to aid the Mancini Company as to whether it is viable to extract gemstones or other valuable minerals from the spoils. If Haranistani government assessment suggests that such processing is viable then it may

> undertake, at its own discretion and risk, extraction processes and pay the Mancini Company 50% of any profit made from selling the minerals and gems.

This is indeed a fine deal and on behalf of the Haranistani government, we look forward to a successful working relationship with the Mancini Company over the next twenty-six months.'

52 – 23rd December 2005, Docklands, London

'Where is everybody, William, the place is deserted.' Chambers asked after he had found his own way to Mancini's office in the headquarters of the Mancini Construction Company.

'It's Christmas, Mike. We've closed for two weeks from midday today, so I guess most of them are down the pub spending some of the bonuses that generous Uncle William here has given them.'

'Been a good year has it, William?'

'I should say so. We're forecasting a 20% profit on the deal with the Haranistanis, which will make for good year-end figures. But that's not all. We're buying the land from Haranistan at the start of the deal and selling it back to them, piece by piece, at a huge profit as we complete each of the buildings for the new town. Although the deal is in Haranistani crowns, they accepted six, £1 million cash payments to their embassy at five crowns to the pound, even though the spot rate this morning was 4.98. That allowed us to make more than 80% of the payment in dirty money now and be paid oodles of clean Haranistani crowns later. We can do the same with the second payment of forty million crowns due in February.'

Chambers felt some concern but decided not to say anything. There would be nothing to gain by spoiling Mancini's good mood on a matter with which he had had no involvement.

'Nice one', he responded, as he accepted a large glass of single malt.

'A quick snifter and just a little bit of business before we all break for Christmas. Have we heard any more from the chancer on Fence-Bay since we decided not to buy his, or is it her, ERECOT with translation services?'

'Oh yes, William, as I think you knew I had when I suggested we meet at a quiet location. At the time I didn't think of your head office as a quiet location, but now I understand. The ERECOT is now on offer for $100,000 as a straight purchase.'

'What's it really worth and can we make a profit on it if we bought it?'

'I'm working on that one, William. Could you use it as a sweetener to get another deal with the Haranistanis? You know the sort of thing, "English philanthropist finds lost ERECOT and returns it to its rightful owners. It's a gift to our great friends the Haranistani people, with whom we have worked co-operatively to enhance its infrastructure", says shy company director William Mancini. You might even get the Order of the Cyclops… Although I wouldn't hold your breath for a knighthood for services to export from a grateful Her Majesty's Government.'

'Stop blowing smoke, Mike. Although I do like the idea of a deal clincher.' Mancini smiled as he whimsically tossed over the idea in his mind.

'By the way, do we have any idea who's selling it?'

'I'm working on that too, William.'

'Alright, keep at it. I might pay fifty grand for it.'

53 – 5th March 2006, King Harani XLV Motorway, Haranistan

Crown Prince Helini's car was second in the line of royal cars following the king to the junction with the newly built motorway that led to the site being developed by the Mancini Construction Company. Ahead of him the lead car contained the king and his special guest for the opening of the motorway, William Mancini. In front of them were two security cars, with two more at the rear of the four car procession. Police motorcycle outriders were to either side of them. They were about five minutes away from the junction. Helini ensured that the panel to the driver's compartment was shut before turning to Mohammed, the only other passenger in his car.

'Feisal, do we really need all this security? Are we that unpopular with our people?'

'My understanding, sir, is no and no, yet our Chief of Security insists on it. It does put on a fine show for the world's press, which has to be good for the country. His Excellency King Harani XLVI, long may he reign, is seen as a prominent world leader, as indeed he is, being properly escorted as he performs his duty in opening this new motorway.'

Helini smiled. In private he had told Mohammed he could simply refer to his father as 'the king', but Mohammed had used the full and correct term expected of every Haranistani when speaking of their monarch. His purpose had been to reflect the majesty of the occasion, which in truth was just a chance to please the king with a royal ceremony.

'Are you preparing the press release, Feisal? If so then please don't forget the spirit of co-operation between Mancini Construction and our hard working Haranistani state workforce to complete this road on time.'

He hesitated and then with a rueful smile added, 'It was on time, wasn't it?'

Mohammed knew that the completion was, in reality, nearly three weeks behind schedule. He could have applied a 100,000 crown penalty from the relevant contract clause but had obtained Helini's agreement to waive it. In exchange, Mancini was funding the opening ceremony.

'Yes, sir. As you said, we co-operated fully with the Mancini Construction Company to ensure this road was completed at the time specified by the contract.'

'Nicely put, Feisal. And now to the opening ceremony. Let's hope my father is on form today and not too long winded. Is it just him who will speak?'

'I'm afraid not, sir. Mancini is going to

speak as well. He will say the first words then ask the king to do the honours. Once it's open we will drive as a cavalcade along the length of the motorway to the site of the new town of Harani XLVI. There will be a reception at the site of the new hotel at the other end. It will give our workers a chance to see their king and cheer him. And cheer you as well of course, sir.'

'Hmm, thanks, Feisal. If they really knew what was going on, it would just be me they'd cheer, but for now we'll let my father take the glory. Things will change soon enough.'

'Indeed they will, sir.'

54 – 5th March 2006, Site of the King Harani XLVI new town, Haranistan

Helini drank a whole pint of orange squash in one go.

'At last, Feisal. I thought I'd die of thirst. My father can certainly go on when he has an audience. It took nearly an hour to cut that damned tape. At least Mancini's speech was short and to the point.'

Mohammed too had drunk deeply from his glass, but was ready to reply.

'The king certainly gave us the full details of what had occurred in the process of getting this road built, sir.'

'Nicely put, Feisal. Now we must move on to the next phase. Have we received the full seventy million for the land yet?'

'Yes sir, the majority of it in sterling cash. We have had to be a little careful not to cause questions on the money markets, but I've been able to use the additional influx of British engineers as a reason for our higher than usual levels of sterling. That, plus using it to fund our embassy in the UK, and holding back the Crowns here in Haranistan, should avoid suspicion. We used the retained money to build up our stock of dollars, euros and gold. We are still holding quite a lot of sterling cash in the

Royal Bank of Haranistan, but that is not known to the money markets, so should not be an issue and it will reduce over time.'

'Good, when do we have to make our first payment to Mancini?'

'If everything is on time, a payment of fifty-five million crowns will be due in six weeks, sir. That's when the hotel is completed and handed over to us. The road has already been paid for by the retention of a payment on the land, so there's nothing now. We agreed with Mancini he would be paid in sterling from the Royal Bank of Haranistan. At the going exchange rate of course.'

'So it's time for our next move?'

'Yes, sir. Our bank has already starting printing money. The presses have been running twenty-four, seven for the last two weeks. At midday today the Crown was down 5% against the dollar on what it was when Mancini paid us and we started printing. By the time it comes to paying our first bill it should have fallen 20 to 25%.'

'So Mancini will only get a payment of about four million pounds, instead of the five point five million he was expecting. How upsetting for the poor man.'

'Yes, sir, but looking on the bright side, he will have done better out of the hotel than he will for the remainder of the contract, when the Crown will have fallen to about 50% of what it was last month.'

'That's a nice way of putting it, Feisal. My concern is what the impact will be on our own people? I don't want riots on my hands.'

'I understand, sir. All our oil revenue is received in dollars, so we will get more Crowns per barrel, which will permit us to increase wages. So working Haranistanis will not suffer. The rich will have to pay more for their big cars, including more tax, which will be good for our exchequer. I propose we cut the purchase tax on cars with engines of between one and two litres to stabilise their prices for lower income Haranistanis. Of course there is no tax on cars less than one litre although their prices will rise, but most will have received pay rises to cope with it.'

'Agreed, Feisal. Will any other Haranistanis suffer?'

'There might be the odd glitch, sir, before salaries adjust to inflation. We will ensure that our construction workers get pay rises, so they don't interrupt the new city building programme, but I cannot speak for the private sector, for example in the docks, where there might be some unrest resulting in industrial action. That might impact the import of construction material for the new city.'

'Oh, dear. Do you think it could cause delays to the programme which will need us to invoke penalty payments?'

'It's your decision, of course, sir. You have shown great generosity by waiving penalties for the lateness of the road. I would counsel against doing so again for fear that Mancini might think he can take advantage of us.'

'Wise counsel, Feisal. It would never do for him to think we're a soft touch. Please see to it that penalty charges are always invoked for any future lateness, although it will mean increased Mancini losses on this contract. Please tell me there is nothing else that will have a negative impact on the poor man's company?'

'I'm afraid there is, sir. All their expenses in Haranistan, like hotel bills, will go up significantly, in Crowns that is, although this will be offset by their getting more Crowns to the pound. It's such a pity they didn't ask us to pay for the contract in pounds, euros or dollars rather than Crowns, but I'm sure they'll have been wise enough to sell Crowns ahead to protect against just this sort of incident.'

'It's not our business of course, but I'm sure you're right, Feisal. They will have thought of it. After all the Crown has never moved more than a couple of cents either way against the dollar for the last twenty years.' Helini face broke into a rueful smile as he thought of how this news would be greeted in the Mancini boardroom.

'Are we sure this contract will break Mancini financially?'

'I think we can say that with some confidence, sir.'

'Oh, I almost forgot; have they found our little treasure trove yet?'

'Not yet, sir. That's located where the last building, the residential block for the miners, will be sited. We don't want them finding it too early and losing interest. This way we'll know they have built the foundations properly. Nice and deep that is.'

'What about the spoil. Anything promising for them to recoup any losses there or to give us clues as to where we should start mining?'

'Nothing from the road, sir, but then again we didn't expect anything in that area. The best places are close to the mountains, where the buildings are being located.'

'Fine, we can discuss the next phase of our plan in the car on the way home.'

55 – 30th March 2006, Mancini Construction Offices, Docklands, London

William Mancini passed Chambers a drink before he started their meeting.

'Mike, to what do I owe the pleasure of this visit?'

'It's the ERECOT again, William. I've found out who's selling it.'

'Really, who?'

'For the moment, can I just say it's a source inside Haranistan and that they have agreed to your price of £50K?'

'Sounds good. How will we arrange the transaction?'

'I'll deal with that in a minute, but it gets better.'

'Better… how?'

'I know how they intend to bring it into the country. I'll arrange for a little light-fingered friend of mine to lift it for you. She'll do it for a grand.'

'OK, if that's really what's going to happen; what are we going to tell the seller is going to happen?'

'We'll say that we'll pay on delivery in a crowded location to avoid any suspicion of foul play. We'll send them a video of us putting fifty grand into a briefcase and locking it in a left luggage location at Waterloo station, six hours before their rep hands over the eye to me and I confirm it's genuine. They'll know where it is so they can watch it all the time if they feel so inclined. When I get the eye, I'll give them the key.'

'How do you give them the key and stop them getting my fifty grand?'

'Easy, by the time we meet, my little thief will already have the eye, so they won't be able to give it to me. No eye, no key, no money.'

'What if they send a team to mug you?'

'William, I'm flattered by your concern for my health, but did you really believe I'd go alone. I'm sure you won't mind lending me a couple of your excellent heavies for the occasion.'

'Do you mean my personal security staff, who are fully vetted, law abiding staff on my payroll? Alright, since it's you. Make sure nothing goes wrong, because I'm holding you personally responsible for this operation, Mike.'

'Understood, William.'

56 – 2nd April 2006, Westminster, UK

Chase sat nervously waiting to be called in by Howard Devereux, the Secretary of State for Defence. It was his second week as a Junior Defence Minister after a spell in the Whip's Office. A Civil Servant invited him to come into the meeting room. Devereux was there with the Prime Minister.

'How's it going, Henry? A bit different from whipping, I imagine?'

'Fine thank you, Howard. Things are coming into place nicely.' He was lying. He was struggling and he knew it, but hoped his audience did not.

'That's good because the PM and I have got something special, which we think will be right up your street. As you know, we retired two Type 42 Destroyers, HMSs Glasgow and Newcastle, from the fleet last year. It's time to sell them and we want the best price possible, but they have to go to a friendly power. We can't afford any backlash. There has been interest from Australia, Haranistan and Peru. The Australians want both and are obviously our best bet, but they're only prepared to pay six million each, whereas the Peruvians will pay ten, but that's just too risky at the moment. Haranistan would be acceptable, but it has indicated it would only go to seven and may only buy one. We would like more, ideally eight if we can get it, and we want to sell both of them. They don't know we won't sell them to Peru. We want you to take charge of the sales and get the best price you can. I must emphasise, we can't be seen to be bribing anybody. Is that clear?'

'Perfectly, Howard, I'll get to it.'

57 – 2nd April 2006, Belgravia, UK

'How in heaven's name are you going to get Haranistan to pay sixteen million for those ships?' Felicity Chase asked her husband over supper in their London flat. She knew he was capable of thinking up creative ways to make things happen, but this would be a tall order. Sir Henry knew it would be difficult as well.

'I do have one idea.'

'Pray tell, husband dear.'

'The ERECOT.'

'What, the eye your great grandfather's team was thought to have found before the collapse of the chamber killed him? The one that little weasel Farquhar was supposed to have possessed but never admitted it? The one that came to light after his death?'

'That's the one. I'm sure the Haranistanis would look very kindly on anybody or any country able to return it to them?'

'But I thought it was shown to be a worthless fake?'

'Not necessarily either a fake or worthless, but not the true eye either way. However, somebody has come up on Fence-bay claiming to have the original and is prepared to sell it for £100,000.'

'Fence-bay?'

'It's a sort of criminal e-Bay, where you can buy stolen goods.'

'How the hell do you know these things?'

'You learn a lot of interesting things in the Whip's office, my dear, including how to recover stolen property that might embarrass a colleague. In our party of course.'

'But neither you nor Her Majesty's Government can be seen to buy stolen goods. So what use is that?'

'We can't, but MI5 can.'

'But you'll still need to prove it's genuine... And have a cover story.'

'Right in both cases, my dear. But remember, I'm the great grandson of Sir Archibald Chase. I would dearly love to return the true eye to Haranistan as part of a celebration to mark the ninetieth anniversary of his expedition in 1917. I could offer a reward for information leading to the recovery and safe return to Haranistan of the true eye.'

'How will you know if it's genuine?'

'I'll ask my friend Professor Arnold Roberts to confirm it. He has contacts in Haranistan. I'm sure between them they can decide if it's genuine. Even if it's not, it doesn't matter provided the Haranistanis *believe* it is. We get it back to them and a grateful Haranistan buys our warships for sixteen million, or thereabouts.'

'Can you really tie the return of the eye to the purchase of our ships?'

'Of course not. But I can show them that if they don't buy our ships then the eye will go to a private purchaser who will put it in a vault somewhere. Then they'll never get it back. It might work... Why, have you got any better ideas?'

58 – 20th April 2006, Crown Prince's palace, Haranibad, Haranistan

Helini held the object up to the light.

'This is a fine piece of work, Feisal. Who made it?'

'Our Crown Jewellers, here in Haranistan, sir. With our gemstone industry, they have some of the finest craftsmen in the world. They have made royal crowns, tiaras and rings for over four centuries.'

'How did they do it so quickly?'

'When the king first conceived the idea of putting it about that the ERECOT had been stolen, he ordered a cover story to make the whole thing believable. This included newspaper and television articles on how our excellent jewellers made a fitting replacement. There were drawings and artists mock-up as well. They even purchased some of the raw materials, including an old piece of ivory. All we had to do was complete the job.'

'What about the ruby? It looks magnificent. Where did it come from?'

'From our own mines, sir. It too was held back as part of the deception. It has an unusual shape that allowed us to polish one end to give a large flattish, round surface to act as the surface of the eyeball. The remainder is much smaller, with flaws. But you can't see them because they are held inside the setting. It's of lower weight and quality than the pigeon-blood ruby in the original, but still gives a quite remarkable effect.'

'Indeed it does. And the ivory case is hand turned from an old piece. Excellent workmanship. Must have been a highly delicate operation. Where did we find the skills to make it?'

'From our dental college, sir. They're used to working in ivory and often set the students competition tasks to improve their skills. One of the leading trainers made it.'

'Very nice. How much is it worth?'

'As a known fake, with this known precedence, skills and materials, and the right level of buyer interest, between forty and fifty thousand dollars at auction. Could be more. If it were believed to be genuine and the sale was a legitimate action by our government, it's almost priceless. It could fetch five million dollars. On the black market, to go to a collector who could never display it or admit ownership of it, probably about half a million.'

'What are we asking for it?'

'£100,000, sir'

'Isn't that a bit cheap?'

'Probably, sir. But it's not about the price, is it? It has to be believable, but we want him to be interested so we can deliver our surprise package with it.'

'Fair point, Feisal. How are we going to deliver the surprise?'

'In a briefcase, sir, timed for maximum effect.'

'Won't they be able to detect it?'

'Chief says he's thought of that, so I'm trusting him. He'll also have a backup method using one of his agents.'

'OK, Feisal. Please explain to the Chief that he is to take full control of this mission. I will hold him personally responsible for its success. No excuses will be accepted.'

59 – 27th April 2006, Crown Prince's palace, Haranibad, Haranistan

Maisie Jennings was reading in one of the harem lounges when Carol Anderson came in.

'He wants you tonight, so you'd better prepare yourself. You are clean, aren't you?' Anderson's tone was matter of fact, although the news came as a complete surprise to Maisie. For two years after her first encounter she had been a firm favourite with the prince, but her star had been waning and she had not been called for over a year. Other girls had come and gone and she had got used to an easy, celibate life, including being a mentor to the younger girls, helping them in the way Anderson had helped her.

'But he hasn't called me for over a year, so why now?'

'Am I suddenly a mind-reader, Maisie? How would I know why he wants you all of a sudden? But we can guess it will involve your smelling very sweet and wearing some nice see-through clothes, which will get removed fairly quickly. Now, as I said, are you clean?'

'Yes.'

'Well, you'd better start getting ready then. You've got an hour.'

60 – 27th April 2006, Crown Prince's palace, Haranibad, Haranistan

Maisie found herself in front of the prince dressed in her normal outfit of see through silk veil, top, trousers and knickers, which were removed in the time-honoured fashion leaving her alone with the prince and standing naked in front of him. She was expecting him to take her across to the bed and to right royally shag her as she described it to herself. To her surprise he did not. Instead he produced a white spherical object about 3.5 centimetres in diameter with what looked like a large ruby set into it. It resembled some strange form of eye.

'Put this inside you and walk around the room.'

Maisie could not believe what she was hearing. What was this? Was he getting kinky in his old age? She knew better than to ask why, obeying the instruction as given.

'Now walk around the room.'

She obeyed, making several laps of the area in front of him such that he could see her at all times.

'How does it feel; could you keep it inside you for a long period of time, without it showing?'

Maisie had not had to talk to the prince

before, so she was unsure how much she should say to him. Anderson had not advised her on conversation because, most of the time, there wasn't any. She decided that the truth, delivered with due modesty, would be right.

'It's a bit sharp, sir, but other than that, there should be no problem. I could probably put something over the sharp bit and then it would be fine.' She thought her response had come out right.

'I'll get some sealing wax put over the ruby.' The prince replied. He hesitated before continuing.

'Maisie, you have behaved well while you've been here and I've enjoyed your company, so I have decided to reward you. I am going to send you on a trip to London.' Maisie had learned not to show her emotions, although the thought of getting away from the mind-numbing boredom of the harem and going to London really excited her.

'I want you to take that eye to London and ensure it gets there without any trouble at Customs. You will deliver it to my contact along with a briefcase that you'll pick up when you get there. I will give you the number and a code for a left luggage locker at Waterloo. It will be much safer if the object is brought into the UK by a Briton, so you will travel under your own name.

We will get you your passport. You will have to write to the Passport Office saying you've lost your birth certificate. We'll post your application from England and provide the references you'll require. You will travel to Riyadh as one of my wives and from there we will take you on a day trip to Abu Dhabi, where one of my men will meet you. From there you will both fly to Paris and then take the train to London. The contact will take you to the delivery point. Once you have made your delivery we will meet up at my apartment in Bayswater. The contact will watch you make the delivery and then take you there. If you do this successfully I will set you up with a flat in England and let you go. Would you like that?'

Maisie was staggered by what she had just heard. She wanted to hug him on the spot, but remembered Anderson's words.

'Thank you, sir, I should very much like that.'

Their meeting ended with the right royal shagging Maisie had expected in the first place.

61 – 29th April 2006, Police Headquarters, Oslo

Ffolkes was feeling uneasy. He hated the idea of being called to a meeting with Commander Magnussen when he did not know the reason for it. Things had been quiet since his return from London, so maybe something else had come up, but if that was the case he would normally just get a phone call. There was no point in speculating, he just had to go and find out.

'Come in, Sven, shut the door and please take a seat.'

'Thank you, sir, how can I be of service today?'

'Sven, you will recall you asked me if I could arrange for you to visit Haranistan and be granted access to the secret location of the tomb of King Harani XVI. You said you wanted to check out something called, what was it? Yes, the ERECOT, so you could help our British colleagues with a couple of their murders and our body on the Lofoten Islands?'

'Yes, sir, I know it was a strange request, but it would have helped. It might still help, but I assumed you'd had no luck.'

'Well, Sven, actually I have, but thing are a bit more complex. Can you arrange for somebody to feed your cat?'

Ffolkes smiled. It had become a bit of a standing joke between them. The Commander, like Ffolkes, was very fond of cats and 'arrange for somebody to feed your cat' meant, 'I'm sending you on a mission, usually abroad, and I'm not sure when you will get back.'

'When do I go, sir?'

'Tomorrow, Sven, but don't be too hasty. I need to explain a few things first.'

'Sorry, sir, please go on.'

'The Haranistanis have granted your request. I think our king's friendship with Crown Prince Helini helped. Anyway, it's all sorted. Here's a letter of introduction from our king, which you may show to Haranistani officials but may only give up to the Crown Prince or King Harani himself.'

Ffolkes did not know what to say. Was the visit really still important now? The case had gone nowhere since he left England and he knew George Peters was busy on other work. He could not say this after all the work that must have occurred behind the scenes to get this visit arranged, so he decided to appear grateful and go ahead.

'What I have just told you, Sven, is the official purpose of your visit, but there is more to it. When you arrive in Haranibad you will be taken straight to our embassy, where you will be briefed by our ambassador. Don't bother asking me about this bit, because I don't know the answer. They won't tell me, which made me instantly suspicious, but I cannot argue when decisions come from as high up as this one did. What I do know is that you are going to be issued with a diplomatic passport, which you will carry in addition to your current Norwegian passport and your warrant card.'

'Two passports. Isn't that a bit strange, sir?'

'More than a bit, Sven. The instructions are to use your normal passport unless the situation demands otherwise. If needed, you are an attaché working out of our Embassy, who is there to assist the Haranistani Department of Home Affairs on security and policing. You've probably already guessed, but it's Crown Prince Helini who's in charge of that department. His top man is a guy called Feisal Mohammed. I imagine one or other of them will make contact with you, but you shouldn't make the first move. If you have no more questions, I'll wish you good luck and let you pack. My secretary has your tickets and diplomatic passport.'

62 – 30th April 2006, Haranibad, Haranistan

As the Norwegian Royal Airways HS748 touched down at Haranistan's King Harani XLV International Airport, Ffolkes thought back on what had been a long, albeit very comfortable, journey. As a diplomat he had travelled first class to Cairo from whence this jet had taken him, plus two other diplomats, on the final leg of the journey. All three sped through Immigration and Customs, and were whisked into a waiting, diplomatically registered, car for the short trip to the embassy. It was already after six by the time Ffolkes was taken to his room by an embassy porter.

'Dinner is at seven-thirty tonight, Mr Ffolkes. It's just the ambassador, our head of security and you tonight, sir. The ambassador's family are on a short holiday back in Norway. The ambassador requests you do not leave the embassy compound this evening.'

Having given this message, the porter left Ffolkes to prepare.

63 – 30th April 2006, Norwegian Embassy, Haranibad, Haranistan

The first course passed with only small talk between the three men and they were well into their main course before the ambassador played Grieg on a sound system. It filled the room as he spoke, softly. Ffolkes strained to hear his words.

'Sven, your appointment with His Excellency King Harani XLVI is set for ten tomorrow. One of our cars will take you from here at nine-thirty. Please take your diplomatic passport. Tomorrow you will be one of our experts on systems for the security of property, whom we have offered to Haranistan as a gesture of goodwill. We've told the king that our intelligence suggests the ERECOT is the target of a gang of jewel thieves who believe the original was recovered and is back where it belongs within the gold statue of the Cyclops; the RECOT I think it's called. The king is adamant the present ERECOT is only a copy, but even that is of great worth. Also, there are many other items of high value in the tomb, so he's greatly concerned by all this. He's accepted our offer of help to add modern security systems, just in case the true location is discovered. He will allow one trusted representative, that's you, to view the site, take measurements and even to photograph what you need to. With this information we can tender for a system from some of the leading security companies. I've asked our security expert to be here tonight to give you a briefing on what to say and the questions to ask. You can do that after dinner. Is this alright and are there any questions for me?'

'It's fine, sir and thank you for all the effort that you, and many others I'm sure, have put in to make this visit happen. Do we know if they will actually show me the tomb and if yes, then who will escort me?'

'I know the king will meet you and they have said you will get a tour of the tomb. Whether he will take you there personally or not, I don't know. We understand he's been in poor health recently, so he might not accompany you.'

64 – 30th April 2006, Saudi Arabia

Maisie was delighted to be wearing western clothes, even if they were hidden under a burka. The eye, coated completely in sealing wax, was nestled safely inside her, making the journey quite stimulating.

"Now, when I wouldn't mind a shag from the bastard, he's nowhere to be seen, but things have to be getting better", she mused to herself. She would not have dared to share those thoughts with her travelling companions, who were the prince's three Haranistani wives. They were already very upset about having to travel with a concubine and pointedly refused to recognise her presence, let alone speak to her. Instead they prattled away with each other in Arabic to ensure she didn't understand what they were talking about. As if she would have cared anyway. They only tolerated her presence because the prince had commanded it.

The party had travelled in the prince's private jet, late the previous evening, from Haranistan to Riyadh, passing smoothly through immigration since the prince's family enjoyed diplomatic protection there. The next leg of the trip was in an air-conditioned luxury bus across the border to the Emirates, where the wives were to be taken on a shopping trip in Abu Dhabi.

Maisie had been told that the bus would stop for a meal break where she was instructed to stay on it until the other wives had left. She was then to leave her burka in the toilet of the bus and go into the service station as a western tourist, where she would be met by a contact who would take her to the airport. Because the Emiratis were far more relaxed about dress for women, she was able to wear a short skirt and tee-shirt, which made her feel much more comfortable in the heat.

She went into the service station building, and immediately headed for the shops. The prince had provided her with credit cards and some cash in dollars. She hardly had time to finish her shopping before she felt her arm being grabbed and heard a voice she thought she recognised.

'Hello, Maisie, it's been a long time. Your car awaits you.'

She turned to the voice and recognised its owner immediately. Her heart sank.

'Mike Chambers. Well, I had hoped the next time we met was because somebody had asked me to identify your body on a mortuary slab.'

'Come on now, Maisie, that's not nice. I took you from the slums of Luton to a life of luxury, so I did you a favour and you should be grateful to me. Look, by way of example, I have this luxury Mercedes for you to travel in and if you promise to behave I'll let you ride in the passenger seat next to me, rather than tied up in the boot.'

She wanted to kick him in the groin, steal his car keys and escape, but sense prevailed. She didn't know how to drive and only had a couple of hundred dollars on her. They would soon be used up, then she would have to use her credit cards and risk being tracked by the prince's henchmen. Her mind went back to the video Anderson had shown her. Such a silly trick would almost certainly end with her receiving the same fate.

'I'll behave', she responded grudgingly as she settled herself into the luxury white leather seat. Chambers pulled the seat belt across her, secured it and then removed a small key, which he placed in his left pocket.

'There you are, Maisie, nice and secure.'

'Charming. Then, you'd better drive carefully, because I don't want to be burnt to death in a car I can't get out of, with you already dead beside me. I don't mind being cremated, but I want that to happen *after* I die.'

'For you, Maisie, I'll be caution personified. I wouldn't expect much in the way of thanks if I returned damaged goods to our dear Crown

Prince, anyway.'

As they pulled away from the service station, the air conditioning brought the temperature right down allowing her to enjoy the luxury of the ride to the airport, although a little voice inside her head said something was wrong.

'So are we going to Abu Dhabi as planned or do you have more surprises for me?'

'You know me too well, Maisie. Yes, I have a surprise for you, but it's a pleasant one. We have an overnight stay in Dubai and if you remain a good girl there'll be sightseeing and dinner as well. The Crown Prince is paying so we can push the boat out a bit tonight. I can't promise the same luxury for the whole trip, so you might as well enjoy yourself.'

Maisie agreed. She knew she had to bide her time.

65 – 30th April 2006, Haranibad, Haranistan

Ffolkes sat back after the security briefing. He would not have believed what he had just heard had it not been for the fact he had a letter to prove it. The security officer swirled his cognac around the bowl of his glass before taking a large gulp. Ffolkes thought he had finished but he spoke again.

'In our experience, this sort of thing doesn't often go without hitches and sometimes they fall apart completely.'

"That's not very reassuring", Ffolkes mused, but said nothing, waiting for the security officer to continue.

'If things don't go to plan, it's always best to have somebody you know you can trust to act as a backup, so we've arranged someone for you.'

'I'm not sure if I should be happier knowing I have backup or more worried by knowing things can go wrong.'

'Fair point, but if you think about it, the fact that things could go wrong is always there, so you should be no more worried than you were. And you should be happier because we are putting backup in place.'

'How will I recognise my backup?'

'That's what we must decide now. Give me a fact about you that few people know. If you hear it from somebody then you know you can trust them.'

Ffolkes thought hard.

'I have a cat called Ignatius. I named him that because it means fiery one and he's certainly has his fiery moments.'

'Perfect. Ignatius; fiery one. Let's hope it won't be necessary.'

'I'll drink to that.'

66 – 30th April 2006, Crown Prince Helini's Yacht, Haranibad Harbour, Haranistan

Mohammed was feeling very nervous as he walked down the gangplank of the Crown Prince's yacht. They were almost at the end of months of planning. He was shown into the lounge where the Crown Prince was pacing nervously back and forth. Wagner was playing loudly over the ship's system.

'Come in, Feisal. Sit down.'

Mohammed sat on the edge of a settee. Helini poured two neat cognacs, passing one to Mohammed.

'I think this is required, Feisal, so please don't decline it.'

Thanking the prince, Mohammed took the drink from him. They said nothing but touched glasses before both drained their drinks.

'Is everything in place?'

'Yes, sir. We are just awaiting the timing from you.'

'Fine. As you know, officially I'm on holiday, sailing tomorrow for a cruise ending up in the United Kingdom. If it all goes wrong and it looks like we're going to be arrested then we'll sail to safety. You will stay on board with me tonight and until it's all happened. You have brought your passport and visas with you, haven't you?'

'Yes, sir. When will it all happen?'

'Tanks will be put on to the streets of Haranibad and all other major cities from 11:00 am. The police will close all banks and public buildings. An announcement will be made at midday including an instruction to everybody to be off the streets by 1pm, when a curfew will start. All access to ports and airports will be closed at 11:00am, but international flights due out before 1:00 pm will be allowed to leave. If all goes well we should be able to lift the curfew by eight.'

'You should set sail at nine tomorrow for your holiday, as planned, sir. For the sake of normality, I will leave this yacht tomorrow morning and go to work as usual. If anything goes wrong you will be clear of our territorial waters and safe by eleven. If it goes as planned you can sail back in after eight to adulation from your new subjects… I can arrange that, but please, do *not* come back until you have had confirmation from me. If I don't call, you'll know there's trouble, but they'll not know you have been warned. You can sail on to the United Kingdom and do your best from there.'

'I agree, Feisal, using that method means my safety is assured, but what will happen to you if it goes wrong? How will *you* escape?'

'Don't worry about me, sir. I have a launch hidden on the coast. I should be able to get to you with it, but if not, then I am just a junior government official who does what he is told.'

'Yes, Feisal. Sounds convincing… I think. On the other matter, have you cleared everything with the Norwegians?'

'Yes sir. Their man will be with the king and queen tomorrow morning.'

'Then let's have one more as a nightcap and then get an early night.'

'Good idea, sir.'

67 – 30th April 2006, Crown Prince Helini's Yacht, Haranibad Harbour, Haranistan

She was already waiting for him in his cabin when Mohammed entered.

'Is he wetting himself?'

'Let's just say he's nervous, but not as much as I am. If it goes wrong he'll just sail away. I'll be executed.'

'Then you'd better make sure it doesn't. You're no use to me dead. You've made me promises in case you'd forgotten.'

'How could I forget? I'll make it official at the first opportunity.'

'That's a nice thought, but we have to get over tomorrow first. On another matter, do you have it?'

'Yes. Here it is.' She handed him a small package. He looked at it, then handed it back to her.

'Did you know we've had some more interest in the UK? We said the price was £100,000 and they didn't baulk. All we have to do is satisfy their experts it's genuine.'

'And how do we propose to do that?'

'There's the interesting bit. We have been asked, via a Professor Arnold Roberts, of Empire College, if we could provide an expert. I thought I'd send our Chief Crown Jeweller.'

'You mean you are going to send the guy who made it to tell the buyer it's genuine? I like it.'

'It's an excellent piece of work and well worth the money, so why not? On another point though, how will you deceive her?'

'Don't worry about her, I've got it sorted.'

'What would I do without you?'

'Go celibate, I hope. Now come to bed. Don't worry about him. He's got his favourite girls tonight, both of them, so he's going to be busy.'

68 – 30th April 2006, Dubai

It had been a long but unadventurous drive to Dubai. Maisie behaved all the way, so Chambers had rewarded her with a shopping trip in the Mall of the Emirates. Although he had a small case, with a few clothes for her in it, things would look much better if they turned up with several expensive suitcases and both appropriately dressed for one of the best hotels in Dubai. Even though the Emiratis were very tolerant, a tee-shirt and mini skirt would not have been right for this hotel. He had persuaded her to buy an expensive day dress, even though she complained that it made her look forty and did he have an older-woman fixation he wanted her to play out.

The bribe of a very expensive and virtually non-existent bikini had sealed the bargain. When the prince was paying, anything was allowed and he did not question it if he got what he wanted, which was for Maisie to deliver the ERECOT and a briefcase to William Mancini. That was precisely what he was there to make her do. Nothing else mattered. The fact that both Mancini and the Crown Prince were paying him was a bonus as long as both wanted the same thing, and in this case at least both thought they did.

He and Maisie had also come to an arrangement, which would ensure she could not escape, in exchange for him allowing her limited freedom of movement. All she had to do was to remain within his sight. She had placed the ERECOT in the hotel room safe and locked it with a combination only she knew. He made her take it out in front of him and accepted it was genuine even though it was covered in sealing wax, because, as she had put it, 'Do you think I'd have carried this thing in my fanny for the last twenty-four hours unless it was the genuine thing? Well, do you? Also I have stripped in front of you, so you know I've nowhere to hide anything. You can look up my arse if you're still not sure.'

He had declined that offer, replying, 'Maisie, my dear, of course I trust you.'

He didn't and never would, because he knew what he had done to her, but failing to deliver the ERECOT was just as great a risk for her as it was for him. And she knew it. She also knew she was close to freedom, so why would she take risks now?

69 – 30th April 2006, Dubai

Maisie was in the shower when Chambers made a call.

'You wanted me to call.'

'Yes, things have changed.'

The voice at the other end sounded different; more assertive maybe, but it was definitely him.

'How, precisely?'

'You're to delay your departure from Paris for a week. You should arrive in London on the eighth. Where are you now?'

'Dubai of course, as we agreed.'

'Then stay there, but pay cash. I've arranged for $10,000 to be put into your account. Do not use his cards. If you already have then check out and move to a different hotel. I don't want any trace of him attached to you or her.'

'Fortunately I haven't, but why no trace of him; what's going on?'

'It's complex.'

'I do complex. That's my job. I deal with complex all the time. Tell me what's happening.'

'Later perhaps but not now. There's one more change of plan. Tell her not to take the briefcase to Mancini, but to his place in Bayswater instead.'

'What about the ERECOT?'

'She should still take that to Mancini and collect on it. You are to make sure she does collect. Do that after she delivers the briefcase. I've got to go now, things are a bit hectic here.'

The phone was cut off before he could respond. It was unavailable when he tried to call back. He picked up the phone again, this time dialling a hotel in Paris. He had just finished that call when Maisie came out of the bathroom wearing only towels. He looked her over before saying, 'It's my turn now and this time you can be the one to look.'

'No thanks, if it's all the same to you.'

'It's not. And that wasn't an invitation.'

'Oh, for heaven's sake can't you trust me to get dressed while you shower?'

'No.'

'So what are you going to do if I make a run for it while you're in the shower? Chase me down the corridors with your dick swinging from side to side?'

'An amusing thought, but no. I'm going to lock us both in the bathroom and take the key into the shower. It's nice to know that some hotels still rely on good, old fashioned keys.'

'Why not just lock the room instead?'

'Because dear Maisie, as you well know, the room doesn't lock from the inside, but the bathroom does. You do want me to be clean and smell nice for our posh dinner date, don't you?'

'Alright, but I'm not washing it for you.'

'Okay, we've reached a deal.'

70 – 30th April 2006, Paris

The phone in the room rang. Fey had been gazing over Paris from the balcony on the tenth story of her hotel and heard it late, but she still got there in time to pick it up.

'Anna?'

'Hello, Mike, how are you?'

'I'm fine, Anna, but I don't have much time to talk. I've had to change our arrangements, but it means you get an extra week in Paris. How do you fancy that?'

'Are you coming back to spend it with me?'

'Sorry, Anna, I can't, but I arranged everything for you. The hotel's all covered for next week and there's a package for you in reception. And no going about your normal business. I don't want you holed up in a Parisian police cell when you should be on the train. Just take a holiday. Must fly, love you.'

The phone went dead. Fey was concerned. Was she being left in the lurch? There was only one way to find out, so she went down to reception.

'Do you have a package for me, Room 1079?'

'Yes, madam. You will need to sign for it, please.'

As she was signing the book in reception

she checked the arrangements.

'Has my booking been changed?'

The receptionist moved to his computer.

'Yes, Madam, your booking has been extended for one week. Your last night will be the seventh of May, with checkout by ten the next morning. Bill to be settled by Mr Chambers. He has given us a credit card authorisation for the room and breakfast plus up to 300 Euros of extras.'

'Thank you', Fey replied as she handed back the book. The receptionist checked it and hesitated.

'Something wrong?' she asked, concerned.

'You have signed it "Anna Fey" madam, but this package is for Mrs Chambers.' Caught out, Fey thought quickly.

'Oh, yes, sorry. My husband and I agreed I should retain my maiden name for business purposes. I run an agency under it. I can sign it as Mrs Chambers if you like.'

'No, that's alright, madam. I remember your being with Mr Chambers and the room number is right. I'll just make a note of it in the book.'

He handed over a large envelope. Fey took it back to the room before opening it. She found a second class ticket on the Eurostar for 8th May and 500 Euros in cash. "Generous", she thought,

"Montmartre, here I come."

71 – 1st May 2006, King's Palace, Haranibad, Haranistan

The Norwegian Embassy car pulled into the palace car park at 9:45am. Ffolkes was the only passenger and a very nervous one at that. He had been going over and over the briefing he had been given by the Norwegian security advisor and he still didn't believe it. He tried to convince himself that his training as a policeman made him capable of dealing with any situation, but surely not this. How would he cope with this? He knew he had no choice so there was no point in fretting. He felt hot and uncomfortable because of the bullet-proof vest he was wearing under a suit the embassy had found for him. Nothing of his own fitted. He had been assured it did not show.

'They've never met you before so why shouldn't you look overweight? If things get to the worst then save yourself and try to avoid a diplomatic incident.' If this was not going to be a diplomatic incident then he did not know what one was. He played over the last instructions.

'Just act normally, the king must suspect nothing. Go in and get the information you want. Nothing will happen until you get back.'

'Mr Ffolkes, please come into the reception room. His Excellency, King Harani XLVI, long may he reign, will be with you soon. Please take a seat. We have put out coffee and biscuits on the sideboard. There is a bathroom over there if you need it.'

"A double scotch might be more helpful", Ffolkes thought, before responding, 'Thank you, that's very kind.'

Having done his duty the palace official left. Ffolkes could not drink, eat or sit, but made use of the bathroom. The palace official returned at 9:59.

'Mr Ffolkes will you come through, please?' He led Ffolkes through to a much larger, highly decorated room where a man in his late sixties and a woman in her early fifties were waiting. Both were wearing western clothes; he a three-piece suit with Prince of Wales check, white shirt, blue tie and black shoes and she a light blue trouser suit, dark blue shoes and a white hijab. The man moved towards Ffolkes offering a handshake. He spoke in English.

'Good morning, Mr Ffolkes, this is my wife, Queen Fatima and, as I am sure you have guessed, I am King Harani. We are very pleased to meet you.'

Ffolkes shook his hand, taking a firm grip to prevent his nervousness from showing. Having told himself to keep calm for what must have been the hundredth time, he responded.

'Your Majesties, thank you for giving your time to help in my investigation and allow me to advise you on security.' His heart sank. Had he already made a faux-pas? Did the king know he was investigating a crime or was he just expected to give advice on security measures? He could only wait for the king's reply, which gave nothing away.

'I'm glad to be able to help our Norwegian friends. Your king and queen have always been very kind to me and my family, so it's nice to be able to repay them with a little help.'

"You just don't know how true that remark is", Ffolkes thought, before the king continued.

'Shall we get to it?'

As he spoke the queen pressed a button on the wall, which, much to Ffolkes' surprise, opened a concealed door to a lift. The queen took hold of the king's arm, helping him make less than steady progress into the lift. As they all entered, the king added, 'We don't even need to go outside. I had this installed last year.'

The lift descended slowly for about thirty seconds before coming to a gentle halt. The doors opened on to a platform where a small rail car, with its door open, awaited them. They all boarded the car. The doors then closed and it began moving into a tunnel.

'This shuttle will take us straight to the

tomb, which is located underground. For obvious reasons, I will not tell you where. It will take about ten minutes, during which time you can tell me exactly what you are hoping to discover that will help you solve your crime.'

Ffolkes felt relieved. So at least the king knew one reason for his trip. He explained about the two ERECOTs and about one being very old, made of obsidian and ivory and the other an obvious, although valuable, modern fake. He watched the king's face for a reaction, which was one of incredulity.

'I've never heard of either of these eyes, but I can assure you that neither is the Eye of the Red-Eyed Cyclops of Thebes, or the ERECOT as my elder son insists on calling it. You are about to see the eye, safely settled in the golden Cyclops and to my knowledge you will be the first foreigner ever to be accorded that privilege.'

This time it was the king's turn to gauge a reaction and he was pleased with what he saw in Ffolkes' face.

'You look surprised, Mr Ffolkes, which pleases me greatly. You have heard the stories of the eye being stolen and what is there at the moment is just a copy. I can tell you this is a fabrication; a fairy story made up by my excellent press department. We wanted to deter thieves and we thought that telling them it was too late might be the best way. When you see what we have in this tomb you will understand why. These are national treasures and it is my duty to protect them for the nation.'

'So, just to confirm, please sir, there has never been a copy made of the ERECOT, it was never stolen and what is there is a complete, original RECOT.'

'That is correct, Mr Ffolkes. But now that I think about it, the story might have caused law enforcement agencies some problems. If the criminal fraternity thinks the true eye is out there then there will be those who want to possess it, and might buy, sell or steal it.'

'Worse than that, sir. They might also kill for it.'

'Really, Mr Ffolkes, there are people who would kill just for a valuable artefact?'

The king appeared surprised and saddened by what he had heard. He was still reflecting on this when the car pulled into a small underground station, where the car doors opened. Ffolkes followed as the queen led the king to a doorway with a closed steel door. The king placed his right thumb of a pad beside the door and announced, 'King Harani the forty-sixth. Three adults.'

The door slid open, allowing access to a small, dimly-lit chamber, with a second door similar to the first, on the opposite side. This time the king placed his left thumb on the pad and looked into what appeared to be a spyhole in the centre of the door.

'Iris recognition?' Ffolkes asked. The king grunted confirmation.

'Only my elder son and I can open this door. I am in poor health now, and the Crown Prince has no children, or at least none of which I am aware, so I will probably have it programmed for my younger son as well, just in case.'

The second door opened into a chamber illuminated by a single lamp above the doorway.

'Look straight ahead', the king advised, but need not have bothered. Ffolkes could see a bright red reflection above and directly ahead of him. It was little more than a metre away.

'It's both magnificent and frightening at the same time, which is the point of it, I guess.' Ffolkes' admiration was genuine.

As his eyes got used to the light he could make out a small circular room, about three metres in diameter, with a second door immediately opposite the first. The walls and ceiling were roughly hewn rock and the floor sand on rock. The only thing in it was a three metre high golden statue.

'Yes, it is. Behold the Red-Eyed Cyclops of

Thebes, which guards this tomb.'

The Cyclops held a huge club in its right hand. It loomed menacingly over the doorway, looking down so that the eye picked up the reflection of the single light. The king continued.

'I know you have come to see the Cyclops and indeed you shall see it, fully illuminated, but firstly let's go through to the tomb of King Harani XVI and see its magnificent treasures.'

Supported on the arm of the queen, he led Ffolkes around the Cyclops and through the door on the other side. He pressed a light switch, which turned on a low level of light in a semi-circular room formed from a natural cave. Immediately opposite was a large stone sarcophagus with a carved figure on its top.

'The body of King Harani XVI has lain undisturbed in there for nearly fourteen hundred years and we desire it should lay there for many, many more years to come. To our knowledge the sarcophagus has never been opened and we intend it never should be. We did tests once, to confirm the presence of a body inside, but that was enough. This is a grave, so we will leave it in peace.' He paused in reverence before continuing.

'Now look around the walls. You will see shelf upon shelf laden with magnificent artefacts made from gold, silver and gems. Please look at them, admire their beauty, but do not touch them, because we would like to keep them free from the damaging effects of skin acids. Corrosion is one of our greatest fears, which is why we keep the humidity low. At this depth, we are nearly fifty metres below ground, the temperature stays constant, so that is not the problem. Normally we would not allow it, but you may take photographs on this occasion. I am told you need them to make your security recommendations. I will turn the lights up gradually so your eyes stay accustomed to it and you will pick up more detail as we increase it. I suggest you take your photos at the end when the lights are at their maximum. Now please, Mr Ffolkes, enjoy your time viewing our national treasures. I hope you will agree with me how important it is to preserve them for generations, rather than defile this mausoleum by turning it into a tourist attraction.'

Ffolkes took his time, admiring many individual items and asking questions about some of them. He had been told to keep the king there as long as he could, ideally not returning before 11:00am. The king proved very knowledgeable on the artefacts, which made his enjoyment the greater. He could have stayed much longer, but could see the king was tiring and he still had the Cyclops to view in full light.

They left the main chamber to see it at 10:45. Ffolkes walked around it several times, taking photographs from all angles. He viewed the eye at the highest magnification available on his camera.

'It's a wonderful statue and the eye is its crowning glory. How did your experts manage to get it in and out without doing any damage?'

The king looked puzzled.

'What do you mean, Mr Ffolkes? We have never taken it out. Why would we? As you said yourself, we would have to damage this magnificent statue to do that. Our experts were able to confirm it contained a pigeon-blood ruby without needing to remove it, so we would have no reason to. Don't ask me about the science they used because I did not understand it, but they were all satisfied by the results.'

Ffolkes looked again at the eye, this time concentrating on the ivory case.

'But if your experts have never taken it out then how do they know about the hieroglyphics on the ivory?'

'What hieroglyphics, Mr Ffolkes. There are no hieroglyphics on the eye, at least not to my knowledge. What made you think there were?'

'But it's recorded on your stamps and coins, Your Excellency. They say that there are hieroglyphics that are supposed to contain a coded message giving the location of the remaining treasure. The treasure that was buried separately from the king for fear of grave robbers. It's supposed to guide the spirit of the dead king to the second hoard should he ever need it.'

'Second hoard? What second hoard? There *is* no second hoard, Mr Ffolkes. You have just seen the treasures of King Harani XVI and they are magnificent and extensive, but there are no more. Are you saying this information came from official government sources, including our stamps and coins?'

'Yes, Excellency. I had assumed the fake eye we received was supposed to have the same information as the true eye.'

The king's face reddened as his perplexity turned to anger. He was getting upset and the queen could see this.

'Please, gentlemen, no more of this. It is disturbing my husband.'

Ffolkes was devastated. He apologised, immediately and profusely, for the misinformation he had been given and fed back to the king, who was recovering quickly.

'No, my dear. No, Mr Ffolkes. It is not Mr Ffolkes' fault. He has no need to apologise. He should not apologise, because he has obtained his information from what should have been reliable sources and yet it is no more than a practical joke. I detect the hand of my elder son in this. He has long been trying to exploit the treasures, history and culture of our country for financial gain, but this has gone too far. I shall get to the bottom of this, mark my words, I shall. But this is an internal matter. Mr Ffolkes you are an honoured guest and should not have been insulted by these fabrications. This tissue of lies and deceit that make us a laughing stock. Let me summarise the truth for you.'

The king held up his left hand to make and count his points on his fingers.

'One: there is only one eye. It is and has always been in the golden statue of the Cyclops, although I admit to putting around the lie that it had been stolen and we had made a copy.

'Two: The treasures of King Harani XVI were *all* placed in his burial chamber along with his sarcophagus. There are no other treasures.

'Three: there is no writing on the eye. It is made with a pigeon-blood ruby contained within an ivory case. Anything else, even if it comes from official Haranistani sources, is fiction and I shall see that the perpetrators of it are punished.'

As he finished the king slumped into the arms of the queen who struggled to hold his weight. Ffolkes was there immediately to share her load. Between them they helped him back to the rail car. The queen looked up to a camera in the car as the doors closed.

'Please open the doors and give him a little time to rest', she asked, looking up at the camera in the car.

The doors reopened as a voice came into the car from a hidden speaker.

'Would you like me to send for a doctor, Your Majesty?'

'No, that will not be necessary. Just give us a little time. I will tell you when you may start the car.'

The queen allowed her husband to recover then signalled that the car could be started. Ffolkes' heart sank in anticipation of what lay ahead.

72 – 1st May 2006, King's Palace, Haranibad, Haranistan

The car carrying the king, queen and Ffolkes pulled back into the palace underground station at 12:15, coming to a gentle stop in the middle of the platform, but the doors remained shut. Ffolkes knew that what he had been told would happen, but had earnestly wished would not, had happened. Looking on the platform he saw about twenty armed soldiers and one civilian dressed in suit and tie. The civilian approached the car door, which opened. He entered and took the remaining seat in the four-person car next to Ffolkes and opposite the king. He addressed the king in Arabic. As he spoke the queen's face went white. Ffolkes thought she was going to faint, but she recovered sufficiently to retain consciousness. The king looked shocked, but retained his composure. He addressed the official.

'Please will you repeat what you have just said, in English, such that my guest understands?'

The official obliged. 'Harani Anshalari, by command of the President of the Revolutionary Council of the Republic of Haranistan, I am arresting you for the theft of funds from the people of Haranistan.'

Ffolkes was dumbfounded. This was not what he had been told would happen. He was trying to decide what to do when the king spoke again.

'Thank you, you have now committed an act of treason in front of an independent witness. That should be enough to convict you.'

As he spoke the doors opened. An army colonel, who commanded the guard, was waiting outside with two of his men. The king addressed him.

'Colonel, arrest this man at once. The charge will be treason.'

The colonel looked sadly at his monarch. Taking his lead from the king he responded in English.

'Sir, I have been your loyal servant as head of the Palace Guard for over five years, but I regret to inform you that there has been a revolution, backed by all the armed services. You have been deposed. I will do my very best to ensure no harm comes to you or the deposed queen, but I am ordered to allow this official of the Revolution Council to arrest you. This is a sad time for me, sir. I doubt we shall ever see each other again and I might not even survive this day myself. May I wish for you a long and happy retirement in exile, which is what I have been told will happen to you.' He offered his hand to the king, who shook it warmly. He turned to the queen, bowed slightly, saying 'Ma'am.' She smiled back, but could not speak. Ffolkes knew his moment had come.

'Colonel, I have here a letter of authority to escort Mr and Mrs Anshalari from here to the airport and from there to Norway, where they will be granted political asylum and allowed to live there in exile.'

He passed the letter to the colonel, deliberately avoiding the official, who had tried to take hold of it. The colonel examined it carefully for what appeared to be forever. He gave an instruction, in Arabic, to the captain standing beside him. The captain saluted and left.

'Mr Sven Ffolkes, attaché to the Norwegian Embassy, please accept my apologies for thc inconvenience these events will cause you. May I please see your passport to confirm your identity?' Ffolkes passed him his pristine diplomatic passport.

'Fine, that's all in order', he replied returning the passport to Ffolkes, but retaining the letter.

'Unfortunately, I cannot say the same for this letter. It reads:

'I, Crown Prince Helini, in my last act in my capacity as Crown Prince, will at 12:00

Haranistani time on 1st May 2006, depose my father, King Harani XLVI, and declare myself King Harani XLVII. The laws of Haranistan as they exist on the date of this letter, shall stand unless and until repealed by me or the new Haranistani government.

'I authorise the Norwegian diplomat, Sven Ffolkes, who carries this letter and is able to identify himself by diplomatic passport, to escort my father and mother to exile in Norway. I command all Haranistanis to assist their transfer and to ensure they remain unharmed. Any person who fails to enact this command will be committing an act of treason.'

'I read out the English translation, but the words in Arabic say exactly the same.'

'That's clear enough isn't it, colonel? May we proceed?' Ffolkes enquired.

'It is, but events have moved on since midday today when the deposing became legal and the Crown Prince became King Harani XLVII. At 12:05 there was a coup d'état that deposed the new king and replaced him with the Revolutionary Council.'

The official, who had been quietly seething, spoke angrily in Arabic, but was interrupted by the colonel.

'In English please, to allow everybody to understand.'

The even angrier official, obliged reluctantly.

'That paper is meaningless. I have orders to arrest the deposed king and queen so please let me get on with it. If this Norwegian gets in my way, then I'll arrest him as well.'

'No. You most certainly will not.' The colonel declared emphatically.

'This man is a Norwegian diplomat. The representative of a friendly nation who is our guest in Haranistan. Need I also remind you that Norway is a member of NATO, whose warships are rapidly heading towards our shores to evacuate their nationals? Do you want to give them an opportunity to invade as well? As yet our new regime has been recognised by nobody, so they could legitimately respond to a request for support from the newly deposed king if wc do not act peacefully.'

'Fine, I'll just arrest these two and be on my way then. You can deal with our honoured Norwegian guest.'

'Colonel, if I may?' Ffolkes spoke up trying to put as much assertion into his voice although deep down he was quaking with fear. The colonel nodded.

'This honest, hard-working and loyal official has been charged with arresting the deposed king. Should we not let him get on with it, because he has first to find the deposed king? Are we not delaying him?'

'He's here, you diplomatic idiot. Now please let me get on with it.'

'No sir, the deposed King Harani XLVII is not here. This lady and gentlemen are Haranistani citizens who have been granted safe conduct to Norway and diplomatic asylum by its king. The text says that all laws stand unless specifically changed by the king or new government. Has the Revolutionary Council changed that command?'

The colonel smiled for the first time in the whole episode. He addressed the official in Arabic after which the official stormed out.

'Mr Ffolkes, you are indeed a resourceful man. I can think of no one better to whom to pass on my responsibility for my past employers, whom I'm happy, in private, to still refer to as their Majesties, because they will ever remain that to me. But we must be quick and devious, so I hope you might have more tricks up your diplomatic sleeve. I have had to agree to retain you all here until this situation is resolved and I fear that resolution will not be in our favour. Will you please all come with me to somewhere a little more comfortable?'

The colonel led them back to the lounge where Ffolkes had first met the king and queen who were now Mr and Mrs Anshalari.

'Mr Ffolkes, there was a witness to that declaration who may yet save the situation. I am going to leave you now, to follow up my earnest wish that he can help. I hardly need to remind you that I have placed guards around this room. You are a diplomat, so you may stay or leave at any time you wish, but my guards will prevent Mr and Mrs Anshalari from leaving. Just one other thing, I have asked for a nurse to check out Mrs Anshalari after the traumatic events of the morning.' Looking over to the former queen, he added, 'Please don't try to refuse, ma'am, because I shall insist.'

73 – 1st May 2006, King's Palace, Haranibad, Haranistan

A woman wearing a long white dress and wimple came into the room carrying a large bag. Only her face was visible, from which Ffolkes guessed her age to be late thirties or early forties. She looked like a Christian nun, which surprised him. Haranistan had complete freedom of religion, but with the majority being Arabic, the most practised faith was Islam.

'I am the nurse who has been sent to look at Mrs Anshalari', she declared in a confident voice as she placed her bag beside the ex-queen and went to roll up the sleeve of her jacket.

'A moment, please', Ffolkes called as he moved rapidly towards her. 'Could I see some form of identification, please?'

'Sir, I am a nun trained as a nurse. I do not carry identification with me. Most people I visit are pleased to see me and find no need of such identification.'

Ffolkes could hear the indignation in her voice.

'If it helps, I can tell you I am from the order of St Ignatius, a Spanish order working here with the Red Crescent.'

'May, I please look in your bag first?'

'Go ahead, but be quick please, I want to

check if this lady is fit to travel and also this gentleman and I don't think I have a lot of time.' Ffolkes checked the bag, to find only what he expected. He looked carefully at her as he responded.

'Thank you. Please accept my apologies for not trusting you. Do go ahead with your examination.'

She did not respond, preferring to begin her work straight away. She worked quickly, firstly with the ex-queen and then her husband. She decided both were fit to travel, provided the ex-king used a wheelchair. After much protestation and diplomatic, but firm, insistence from Ffolkes, he agreed.

The nurse left them for what seemed to Ffolkes to be a very long time, but was in practice only a few minutes. She returned pushing a wheelchair and accompanied by the colonel. She began settling the ex-king into the wheelchair. He fussed and complained but, cajoled by both his wife and the nurse, he eventually consented, making himself comfortable in the chair. The colonel addressed Ffolkes.

'Mr Ffolkes, I said I was going to check something with the other signatory on your letter of authorisation, whom I'm glad to tell you has influence within the new regime. He cannot as yet agree to the release of Mr and Mrs Anshalari, but he has agreed for them to be taken to the airport, pending a final decision. The roads will be closed very soon and a curfew put in place, so we must move now. I have arranged for an ambulance to take them, together with this nurse, to the airport. I will also escort your embassy car in the same convoy. Let's get going before the situation changes. There is no time to lose.'

Ffolkes knew he had very little choice, but tried one thing to test the colonel's level of co-operation.

'May I travel in the ambulance as well, please?'

'You may, Mr Ffolkes, but please ask your driver to come with us in our convoy, for two reasons. One, I cannot guarantee his safety if he tries to return to the embassy unescorted; and two, I may have to ask you to transfer to that car, with its diplomatic immunity, if we run into any trouble. Now let's be going.'

74 – 1st May 2006, Haranibad, Haranistan

A convoy left the palace with the colonel's armed Land Rover leading, followed by the ambulance carrying Ffolkes, the ex-king and ex-queen and the embassy car bringing up the rear. It had only reached the bottom of the first street when it encountered a roadblock. The corporal in charge ordered them to stop before approaching the front passenger side where the colonel was sitting. Ffolkes could only watch from the ambulance, with his heart thumping and his fingers crossed. After nearly two minutes of discussion between the two there was still no movement. The colonel, in a rage, opened the door, forcing the guard to jump aside quickly to avoid being knocked over.

'Corporal, I am giving you a direct order to let this convoy pass. I shall not repeat it. Either we go through now or I will have you arrested for insubordination. Now stand your men aside.'

The corporal saluted and signalled his men to move aside. The colonel wasted no time getting back into his vehicle, allowing the convoy to move off without further delay. Ffolkes breathed a sigh of relief as they joined the main road to the airport. Apart from military vehicles, there was nothing on the road so they moved quickly, reaching the exit for the airport in ten minutes. Ffolkes' heart sank as they encountered another, much larger roadblock with two machine gun posts and a tank protecting it.

An officer, escorted by two armed soldiers, approached the Land Rover. The colonel was out of it and walking towards the soldiers before they reached the convoy. One of the soldiers raised his gun and aimed it at the colonel, who moved forward without flinching. The officer barked something in Arabic, which cause the soldier to stop, but he kept his weapon pointed at the colonel as they met. The officer spoke briefly before the colonel showed him a piece of paper, which Ffolkes took to be his letter of authority. Both men approached the ambulance followed by the two armed guards. Ffolkes wound down the window as the colonel arrived.

'Mr Ffolkes, I have explained to the duty officer here that we are escorting a diplomatic party from Norway that is leaving from the airport with two Haranistani citizens, who have permission from the Revolutionary Council to leave with you. I have shown him your letter of authority, but he wishes to confirm with the signatory from the Revolutionary Council that all is in order. This includes verifying your diplomatic status. Will you come with us please? These guards will stay with our convoy, but are commanded not to enter any vehicle provided no occupants attempt to leave or the vehicles start their engines. I will explain this to the occupants of the ambulance, will you please give the same information to the driver of your embassy car.'

Two minutes later and having followed the colonel's instructions, Ffolkes found himself, together with the colonel, the officer commanding the guardhouse and an armed soldier, in a small transportable cabin set out as a guard house.

The colonel addressed Ffolkes. 'This officer would like to see your diplomatic passport, please?'

Ffolkes handed over the pristine passport to the officer, who examined it carefully. He then spoke to the colonel. There followed a heated exchange, which ended when the colonel appeared to agree to something. He turned to Ffolkes.

'This officer believes your passport may be a forgery. He says he intends to search you, but I have explained that he has no right to search a diplomat, who has both immunity and free right of passage within our country. He is not satisfied so, I have agreed to ask you if you are prepared to submit to a search, even though you are not obliged to.'

Ffolkes thought what they might find, rapidly concluding that his ordinary passport would give credence to the officer's claim. 'Certainly not. This is a flagrant breach of my diplomatic status. It is equivalent to an act of war. I shall not submit to this. I am a Norwegian diplomat who has the right to unhindered movement within this country. I am on a mission sanctioned by both the Norwegian and Haranistani governments to escort two Haranistani citizens to Norway.'

Although Ffolkes spoke in English, the officer appeared to understand what he said. He spoke to the colonel then reached for the telephone. The colonel explained to Ffolkes that the officer was checking with the signatory from the Revolutionary Council. Ffolkes doubted that he would get through to him and was not surprised when the officer appeared to be stalled in his attempt. After several exchanges, with the officer getting angrier and raising his voice on each occasion, the colonel asked for the phone. He began more calmly, although with greater authority. He spoke in English to allow Ffolkes to understand. He gave his rank and stated his position as the commander of the palace guard, but did not elaborate further on his role at the palace or state that the ex-king was present in his convoy. After a short exchange he stopped speaking and appeared to be waiting for somebody at the other end.

Two minutes passed before the colonel responded, 'Hello' then after a short pause and with trepidation, 'Yes sir, I will pass you over to him.' He handed the phone to Ffolkes.

The voice at the other end spoke before Ffolkes could say anything. 'I understand you are the Norwegian diplomat who was asked by the deposed king to escort Mr and Mrs Anshalari into exile in Norway. Although this request was not made by the Revolutionary Council, we are prepared to consider it. While we do so, I am prepared to let you take them to the airport to await our decision, provided I can satisfy myself that you are who you say you are. Please answer my questions truthfully because, if I suspect you of lying, I shall have you all detained while we investigate. Do I make myself clear?'

'Indeed you do, sir, but may I ask to whom I am speaking, please?' Ffolkes could feel himself shaking and beads of sweat run down from his armpits as he responded, although he made every effort to be assertive in his response and not show his fear.

'Until we can hold a fair election, I am the

acting head of the Revolutionary Council. Will you please give me your name and occupation?' Ffolkes found his matter-of-fact tone reassuring, leading him to conclude that complete honesty would be required to get them all through.

'Sven Ffolkes, Norwegian Diplomat.'

'Fine, what is your role and how long have you held your diplomatic passport?'

'Formally, my role is as an attaché here to offer consultancy to the Haranistani government on security of its national treasures. In truth this is a cover story, agreed with the former Crown Prince Helini, to allow me to make contact with ex-King Harani XLVI and his ex-Queen and escort them safely into exile in Norway. I was only given diplomatic status for this mission and expect to relinquish it at the end of the mission. My instructions are to use my diplomatic passport for this role only and to use my ordinary passport for all other encounters.'

'And what was your role before becoming a diplomat?'

'I was, and indeed still am, a police inspector with the Oslo Police force.'

'Thank you, Mr Ffolkes, for your total honesty, without which I would have had you detained. Do you have your ordinary passport and police warrant card with you?'

'Yes sir.'

'Are you prepared to show them to my duty officer?'

'Yes, sir.'

'Then please pass the phone to the duty officer.'

Ffolkes did as instructed. The duty officer listened, confirmed he had understood his instructions and terminated the call. He spoke to Ffolkes in broken English.

'May I see ordinary passport and warrant card please, Inspector Ffolkes.'

Ffolkes handed them to the officer and waited.

'Thank you, Inspector. You may now proceed to airport. You are to wait in First Class Lounge for further instructions.'

Two minutes later the convoy arrived at the back of the airport terminal. The colonel, in the lead vehicle, pulled forward to allow the ambulance to get as close as possible to the entrance. The ambulance reversed back and left, putting it at right-angles to the colonel's Land Rover, facing away from a set of plastic doors designed to allow easy access for fork-lift trucks, but also being suitable for wheelchairs. The embassy car stopped behind to allow the ambulance to leave after it had disgorged its occupants; an old man in a wheelchair, a nurse pushing it with a middle-aged lady beside her and a very worried-looking Ffolkes following them. All the doors of the embassy car opened and three large men, in traditional Arabic dress and wearing sunglasses, who had previously been hidden from view, jumped out to prevent anybody following them.

'Who the hell are you? Get out of my way.' The colonel barked in Arabic. He was in no mood to be prevented from following his charges, who had by then disappeared behind the plastic doors. The first man responded, also in Arabic.

'Diplomatic protection. We have Norwegian diplomats who will be leaving the country before the airport is closed.'

'Do you think I don't know that, man? Did you think I was just out here plane spotting? Now out of my way before I have my squad remove you.'

The man held up his hand.

'Just a moment, sir, while I confirm what I should do.' He spoke into a microphone clipped over his head.

'We have a military escort with this group. What action should we take?'

He awaited a response through his earpiece. The colonel, stunned by this action, also waited. Five seconds later the man responded to the unheard message in his earpiece.

'Got that, we are to stand down and leave this to the military escort. Very good, sir, out.' Turning to the other two men he added, 'Okay, we're out of here; it's down to the colonel now.' With that, all three returned to the diplomatic car, which left without further ado.

75 – 1st May 2006, Haranibad Airport, Haranistan

Ffolkes paced nervously about the first-class lounge. Out of the window, looking down, he could see an almost deserted departure concourse. It was 12:40 pm and the airport was due to close at 1.00 pm. Apart from his Royal Norwegian flight, which he expected to board imminently, there was one other departure, an El Al flight to Tel Aviv, still due out before closure.

Inside the lounge with him were: a man in the wheelchair wearing a three piece suit in Prince of Wales check, a lady in a blue trouser suit and white hijab and an overweight, middle-aged lady with short dark hair wearing a bright orange trouser suit, white blouse and blue and orange striped neck scarf. She was carrying a black leather briefcase.

Everybody was looking out at the concourse, with their backs to the door. He could see nervous passengers in the lounge pressing towards the departure gates waiting for the first call of the El Al flight. Slightly to one side was an old man in a wheelchair, with his right leg up in plaster and a drip attached to his left arm. He was wearing a dressing gown over striped pyjamas, with a blanket across him. He appeared to be asleep, or he may have been drugged. A nurse in a smart maroon uniform was beside him.

An announcement, in Arabic, came over the public address system. In the lounge, the lady in the orange trouser suit headed straight for the door, pushing past the colonel and one of his soldiers as they came in. The announcement was repeated in English.

'This is the first call for passengers for El Al flight 8718 to Tel Aviv. Would passengers with special needs and those with small children please board now?'

Ffolkes saw the nurse push the man in the wheelchair to the front of the queue. He moved over to address the colonel.

'Colonel, do we have any news of when my flight can leave, please?'

'I'm sorry, Mr Ffolkes, I am still awaiting clearance. I have checked with the tower and they will still let your flight leave, providing it is only carrying foreign diplomats, and Mr and Mrs Anshalari if I get clearance, even if we pass the one o'clock deadline. In the meantime you are comfortable and secure here. My men are covering all the entrances and I will stay with you. All we can do is wait.'

'Thank you, colonel.'

Ffolkes waited nervously. He looked over

to the El Al flight where he saw the man in the wheelchair and his nurse pass through the gate. The lady in the orange suit was being checked through into first class. The call for all passengers on the flight was made. He watched the scramble as everybody tried to board at once. The nervous crew opened as many boarding points as possible, spilling over into the next gate, which had no flight waiting. Judging by the speed they were getting passengers through, he doubted the checks were very thorough. Five more minutes passed, during which time the queue had dwindled to almost nothing. It was now 12:50pm.

The colonel's radio broke into life. He answered it in Arabic. Ffolkes could not understand what he said, but he looked worried. All his facial expressions told Ffolkes he did not like what he was hearing. Just then the door burst open. An Arabic man, wearing a suit and tie, entered followed by two armed civilian police. The soldiers moved to prevent them going further, but the colonel intervened before any conflict started. Ffolkes recognised the man in civilian clothes as the one who had tried to arrest the ex-King at the palace. The colonel exchanged a few words with him in Arabic then approached Ffolkes. The man waited.

'Mr Ffolkes, this official has warrants for

the arrest of Mr and Mrs Anshalari. I can be of no further help to you and must leave now. He will take charge from here on.' He shook hands with Ffolkes and stood back. Ffolkes had just watched the gates of the El Al fight close. The official approached Ffolkes.

'Mr Ffolkes, I shall now take Mr and Mrs Anshalari in custody. You and any other diplomats may leave; your flight has been cleared.' He went across to the man in the wheelchair and the lady beside him, without waiting for an answer.

Despite this, Ffolkes responded. 'Excuse me, but there is no need for you to worry, I can see Mr and Mrs Andreessen on to the flight from here.'

'Please, Mr Ffolkes, do not impede me now, I don't want a diplomatic incident. Just go and let me arrest these two.'

'But they are Norwegian diplomats. You have just said we could leave.'

While they had been speaking the lady had reached into her handbag to produce two Norwegian diplomatic passports. Ffolkes watched the El Al jet taxi out towards the runway. The official snatched the two passports and looked at the photographs. Ffolkes could see his face sink. He went around to look at both of them, just to confirm what he already knew, which was that they were not the ex-king and queen.

'Where are they', he demanded at the top of his voice, which was just audible over the sound of the El Al jet taking off.

'Where are who?' Ffolkes enquired innocently.

'Mr and Mrs Anshalari of course. Where are they?'

'I'm sorry, but I have no idea. Your nurse took them away as soon as we arrived in the airport. I was told that the king, sorry Mr Anshalari, was unwell and needed treatment. I have not seen either of them since then. I assumed he was in a sick bay close by while we waited for clearance.'

The official turned to the two police.

'Find them.' He screamed in Arabic.

Both left immediately. The official then drew breath ready to address Ffolkes. The colonel, who had been watching the incident unfold, moved forward in case there would be trouble.

'Mr Ffolkes, you and Mr and Mrs Andreessen should leave the Democratic Republic of Haranistan now and I strongly advise that none of you ever returns.'

Ffolkes nodded but did not reply. He went over to the wheelchair to push Mr Andreessen through the departure gate while Mrs Andreessen held on to his arm.

Only when they were safely seated on the plane and flying over the Red Sea did they smile and raise a glass to each other on a job well done.

'Friends, let's not forget the colonel. Let us drink to his surviving this whole episode.'

76 – 1st May 2006, Crown Prince Helini's Yacht, Red Sea

Helini was very concerned. It was after four o'clock and he had heard nothing from Mohammed. He had sent his declaration to the leading international television stations and tried to get news from them, but all were reporting a confused situation. They knew he had deposed his father, but other things had happened since. He turned to the BBC World Service, where its reporter was doing a piece to camera from a hotel in Haranibad.

'I am speaking to you from my hotel foyer because there is a curfew. Nobody is allowed on to the streets and there are tanks and armoured personnel carriers out there to enforce it. The situation is far from clear. At noon today, local time, Haranistani state television and radio broadcast a statement from Crown Prince Helini saying he had deposed his father and declared himself King Harani XLVII, absolute ruler of Haranistan. The statement said all existing laws of Haranistan would continue unless and until repealed by a new government which he intended to appoint within the next twenty-four hours. Since then there has been only confusion. King Harani XLVI and Queen Fatima are rumoured to be in hiding and there is no sign of the Crown Prince. His last known whereabouts were yesterday evening when he set sail on his yacht for a two week holiday. His younger brother, Prince Stephan, King Harani XLVI and Queen Fatima's only other child, is known to be in England, where he is studying to be a doctor, but he too is in hiding and not available for comment. We are hearing rumours of a second coup, deposing the new king and declaring Haranistan to be a democratic republic, but I must emphasise that nothing is clear.'

The picture then went back to the studio where the news anchor summarised the facts but added nothing to what the correspondent had said.

On board the yacht, in addition to the Crown Prince, his security detail and the crew, were Carol Anderson and two eighteen-year-old abducted Russian concubines. The phone rang in his stateroom.

'Excellency, there is a Royal Haranistani Navy destroyer ten nautical miles away on our port side. The captain has asked us to heave to, such that he can send a boarding party. Shall I comply?'

'Absolutely not. Can you patch the captain through to me?'

'I can try, sir, but it might be easier for you to come to the radio room. It is just along the corridor from you.'

'Okay, tell the captain I'm coming. Please check the location of the nearest ship of the International Protection Fleet.'

Helini put on the headphones as soon as he arrived.

'Hello, captain of Royal Haranistani Navy destroyer, this is King Harani XLVII, your supreme commander. I order you to return to Haranistan and await my further orders.'

'I'm sorry, sir, I am in command of a destroyer of the Democratic Republic of Haranistan and I have orders to board your yacht and bring it and all its passengers back to Haranistan.'

'Captain, you are flying the flag of the Royal Haranistani Navy and I am its supreme commander. I repeat my order to you to return to Haranistan and await my further orders. I am warning you that failure to comply with this order would be an act of mutiny, punishable by death.'

'I'm sorry, sir, *I* must repeat, I am in command of a destroyer of the Democratic Republic of Haranistan and I have orders to board your yacht and bring it and all its passengers back to Haranistan. Should you fail to heave to, then I will board your yacht by force if I have to.'

The captain of the yacht, whispered to Helini.

'Sir, there are two cruisers from the International Protection Fleet within fifteen nautical miles on the starboard bow, but they tell me they cannot interfere in a domestic Haranistan matter.'

'Tell them this isn't a domestic matter. We are being threatened by international piracy. This ship is registered in the Bahamas and flying its flag. Strike any Haranistani flags and tell them. Do it now.'

'Hello, captain of the Royal yacht, this is your final warning to heave to and allow my party to board or I will do so by force.'

Helini replied, 'I am going to heave to in order to protect the lives of those on board here, but I must warn you that this ship is registered in the Bahamas and what you are proposing would be an act of international piracy. I have sought the intervention of the International Protection Fleet which is within fifteen nautical miles of us.'

The captain of the Haranistani destroyer replied, 'Prepare to be boarded.'

Helini watched nervously as the destroyer headed towards him.

'Anything from the International Protection Fleet?'

'They're checking sir, but while they are doing that they are diverting a cruiser towards us. They have suggested we move across to join their convoy.'

'I think we might get blown out of the water if I tried that. Keep in contact with them and let me know of any developments.'

Helini returned to his conversation with the Haranistani destroyer.

'Captain, I remain stationary, but I advise you not to attempt to board this ship. I cannot be responsible for the safety of your crew should you ignore this warning. As I speak a cruiser from the International Protection Fleet is heading towards us.'

'I note your statement, sir. Please stay heaved to. I am launching two craft with armed crews now.'

Helini looked up to see the two boats heading straight towards the yacht. He estimated they would be close enough to board within five minutes.

'Prepare the anti-boarding defences and advise everybody to stay below. There will be no other resistance. I don't want anybody to get hurt.'

The two boats pitched and rolled under the force of the yacht's defences. A loudspeaker called out from the lead boat.

'Turn off your defences or we will open fire.'

Helini ordered his captain to comply and heard the ship go quiet. When he looked back at the two boats he saw they were still pitching violently. He did not understand why until he looked up to see two helicopters directly above them. He heard a loudspeaker as well, but this time from directly overhead.

'This is the commander of the International Protection Fleet. You are attempting to board a ship registered in the Bahamas without its master's permission. This would be treated as an act of piracy and we will open fire should you attempt it. Turn your boats around and return to your ship. Comply immediately and do not fire. I should warn you that your ship is within range of our cruiser. We will not hesitate to fire on it should you disobey the command.'

Helini watched with great relief as the two boats turned around and began the return journey to their ship. The radio came to life again.

'This is Captain James Broadlow, commander of the International Protection Fleet. Please steer 200 degrees at ten knots to join our convoy between the tanker and the cruise ship. The cruise ship will slow to give you a line of clear water. Welcome to our protection.'

A very relieved Helini responded, 'Thank you, captain, I will comply with pleasure.'

77 – 1st May 2006, Crown Prince Helini's Yacht, Red Sea

'Carol, I have a problem. I would like to go to the UK, but I could be arrested if you wish to charge me with abduction. What would you have me do?'

Anderson was nervous. She knew he could have her killed and dropped overboard with the minimum of fuss. This would have been his safest method. It would be of no benefit to her if he did and somebody sought to bring him to justice for it, which was probably the reason why he was hesitating.

'Sir, it wasn't you who abducted me and as far as you knew I came to Haranistan voluntarily. You have treated me well. I would love my freedom and I expect you to set me free when I arrive back in the UK and also to help me explain why I have no passport. I can ask no more than that.'

Helini handed Anderson a parcel.

'Go on, open it.'

In the parcel she found a passport, bank card, credit card and bank statement all in her name and the details of an apartment in Notting Hill. The bank statement showed £1,000 in a current account and a further £10,000 in a savings account.

'I will arrange for the apartment to be transferred into your name when we get to the UK. Let's just call it back pay shall we?'

'Thank you, sir. Might I ask what will happen to the Russian girls?'

'Dear Carol, always caring for her charges. They'll stay with me at least until I know what is going to happen to us. I can then agree with them what they would like to do.'

'I understand, sir. Would you like me to tell them?'

'Yes please, Carol, you still have charge of them until we reach the UK, which I expect to be on 8th May, because I intend to reach it without going through any other territorial waters. That means going around South Africa. I hope you will enjoy our last cruise together.'

'I'm sure I will, sir.'

78 – 1st May 2006, 35,000 feet over the Red Sea

The flight attendant came over to the man who had boarded the plane in a wheelchair. Since then the nurse had removed the drip, which was only a dummy, and the bandaging from around his head, before she had helped to seat him in the front of the economy class section of the aeroplane. She was still sitting beside him when the attendant appeared.

'We are clear of Haranistan airspace now, sir, would you like to join your wife in first class? There's a change of clothing waiting for you there, courtesy of the Norwegian government.'

'Thank you, that is very kind of them and yes, please, I should very much like to do just that.' Turning to the nurse he added, 'Would you come to talk to us in about ten minutes please, I should like to learn who you are and why you have given my wife and me so much help.'

'My pleasure, sir. I'll see you in ten minutes.'

Freshly changed into suit and tie, the man joined his wife, the lady in the orange trouser suit who had been in the lounge immediately before the flight was called. Since then she had removed the padding that made her appear overweight and changed into a blue trouser suit that fitted her much better than the orange one. He sat beside her, kissing her warmly before he got comfortable.

'Champagne, sir?' He had not noticed the flight attendant arrive as he seated himself.

'Yes, please, but only when my nurse arrives and may we have a glass for her as well please?'

'No problem, sir, here she comes now.'

The nurse arrived and following an invitation, sat opposite the couple. She picked up her glass.

'A toast to your new lives, Your Excellencies.'

'Mr and Mrs Anshalari, please', the lady responded.

'As you wish, ma'am. It's probably easier than being called ex-queen and also more anonymous if that is what you wish. I wish you a very pleasant retirement in Norway.'

'Much as we are both very grateful for it, why did you help us?' the ex-king asked.

'Because the Norwegian government requested the help of the Israeli government to get you out safely. Its diplomat, Mr Ffolkes, is an excellent detective and an ingenious man, but he doesn't have the resources, training or experience that my team has.'

'So who are you? We should love to know the name of the lady who helped us and indeed why the Israeli government helped an Arabic head of state.'

'My name is not important, sir. Please just call me Miriam. As for why my government helped you, it was because you were the Head of State of a friendly nation who needed it. Israel is at peace with many Arabic states including Haranistan. We regard many of them, again including Haranistan, as our friends. A lot of people do not realise that many Israelis are Arabs and all we desire is to live in peace with one another.'

79 – 4th May 2006, Walthamstow

George Peters was working quietly in his office when the phone rang.

'Inspector Peters?'

'Yes.'

'It's Ian Gordon from Serious Crime. Do you remember we talked when you started your investigation into the murder of Charles Mancini?'

'Of course, Ian, how are things?'

'Something's come up that might be of interest to both of us, but I'd rather not say anything over an open phone. Can we meet, I'm at New Scotland Yard?'

'You're in luck, I'm due up there this afternoon to brief Superintendent Forest on that other little matter.'

'Great, I'll get myself invited to join you after your meeting.'

80 – 4th May 2006, New Scotland Yard, London

Forest called Gordon to join him and Peters in his office.

'What've you got for us, Ian?'

'It might be nothing, sir, but here goes. We've been doing a lot of digging on Mike Chambers. He's one of William Mancini's senior henchman. We thought we might get to Mancini through him. We're determined to try all angles. We think Chambers was into abduction in his earlier career, about ten years ago. He might even still be at it. Could be a side line and have nothing to do with Mancini, but even if it's not, we'll keep it on him for when we nick Mancini. Anyway, several teenage girls from the South East area went missing over the space of a year in 1996 - 97 and nothing has been heard of any of them since. That is until last month, when we received a passport application from one of them.'

He handed Forest a copy of a passport application form.

'She's Maisie Jennings, who disappeared from Luton on her sixteenth birthday in September, '96. The application came from Luton with all the necessary details except her birth certificate, which she claimed had been lost. Passport Office issued a passport for her and at our request put a watch on it.'

'What's her relationship with Chambers?'

'She met some friends on the evening she went missing. We've been able to talk to them and all are consistent on what happened. They left her with a guy called Mike, whom she had only met recently. They were all sixteen or seventeen with hardly any money, but Mike was older and as one of them put it, he was loaded. He bought Maisie a really nice watch. None of them ever saw her after that. From the descriptions, we think it was Mike Chambers and he was responsible for her disappearance.'

'Did anybody else see her? Family perhaps?'

'No. Same story. She lived with her mother and her mother's boyfriend. The mother's an alcoholic and not with it most of the time. Didn't even report the girl missing.'

'What about the mother's boyfriend?'

'Guy called Bill Sampson. No form. He seemed to like the girl. I don't mean in a sexual, harassing way, but just sort of a friendly, avuncular figure. Tried to mediate when she and her mother argued. He was the one who eventually reported her missing. Locals checked it out with neighbours just in case he was spinning a yarn, but they all said he was kosher.

Jennings' friends thought he was alright as well. One of her female friends said she would have known if he'd tried to mess with Maisie.'

'So you think he has nothing to do with it and that Chambers was responsible for her disappearance?'

'Things seemed to be pointing that way when we got a massive break. Jennings' passport was used on 30th April to enter the United Arab Emirates, by car, from Saudi Arabia. But it gets better. I just love the Emiratis. They have video records of all vehicles entering through their land borders. They sent us the film of two people crossing the border in a Merc. The driver looks like Chambers and the passenger could well have been Maisie Jennings. The trouble is, nobody's seen her for ten years, so we couldn't be sure.'

'So, if this is her and she was abducted by Chambers, then what the hell's she doing swanning around Saudi and the Emirates with him in a Merc? Could Jennings be dead and this girl is using her passport? Because Chambers knows she's dead, probably because he killed her?'

'Those were our first thoughts as well, George, but then we took a very close look at the footage. It looks like her seatbelt has a key to lock it into place, so she's not there willingly; as you would expect if he did abduct her. Based on this we showed the film to Bill Sampson and Jennings' old friends. They all say there's a strong likeness and it could be her, although the girl in the film is thinner.'

'So where's she been for ten years. A Saudi harem?'

'Harem's a very good bet, but it doesn't have to be Saudi. There's also Haranistan nearby and we know its Crown Prince has one. We also know, please don't ask me how, that he likes dark haired, teenage white girls, so Jennings would have fitted the profile when she was abducted.'

Peters appeared to be thinking deeply. Forest was the first to notice.

'Something ringing a bell, George?'

'Yes, sir. This is not the first time Haranistan has come up in my investigation. We came across it in connection with a famous and very valuable artefact called the ERECOT. It was supposed to have been stolen many years ago, and is now being offered on Fence-Bay. It could be nothing, but you've got me interested. Funnily enough Inspector Ffolkes, our Norwegian colleague in whose patch Charles Mancini washed up, is over there now. The king has granted him special access to a tomb in a secret location known only to the royal family. I haven't got a clue how he managed it, but I'll try to get a call through to him to do a bit of digging. Do you have any more on this Maisie Jennings, Ian?'

'I've saved the best bit to last. We got our agents in Dubai to see what they could get. Chambers and the girl are in the same room in one of the top hotels. It's twin beds, not an intimate relationship, but we were able to get DNA and fingerprint samples from the restaurant. She doesn't have a criminal record, so we don't have fingerprints on file to compare against, but the mitochondrial DNA is a match with her mother. She has no siblings or female cousins so it's definitely her.' Gordon's face portrayed a note of triumph as he delivered this message.

'Well, well, well. We have Chambers in the company of a, probably unwilling, woman whom we think he abducted ten years ago and who has been missing, maybe in a harem, ever since. We don't even need to ask why, if we can get the two of them we can probably get her to finger him for abduction and might even get news on some of the other girls who've gone missing. Are they still in Dubai?'

'Yes, but they are both booked on a flight to Paris on 8th May, then the Eurostar to London the same evening.'

'Can we be that lucky? I'll have somebody waiting for them should they come. I assume that's what you'd like me to do. Are you still keeping close tabs on them in Dubai?'

'Yes please and yes, George, and here's hoping for a result. I'll keep you posted if anything changes.'

Peters tried to phone Ffolkes several times that night and the following morning but kept getting the message, 'All lines into Haranistan are busy, please try later.' He prepared a text, hit the send button and hoped for the best.

81 – 7th May 2006, Notting Hill, London

Anderson sat in a chair in the flat in Notting Hill that Helini had given her. She reflected on what had happened since his yacht had docked in Dartmouth. She had spent her last few days on the yacht learning all she could about the UK, so she could pick up her new life with the minimum of fuss and without appearing out of place.

On arrival at Dartmouth she had slipped ashore dressed as a cleaner while Helini was busy with immigration and customs. At that point all she had were the clothes she stood up in, the address and keys to the apartment Helini had given her, money and the package. She took a bus to Torquay, bought some clothes in a department store and then travelled by local train to Exeter. After changing in the toilet she became an anonymous lady on a day trip to London. She had even bought a return ticket to avoid arousing suspicion.

At Paddington she decided to pitch straight in to London life so, walking past the taxi rank, she took the Underground to Notting Hill, where she bought herself a book of London street maps. It had already returned its value in helping her to find the flat.

It was then time to eat, followed by some

sleep, before an important appointment planned for the next day. To her surprise she found basic supplies in the fridge and a well-stocked freezer. As she looked at the instructions on one of the packets from the freezer she told herself, "I'm an intelligent lady. I can work this out." She had had the good sense to visit the galley on the yacht, where the cook had explained the purpose of a microwave and how to use it. She had put this knowledge to the test and survived. Her first day of freedom had been rewarding but tiring. She put her precious package into the safe and retired to bed happy.

82 – 8th May 2006, Eurostar to Waterloo, London

Maisie's level of excitement at the thought of being free and back in the UK had risen steadily during what had otherwise been an uneventful flight from Dubai to Paris. Despite this she had a nagging doubt about how Mike Chambers would react to her being let go. Apart from allowing her to satisfy the call of nature, he had not left her side for the whole time. He had even insisted she go to the toilet just before the plane landed so she would not be out of his sight at any point in Charles de Gaulle airport or the Gare du Nord. He had booked a car to take them from the airport to the station where, to her chagrin, they were able to board the train straight away. Chambers had taken away her passport and the dollars and credit cards the prince had given her, replacing the money with twenty five euros and forty pounds. He explained that Maisie was not rich and did not have a bank account, so had no credit cards.

'Sorry love, it's second class from here on. We are just boyfriend and girlfriend travelling home after a romantic weekend in Paris and we don't have much money left', he told her as they settled into the two rear facing seats in a block of four with a table in between. Chambers took the outside seat. He stowed their luggage behind the seat. Sitting opposite them was a man in his forties, occupying the window seat. His only luggage was a briefcase from which he produced a laptop. He placed it on the table in front of them and began working. Beside him was a woman in her twenties. She had only a coat and a small rucksack, both of which were on the luggage rack.

Maisie was feeling nervous so she shrank into her coat by the window. She could not understand why, but she did not trust the girl opposite. She knew she was carrying something she dare not lose and somebody might want to steal it. She reached into her coat pocket to pull out the large spherical boiled sweet she had bought at the service station. She remembered being told that these sweets were called gob-stoppers. Her mum said she used to buy them for an old penny, grumbling that she had to pay ten pence each for the ones she bought for Maisie. What would she have said about having to pay a dollar for one in an Emirati service station? Keeping it in the packet so her fellow travellers could only make out its size and shape rather than what it was, she rolled it around in her hand for a few moments and then put the packet back in her coat pocket.

Two minutes later she took off her coat and

put it up on the rack. It was then she noticed that her coat was identical to one already on the rack and presumably belonging to the girl opposite. So she was planning to steal the prince's property, was she? Whatever her plan, she would likely end up with something she wouldn't want to talk about, while his property, her deliverable, rested securely within her. She took out the book she had bought at the service station and read for the rest of the journey.

83 – 8th May 2006, Waterloo, London

As the train pulled into Waterloo, Maisie noticed the girl opposite had already gone and the man had packed up his laptop. He left as she reached up for her coat. When she tried to put it on, she realised it was too tight for her. The girl opposite had taken hers and left her own. So she thought she'd got the ERECOT did she? No chance, but Maisie still needed to put on an act.

'That girl's taken my coat and left hers. Where is she, Mike?'

She did her best to appear distressed.

'She's already gone, I'll see if I can catch her before I go. You get the luggage and the other coat, just in case I can find her.'

The train had already stopped. Chambers' chase was hampered by the corridor being full of people trying to get off. He soon returned.

'It's hopeless, she must be well gone by now. Is there anything in that coat to identify her?'

Maisie checked the pockets.

'Nothing'.

'Was there anything in your coat she might find?'

'Nothing, I was only given it yesterday.' Maisie lied, knowing it contained the wrapping from the sweet she had bought at the service station.

'Then, don't worry, I'm sure his lordship, sorry Excellency, will buy you another coat for being a good girl. You still have the package, I assume?'

'Of course I do. You don't think I'd be stupid enough to leave it in my coat on the luggage rack do you? Now let's get this over with.'

Chambers looked worried as he took Maisie to left luggage and waited while she found the locker, entered the passcode and removed the contents. She found herself holding a locked, black briefcase on which was written:

Property of Crown Prince Helini of Haranistan. The contents of this briefcase are subject to diplomatic immunity and should not be examined by any non-Haranistani nationals. If found please return to Crown Prince Helini at 21 Bayswater Road or to the Haranistani Embassy. A reward of £100 will be paid to anybody returning this case, unopened, to either address.

'It's a pity I not taking it to the prince, I could have made an extra hundred quid.' Maisie quipped.

'Funny you should say that Maisie, because there's been a change of plan and that's precisely what you're going to do.'

'Here comes one hundred quid, then. Let's get to number twenty-one Bayswater Road before he changes his mind.'

84 – 8th May 2006, Empire College, London

She made a final adjustment to her wig and replaced her sunglasses with clear ones. It was precisely 10:00 am when she entered Empire College.

'Professor Roberts, please?'

'Certainly madam, may I have your name please?'

'Miss Erecot.'

'Pardon, madam, would you repeat that?'

'Yes, of course, it is a little unusual. It's Erecot, that's E, R, E, C, O, T.'

The calmness of her voice hid the inner turmoil as she awaited the climax of the mission. Five minutes later she was shown into Roberts' study. He introduced her to the other two people in the room.

'Miss Erecot?'

She could detect a slight note in his voice, which she interpreted to mean he knew it not to be her real name, but he would rather not admit it. As far as he was concerned, and his reputation depended upon it, this was a legitimate meeting where a legally permitted transaction was about to take place.

'This is Sir Henry Chase, who is sponsoring the reward for the safe return of the artefact and this gentleman is from the Royal Haranistani jewellers. In view of the situation in Haranistan at the moment he prefers to remain anonymous. Do you have the artefact with you?'

Her heart was racing as she took the package from her handbag and passed it to the jeweller. He removed it from its felt bag, examined it carefully with an eyeglass, measured it with callipers and then very carefully unscrewed the ivory case. He examined both the case and the ruby inside before reassembling the whole piece. Eventually, he spoke.

'Beautiful… Magnificent. I never thought I'd ever have the privilege of seeing it, let alone helping to repatriate it to its rightful place in the golden stature of the Cyclops in Haranistan. I have no doubts. This is the true eye of the RECOT.'

He handed it back to the lady who had deliberately put out her hand to take it, rather than let either of the others take hold of it.

"Nicely done", she thought, "Just the right level of show to make it believable."

Chase and Roberts shook each other's hands enthusiastically.

'Can I have the reward money now, please?'

'But I don't carry that sort of money with me.' Chase protested, although she detected that his objection was not genuine. She was in no mood to be messed about.

'I'm not taking a cheque. I'll leave this room with either the money or the artefact. It's your call and either way you'll never see me again.'

'Hold it a minute.' Chase protested as he took out his mobile phone. One call later he turned to her.

'It'll be here in five minutes. Just time for a coffee.'

'Not for me, thank you, but don't let me stop you.'

Six minutes later she left in a waiting taxi, with a briefcase containing £100,000 in used notes.

85 – 8th May 2006, Brixton, London

The chauffeur smiled and moved quietly behind Fey.

'King Kong, eh?' he began as he put his hands on each side of her, just above her waist. He slid them slowly up the sides of her upper torso, gently tapping each of her ribs as he went.

'I may not be allowed to touch your face but I can still make a very nasty and painful mess of these. I'll break them one at a time and when I've finished you won't have enough breath left to tell me where it is. So tell me where the ERECOT is while you still can.'

'Please don't hurt me', she pleaded, 'I can be very nice to you if you like.'

'Where is it?' he whispered in her ear as his hands moved to the cord binding her wrists and ankles to the back of the chair.

'I don't know, honestly, the bitch must have palmed it when it looked like she was putting it in her pocket.'

Her voice was barely audible through her sobs.

'Louder', he whispered, 'Say that again as loudly and painfully as you can.'

She hesitated, trying to understand what he wanted of her.

'Do it, and then scream', he commanded

and she obeyed. As she was screaming he untied the cords and clapped his hand over her mouth.

'Scream, again', he commanded, 'but say nothing or we're both dead.' As she screamed for the second time he moved away to a cupboard and brought out a bullet-proof vest.

'Put this on'. He commanded, tugging her arms into it and zipping up the front. 'Now get dressed as best as you can and for heaven's sake, keep screaming'. He pulled out his mobile and turned it on, but to her surprise he did not make a call. Instead he turned the nearby table on its side and pulled her behind it, wrapping himself around her to increase her protection.

After a moment's silence the air was full of blaring sirens. Red and blue flashing lights filled the previously darkened room. She could hear the sound of helicopters overhead before a crashing noise as the windows caved in. Two smoke grenades went off as men wearing gas masks took positions all over the room. Before she could react to this, she was separated from the chauffeur, with her hands cuffed behind her back. The chauffeur was also handcuffed as the men in masks spread our around the room.

She heard one shout, 'Subjects secured' before she passed out.

86 – 8th May 2006, Waterloo Road, London

'Inspector, she's passed through passport control and customs, and picked up a briefcase from the left luggage lockers. Hang on a minute, there's a guy with her. It's Chambers. What do you want me to do, sir?'

'Follow them both to see where they go. Do you have somebody with you, Evans?'

'Yes, sir, Jackson is here as well, so we could cope with them splitting up. They're taking a cab, sir, we're following them.'

'Good, keep reporting in. I'll send armed back up. Chambers is known to carry firearms. Don't approach him or her as long as they're together.'

'Roger that, guv. We're crossing Waterloo Bridge now.'

Before this operation started Peters had set up a video link to Ffolkes in Oslo.

'I've got a strange feeling about this, Sven. Your body was Mancini's brother and Chambers is one of his henchmen. I think that there's a connection.'

'I agree, George, but I don't know how this girl, Maisie Jennings, fits into things. Why are we interested in her and what do we know about her?'

'We know Chambers was responsible for

abducting her from the UK ten years ago and she hasn't been seen from then until last week. Initially we were only interested in Chambers because of his association with William Mancini and knowing that Mancini is looking for revenge for the murder of his brother. We think Chambers might be the one who will enact that revenge, but on whom we don't know. We have been following Chambers for the past few days. He flew to Paris, with another girl, Anna Fey, who's a professional pickpocket. That was a week last Saturday. They checked into the bridal suite of a posh Paris hotel and behaved as a honeymoon couple. We wondered if this was a genuine honeymoon, but our checks found no wedding of a Mike Chambers or Anna Fey over the past three months, so we guessed it was a front and as usual he was up to no good. They stayed together until Thursday, when he left her and flew to Dubai, where we lost him. My man kept an eye on Miss Fey, who returned on the Eurostar today. He caught the train with her and even managed to sit next to her. You can imagine his surprise when who should he find sitting opposite them but Chambers and this girl, Maisie Jennings. They flew into Paris from Dubai together and went straight to the Eurostar. Interestingly, Dubai is where Maisie Jennings' passport was first used.'

'How do you mean, "First used", George, surely it must have been used first when she left the UK?'

'That's the interesting thing, Sven. Maisie Jennings was reported missing ten years ago. She went out to celebrate her sixteenth birthday, in Luton, after arguing with her mother. She met up with some friends who had a drink with her and a new member of their circle… you've guessed it, Mike Chambers. The local police interviewed him, but there was nothing to go on. She couldn't have left the country legally because she didn't have a passport, so we alerted the Passport Office. Three months ago, Jennings applied for a passport, claiming her birth certificate had been lost. The letter was posted in Luton and had photographs, together with certifications of true likeness etc. so they issued her a passport, but put a special trace on it. Our team was informed and we were alerted about its use by Dubai emigration yesterday.'

'So where has she been all this time?'

'That's what we would like to know, but we want to separate her from Chambers before we pick her up.'

'Do you intend to pick up Chambers as well?'

The radio crackled, 'Evans here sir, they've travelled north past Buckingham Palace and are now going up Park Lane. Your armed unit has just joined us. It gave the Palace police the willies I can tell you. They deployed two units and won't stand down until they know we have the situation covered. You may get a call from them, sir'

'Thanks for the heads up, Evans, I'll tell the armed unit to stay with you.'

Peters returned to his conversation with Ffolkes.

'Not if I can help it, because I don't want to alert him that we're on to him, so we'll only pick him up if we have to.'

'Evans again, sir. The taxi's done a U-turn in Bayswater Road and stopped outside number twenty-one.'

'That Crown Prince Helini's London pad. We should have uniform close by. I'll get the armed unit to stand by.'

'Hang on guv, she's the only one getting out. The taxi's leaving with Chambers inside.'

'Armed unit, follow that cab. Evans, pick her up now.'

'Roger that, guv.'

Evans ran as fast as he could, but Maisie Jennings had already knocked on the door. He saw her at the same time the door opened and she saw him. She tried to go in, but the security guard wanted to check her out first.

'No time for that now, this is for his Excellency, I'll come back for the reward later', she said as she shoved the briefcase into the guard's hands and ran off as quickly as she could. The guard closed the door just as Evans passed it.

'Evans, Jackson, get the girl, but don't go into the apartment. I don't want a diplomatic incident. I'll go through the proper channels first.'

'Guv, this is Jackson, I'm in the car and Constable Evans is chasing the girl. I can see them both and he's closing in on her. The armed unit is following the taxi and I'm tagging Evans.'

The next thing Peters head over the radio was a huge explosion. Jackson yelled into the phone.

'Holy shit, I think a bomb's just gone off at the Crown Prince's apartment. Evans has got the girl. The explosion must have blown him right into her.'

Peters reacted immediately.

'Armed unit keep on Chambers. Don't let him out of your sight but don't arrest him unless you have to. Get the bomb squad there now. Inform the diplomatic protection squad and get the most senior officer we have on duty briefed that we will have a major diplomatic incident. Also get the emergency services in there. Oh, and get that girl to the safe house, now.'

87 – 8th May 2006, Waterloo Road, London

Maisie's head was ringing from the explosion and she had a heavy man on top of her. She remembered he had been chasing after her before the explosion, which had knocked him into her and both of them on to the pavement. She just had time to feel herself to ensure she still had the ERECOT before she felt both arms being pulled behind her back and being handcuffed together.

''Ere, what's your game, mate? Let me go before I scream for the police.'

'No need for that, Miss Jennings, I am the police and we would like to talk to you, but not here if you don't mind because things could get a little hectic.'

As he spoke a car pulled up alongside them. Evans bundled her into the back and sat beside her after which the car sped off. Evans showed her his warrant card.

'I am PC Evans of the Metropolitan Police murder squad. Driving us is PC Jackson.'

Jackson spoke on the police radio.

'We have Miss Jennings, where would you like us to take her?'

The radio crackled as the base station responded.

'Take her to Unit B, Jackson. We're using

Unit A, so we can double up on the protection team, but make sure our guests don't meet.'

'Got that, sir. We'll get there as soon as we can. I'll call back when we arrive.'

Maisie was so stunned she almost wet herself.

'Murder squad? I don't know anything about a murder. I've just arrived in London from Paris, so what do the police want with me?'

'We know that, Miss Jennings, but we would like to know where you were before you got to Paris and come to that the ten years since you were reported missing from Luton. Also why you have just delivered a bomb to a property owned by Crown Prince Helini of Haranistan?'

88 – 9th May 2006, Charing Cross, London

Anna Fey came around slowly as she heard voices a little way away. She began to assess her situation. She was lying in a bed with covers over her. She could feel the sheets touching her unprotected breasts.

"Not again" she thought before realising she was wearing knickers, although that was all. "However, that's better than before, and I'm not tied up".

'Would you like a drink, dear?' She opened her eyes to discover the voice belonged to a uniformed WPC in her fifties who was sitting next to the bed. As she sat up and pulled the sheet to her neck, the WPC poured water into a plastic cup.

'I'll get you something to wear, before they talk to you.' She handed her the cup, then moved to an adjoining room. Fey half thought of running, but decided she would not get far with no money, barefoot and wrapped only in a sheet. Whatever her fate, she would have to accept it. The WPC returned, with a bathrobe and slippers.

'Not exactly flattering, but at least it will keep you warm and covered up.'

'Thank you,' Fey replied as she dressed herself, 'That really is quite an improvement, I can assure you.'

There was a knock at the door. The WPC confirmed with Fey that she had dressed and was ready.

'You can come in now', she called. The door opened and the chauffeur entered.

'You again', Fey's voice expressed a good deal of surprise mixed with not a little trepidation. 'I still have to work out whether you're my torturer or my hero.'

He smiled, with flashing white teeth.

'How are your ribs? Should give you a clue.'

She felt around and suddenly hit a tender spot. It made her wince with pain.

'Well, if you did hit me, it would appear it was only once, although you made a good job of it. Since I am alive and not in too much pain, I guess you must be my hero.'

'Thank you and just for the record it wasn't me but a bullet that bruised your rib. I'm really glad we got that vest on you otherwise it would have been much worse. I'm not happy with the SWAT team though. I had you well protected before they pulled you away from me. They let one of Mancini's heavies get a shot in, which hit you. Mind you it's the last thing he ever did, the stupid idiot. Oh, the doctor says your rib isn't broken, but you will probably get a colourful bruise over the next few days. Since we didn't get around to being introduced properly, my name is Sergeant Danny Phillips of the Metropolitan Police.'

'If I'd known we were to be formally introduced, I would have dressed for the occasion.' Fey quipped.

Phillips laughed out loud, admiring the fact that she could retain her sense of humour after all she had been through. His laugh made her laugh and then cough as her bruised rib objected to the exertion.

'By the way, where is it?' he asked.

She pulled a face, recognising he was not being serious.

'As you well know, Sergeant Danny Phillips, I don't have it and I don't know where it is. If I did, I would've told you before, as I rather like my ribs the way they are now and my face as well come to that.'

'So do I', he replied, letting the words hang for a second before continuing, 'and yes, I know you would've. You're a small time thief and pickpocket, who never uses violence. Two convictions for theft, with a suspended sentence last time. So how did you get mixed up with the Mancini gang?'

'You really do have an interesting chat up line, Danny Phillips. That'll certainly put a girl at her ease. Are you going to lock me up for stealing a coat?'

'I really don't want to, because we've had a success today. With what we got now, we should be able to put William Mancini away for a bit. If you co-operate with us we'll not only not charge you, but we'll also put you into witness protection with a new identity and a new life, with no criminal record. For now though, you are safe with us and all I need to know is how you got mixed up with Mancini.'

'I'm happy to tell you. It was an offer from my new, and now very ex, boyfriend, Mike Chambers. Can you lock him up as well?'

'That'll be my pleasure, if you'll testify against him. Let's leave it at that for the moment, I'll let you get dressed for our formal introduction and then we'll take you to a safe house.'

89 – 9th May, 2006, Wimbledon

Maisie had slept fitfully, but felt much better. WPC Sheila Jones had given her breakfast.

'Do you feel up to being interviewed, dear? Inspector Peters would like to talk to you as soon as he can. It's very important if we are going to catch the people who did this terrible thing.'

'But I'm innocent. I had no idea what was in that briefcase. It must have been Mike Chambers. He told me the plans had changed and I had to take the case to the prince.'

'Don't tell me, dear, tell Inspector Peters. If you've done nothing wrong then you've nothing to fear. I'll be with you all the time. Now can I say you're ready to talk to him?'

Maisie nodded, fighting back tears.

'Miss Jennings, I'm Inspector Peters of the Murder Squad. WPC Jones you know already. All I want to do for the moment is to talk to you. You are not being charged with anything and you're not under caution. If you want to take a break at any time then say so, but the more information I can get and the quicker I can get it, then the sooner I can bring the killers of Crown Prince Helini, or King Harani XLVII of Haranistan as I should say, to justice. Do you understand?'

'Yes. Is he dead? Did the bomb kill him?'

'Is who dead?'

'Crown Prince Helini, of course.'

'Yes, he is, along with two of his staff. There are also three injured.'

'I can't say I'm sorry for him, but I am for the others.'

'Tell me why.'

She told Peters the whole story from her abduction right through her time in the Harem until the offer he made her to go to London if she took the ERECOT with her.

He explained to her how Helini had seized power and proclaimed himself king, only to be deposed immediately afterwards in a coup d'état.

'Thank you, Maisie, with what you have told us, we have enough to put Chambers away for abduction. Will you testify against him?'

'Yes, I'd love to see that bastard put away for a very long time.'

'It may mean us putting you into long term witness protection and even changing your identity.'

'Since I don't really have an identity at the moment, that's unlikely to be a problem.'

'I'm pleased to hear that. We might also be able to do him for murder as well if we can prove he knew there was a bomb in that briefcase, but all in good time. Please tell me about this object the prince asked you to carry for him, the ERECOT, I think you called it.'

'Yes, it's weird. It's like a large eyeball with red centre. The white section looked like ivory. He said it contained a valuable ruby. He wanted me to take it to this guy called William Mancini, in London. I had to collect the briefcase and deliver it to him as well.'

'So the briefcase was meant for Mancini. Why did you take it to the prince's house instead?'

'It was Chambers. He told me there had been a change of plan. He had a phone call while I was in the shower in the hotel in Dubai. He didn't know I'd overhead it. But I'm sure it was the guy that made that call who told him of the change of plan.'

'Do you know who was on the other end of that call?'

'No, sorry, I was in the bathroom. I think it was a man's voice. All I can say is Chambers was fairly informal with him, so it probably wasn't the prince.'

'Can I have this ERECOT, please?'

Maisie blushed, making Peters realise where it was.

'Oh, sorry. I'll leave the room. I know

you've been through a lot already, but I'm going to have to ask WPC Jones to take it from you and put it in an evidence bag. It's the rubber gloves I'm afraid.'

Peters left, feeling embarrassed for the poor girl.

90 – 9th May, 2006, Wimbledon

Anna Fey felt relaxed for the first time in several days. She was warm, clothed and sated from a very good meal.

'So, Sergeant Phillips you're a very good cook as well as my knight in shining armour, fearsome interrogator and somebody who can whistle up a fully armed police SWAT team without making a phone call. Is there no end to your talent?'

'Please call me Danny. I am just an ordinary copper doing his duty.'

'And do ordinary coppers do their duty twenty-four, seven then, Danny? I haven't yet seen you take a break.'

'I had a short break while you were recovering from the raid, but I'll be with you now until we can ensure you no longer need protection. Do you feel up to talking about how you got involved in this?'

Fey rubbed her rib, where the bullet had hit. Phillips could see it hurt her quite a lot, but she put a brave face on it.

'This is a little sore, so I might cough a bit as we talk, but apart from that, where do you want me to start?'

'I'll call in WPC Jones, that's Sheila. She'll take notes. We have enough time to go through the whole story, so please start with how you met Mike Chambers.'

Fey's eyes narrowed when she remembered the man who had got her into this. She had trusted him and he had let her down badly. She could have died very painfully and she doubted whether he would even have known, let alone cared.

'I was in a crowd at a Chelsea game doing what I do best, having just acquired a purse from a rather silly girl who was looking doe-eyed at her boyfriend. A voice called out, "Hey, I saw that, stop that girl". I was worried I'd been spotted when this guy, who turned out to be Mike Chambers, grabbed my arm, said "darling, there you are". He took me out a side exit and into a taxi before you could say knife. He must have known what I'd done, but he didn't seem to care. He took me to a really swish restaurant and then back to his penthouse flat overlooking the river in docklands. You can probably guess what happened next, but let's just say for the record that I stayed the night.'

'That works for me. Do you remember the address?'

'I only went there the once, but I think it was called Allenbury Towers, or something like that.'

Phillips turned to Jones, who had been

noting what was said as well as recording it.

'We know it. It's one of Mancini's places. There's somebody watching it; if he turns up there, we'll have him. Please carry on.'

'Well, we had a couple more dates, both at expensive restaurants. At the end of the second one he asked me if I fancied a week in Paris. I'd never been to France, so I accepted like a shot. We had a posh hotel room as Mr and Mrs Chambers, on honeymoon. After a couple of days he asked me if I would do this job for him. I was to return on Sunday evening, without him. He wanted me to steal this object he called the ERECOT, from a girl who would be travelling back with him on the Eurostar that evening. He gave me a second class Eurostar ticket and said he and the girl would be sitting opposite me. I was not to let on I knew him. I should have been suspicious because not only did he know the girl's travel arrangements, but also knew the type of coat she'd be wearing. However he had been really kind and I was getting used to the good life. He also said I would get a thousand pounds for the safe delivery of the ERECOT.'

'Did he tell you what the ERECOT was?'

'He told me what it looked like. It was like a large eyeball made of ivory, about three point five centimetres in diameter with a ruby centre about half a centimetre across. I never actually saw it, but I did see that girl holding something round in a paper bag when she put her hand in her pocket. She must have seen me looking and palmed it, the crafty bitch.'

'What happened to Chambers?'

'He left me on Thursday, but paid the bill till Sunday and gave me some money to enjoy myself. He said he would meet up with me again outside the station at Waterloo, but during the trip I was to act as if we were strangers. You can imagine my surprise when you showed up instead.'

'Tell me about the trip back from Paris.'

'The first thing I must tell you is that it was a week later than we had originally planned. I should have been going home on the first of May, but didn't leave until the eighth. Mike called me the day before to say the plans had changed and I could have an extra week's holiday in Paris. Not too shabby, I thought. Anyway, I digress. I was the first to arrive in my block of four seats. I had an aisle seat facing forward, so made myself comfortable with my magazine. The next to arrive was this guy who was by himself. He had the window seat beside me, so I had to get up to let him in. Mike Chambers and the girl turned up together while I was waiting to sit back down. She took the window seat, so I was sitting directly opposite

Mike, but he showed no sign of recognising me. The girl looked a bit nervous. She shrank into her coat in the corner, which was surprising because it was quite warm on the train. She was fumbling with something in her right-hand pocket. Eventually she took out a small package, removed her coat, put the package back into her coat and then put the coat on the rack. At least I thought she'd put the package back in her coat but, as I said, she must have palmed it at the time. She was good enough to fool me.'

'Do you think she suspected something?'

'She may well have done because she was definitely nervous.'

'Did you leave your seat at any time?'

'Yes, once, to go to the toilet.'

'Did anybody else move?'

'Not when I was sitting there they didn't. The guy beside me fell asleep. Mike and the girl chatted for a bit and then she read her book. He just sat there looking out of the window.'

'Anything else of interest?'

'Not really. We all brought drinks when the trolley came around, but that's about it.'

'How did you manage to change coats?'

'As we got close to Waterloo, I kept looking at my watch to make them think I was in a hurry. When we reached Vauxhall I got up, grabbed her coat and my bag, and walked towards the front of the train. She had her head in the book so didn't see me make the switch. By the time the train stopped in Waterloo I was near the first door of the front carriage. I was out like a shot and one of the first to get through passport control. I headed straight for the taxi rank, but you were kind enough to give me a lift and save me the fare. The rest, of course, you know.'

91 – 9th May, 2006, Wimbledon

'It's what?' Peters screamed down the phone. He was livid and he did not care who knew it.

'It's a golf ball covered in sealing wax, sir.'

'Anything else?'

'We took DNA samples before we removed the sealing wax. They're a match for the ones from Dubai. It's definitely the same girl.'

'That's something, I suppose. Just wait until I have a word with her.'

Peters was about to rush in and give Maisie hell, but held off. He had promised to give Ffolkes a call, so thought he would do that first to let himself cool down. Ffolkes answered straight away.

'George I've been awaiting your call. We got cut off after the explosion. I saw pictures of it on television. I guessed you must have had your hands full, so I thought I'd wait for you to call me. How is it going with the Haranistanis?'

'They're not saying a lot, which is a bit of a surprise, but I guess they've got bigger problems at the moment, what with the revolution. Oh, on that matter, congratulations, I understand it was you who got the king and queen out. How are they settling into life in Norway?'

'Not me, George, I was just caught up in it.

I didn't have a clue what to do. Catching murderers is more my thing. Between you and me, we can thank Mossad, although nobody's admitting it publicly and they're not likely to. I, as the representative of the Norwegian government, have to be the official face of this success. It's a bit embarrassing really, but the Commander says it won't do my career any harm. That's good providing he never expects me to do it again. As for the king and queen, I'm not sure if it's sunk in really; not with him at least. She seems to be accepting it and if anything she's quite relieved. Anyway, George, it's nice of you to ask, but I'm sure that's not why you've phoned. What news do you have for me?'

'We've got Maisie Jennings in a safe house. She's given us enough to put Chambers away for a long time and we've got him in custody. We took him from one of Mancini's properties. That's a useful connection, when it comes to building a case against Mancini.'

'But there's something annoying you isn't there, George? I can tell from your voice.'

'There certainly is, Sven. Jennings told us she was carrying an ERECOT, which she was going to deliver to Mancini. She even described it. Big ruby, yellowing casing with no marks on it. When I asked her to give it to me, she gave me a golf ball covered in sealing wax. Little minx must have it hidden somewhere and thinks she can keep it for herself. I'll put her right about that, I can tell you, Sven. I'll put the fear of god into her, I will, make no mistake.'

'Easy, George, easy. You might be right but let's think about this. Is she going to be stupid enough to tell you she's carrying a valuable ERECOT and then give you a golf ball? She'd know how you'd react. Just like you have in fact. Maybe she thinks she can lie her way through it, but isn't it much more likely she didn't know either. If the girl saw the ERECOT and then took something covered in sealing wax, then ask her why. Even if she didn't know she'd been given a substitute, she might be able to tell you who took the ERECOT. At least start by giving her the benefit of the doubt. You can always come in heavy later if you're convinced she's lying to you. You'll know, because you're too good a copper not to.'

'Thank you, Sven. Now I know why we need to keep talking to each other. I'll be nice to her just in case she's an innocent who's been duped.'

'One other thing, George. You said, yellowing case with no hieroglyphics, yes?'

'Yes?'

'Even if it's as she described it, then it's still

a fake, but a good one and probably looks like the original, which none of the others we've seen or heard about has. We know anything out there is a fake, because I've seen the original. Its case has yellowed and it doesn't have hieroglyphics. How many more of these things are going to turn up and what are they for? This one is different and intended to pass as the original, but what's the purpose of the others? It's these hieroglyphics that are really getting to me.'

'I'll see if she can shed any light on that too, Sven.'

92 – 9th May, 2006, Wimbledon

'Miss Jennings can you describe this ERECOT to me again, please?'

'It was like a large eyeball made of a yellowing material. Looked like ivory, but I'm not sure. Then there was a ruby representing the eye.'

'How large would you say? Size of a large marble, or bigger, say a golf ball or bigger still, like an egg but round?'

Maisie thought about it.

'Golf ball, I'd say?'

'A golf ball covered in sealing wax?'

'Yes, that'd be about right, why is it important?' Maisie was beginning to look worried.

'Because that is precisely what you gave me, Miss Jennings.'

'Very good, Inspector. Now pull the other one.'

'Miss Jennings, I am not joking and I will throw the book at you if you don't start co-operating. What you gave me was a golf ball, covered in sealing wax.'

'What? You're not kidding? A golf ball. A bloody golf ball? I've been carrying an f'ing golf ball inside me for the last week? But I saw it before the sealing wax was put on it.'

'Why was sealing wax put on it, Miss Jennings?'

'For comfort, Inspector. It was a bit sharp as it was, so he said he'd have it covered in sealing wax. It was much better when I tried it, so I didn't check that there was an eyeball thing underneath, I just trusted her.'

'Her? I thought you said that the prince put the sealing wax on it.'

'It was his idea, but Carol got it done. It was her who gave it back to me, covered in wax. She must have kept the eye, the crafty lady. Good on her for pulling a fast one on him. I wonder what she's going to do with it. Come to that, I wonder what's going to happen to her now he's not around.'

'Do you know what it was for and why he wanted to deliver it to Mancini?'

'No, Inspector, he never said anything to me. I was just a concubine who had to do as she was told or be punished. There was never any discussion or explanation. Carol might know something, but it's just a guess. Mike Chambers is probably your best bet. He was involved in the delivery.'

93 – 10th May 2006, New Scotland Yard

Peters was feeling very pleased as he began the interview and he did not care if it showed. He and his team had worked hard for this result.

'It is 10:27 on 10th May 2006. Interview of Michael Allen Chambers who is charged with the abduction of Miss Maisie Anne Jennings between the 26th and 28th day of September, 1996. Those present, in addition to Mr Chambers, are Inspector George Peters and Sergeant Brian Reeves of the Murder Squad and Mr Alexander Dixon who is the solicitor representing Mr Chambers. Also in attendance to observe this interview is Inspector Sven Ffolkes of the Oslo Police Force. Inspector Ffolkes is running an investigation into the murder of a British subject whose body was found in Norway and which may be related to this case.'

He began his questioning. 'Mike Chambers do you have any objection to Inspector Ffolkes' presence or to being asked questions by him that might help his investigations?'

Chambers turned to his solicitor, who nodded.

'I confirm I have no objections to Inspector Ffolkes' presence or to his asking me questions.'

The solicitor spoke. 'Inspector, my client

intends to plead guilty to the charge of abduction and is prepared to help the police in other matters where he can. We expect this fact to be presented in court, such that his co-operation can be reflected when it comes to sentencing.'

'I am happy to do that, but I must make it clear that I am offering no form of immunity to Mr Chambers.'

Chambers became impatient. He interrupted before his solicitor could respond.

'I know that, Inspector, so can we just get on with it?'

'Of course. Mike, do you have any information about the disappearance of Lenny Clark on or about 11th December 2004?'

'Yes. Lenny Clark was murdered by Charles Mancini. He went to see Mancini at his home in Tenterden that night asking for help to hide from the police. Mancini took him to the site of the new M25 Motorway Service Station in Surrey, where the Mancini Construction Company is one of the contractors building the shopping area on the clockwise side. He killed Clark there and buried his body within the foundations.'

'How do you know this, Mike?'

'Because I was there. I tried to persuade Charles not to do it, but he was a real hothead.

He put a bullet in the back of Clark's head before I could stop him.

'Why did he kill Clark?'

'He was angry with Lenny for botching the theft of Alice Adams' ring. He just wanted the ring without any fuss, but Lenny went and killed the poor girl. That put a lot of heat on Charles and also meant he couldn't sell the ring when he found out it wasn't what he wanted.'

'In what way wasn't it what he wanted?'

'He was trying to get hold of a valuable artefact, the ERECOT, or more precisely the gem from it, which he thought Alfie Farquhar had inherited from his great-uncle. It was supposed to contain a pigeon-blood ruby and also a coded message within hieroglyphics written on the ivory casing. He thought the ring was made with this ruby, but it wasn't. It was a nice piece, but not that valuable and, because of the heat, he couldn't even get rid of it to get some of his money back.'

'How did William Mancini react when he heard his brother had killed Clark?'

'He was annoyed, because he's trying to move the family into legitimate businesses, but he didn't do anything about it. He certainly didn't kill Charles, or have him killed, if that's what you are thinking.'

'Do you know who did kill Charles

Mancini?'

'Not for sure and I don't have any names, but I can tell you that Charles Mancini killed somebody else and buried him in the same part of the Service Station. It was an Asian guy who was claiming to have the ERECOT and was prepared to sell it. He met up with Charles and showed him this thing, which was an obvious fake. He said he wouldn't be stupid enough to bring the original, but the fake had identical markings and he could interpret them. They were supposed to lead to a second hoard of treasure not buried in the tomb of King Harani XVI. That hoard is supposed to be much bigger than the one buried in the tomb. It's possible those who sent the Asian guy killed Charles in revenge for his murder.'

'Why did Mancini kill him rather than let him lead them to this hoard?'

'Charles thought the guy was a chancer who was taking the piss. He had him tied to a chair while trying to get the translation out of him, but the guy just kept shtum. He decided he could get the hieroglyphics translated himself, so didn't need the guy. As I said, Charles Mancini was a hothead. He killed this guy in the same way as he did Lenny, again before I had the chance to talk him out of it. He used the Smith and Weston thirty-eight that he carries with him all the time. It made one hell of a mess I can tell you.'

'So you think somebody associated with the Asian man Charles Mancini killed was responsible for killing him.'

'It's all I can think. Charles killed this guy just after New Year in 2005 and he disappeared later that year. I know William was angry with him, but he wouldn't have killed him for it. He just wanted Charles to sort things out and find the treasure.'

'If we take you to the service station site, can you show us where the bodies are buried?'

'I think so. I'm certainly prepared to try.'

'Moving on to the events of last week, which culminated in a bomb going off at twenty-one Bayswater Road. Can you tell us what you were doing, why you were with both Maisie Jennings and Anna Fey and why you told Miss Jennings to take the briefcase containing the bomb to Bayswater?'

Chambers learned across to whisper to his solicitor, who then spoke.

'Inspector, my client will answer your question, but we wish to make it clear that he was not aware of there being a bomb in the briefcase.'

'I understand. Mike, will you please, during your explanation, say what you thought was in the briefcase?'

'I'll deal with that first. I thought they were papers relating to the contract the Mancini Construction Company has with the Government of Haranistan. I received a call from an agent of the Crown Prince telling me not to deliver the briefcase to William Mancini, but instead to return it to the Crown Prince's Bayswater apartment. He said there were errors in the papers and they needed to be corrected before being sent on to William. Maisie was still to deliver the ERECOT to William and pick up a receipt for a payment of 500,000 Haranistani Crowns, that's about fifty grand, against the contract.'

'Tell me more about this ERECOT.'

'The Haranistani Government said it was the genuine article, which it had removed from the golden Cyclops. That's why it had to be smuggled out of Haranistan and into the UK. William saw an opportunity to save money so we arranged to have Anna Fey steal it. Maisie could then not deliver it to him, so he'd save fifty grand and just pay Anna a grand for her work.'

'Did you ever see this ERECOT?'

'No, but Maisie must have. She was carrying it after all.'

'Are you sure Maisie was carrying the

ERECOT?'

'Well, as I said, I didn't actually see it. Most of the time it was inside her, if you understand my meaning. I did see something of about the right size when she took it out, but it was covered in red wax. She was frightened I'd steal it from her, so she put it in the hotel room safe and set the combination. I wasn't allowed to know what the combination was. Whatever it was she was carrying, she thought it was valuable and that the prince would have her killed if she didn't deliver it as instructed.'

'Would Maisie have known there was a bomb in the briefcase?'

'I don't see how she could have. It was in a diplomatic briefcase owned by the Haranistanis, so we both assumed that they put it there and it was their man who made the change of plan. I think they intended to kill William, with Maisie as collateral damage. They couldn't really let her free in London for fear that she would say where she had been for the last ten years. I wasn't keen on her being freed either because she could finger me for abduction, which is why I'm in this mess now.'

'That's a fair point. So why did they change their minds and send the bomb to their own Crown Prince?'

'Haven't they just had a revolution?

Perhaps they just wanted rid of him rather than put him on trial. That's my best guess, but why don't you ask their new president?'

'Nice thought, but there's a fat chance of that happening. If I can take you to the service station now, let's see if we can find those bodies.'

94 – 15th May 2006, Government Offices, Haranibad

Chase felt nervous as he awaited his first meeting with the new president. He had had initial meetings at ministerial level to discuss the purchase of the two Type 42 destroyers recently decommissioned by the Royal Navy. Although the talks had gone well there were still outstanding issues, not least of which were the price and the fact that the UK had not yet recognised the new government in Haranistan. He had promised the Secretary of State for Defence he would get at least £8M each for them. Recognition of the new government had not been discussed, but he could argue it was a requirement of selling ships to them.

'Please come this way, Sir Henry.'

The official was polite, but gave nothing away. Chase followed him into a small stateroom where a man waited for him. Looking around the room it was obvious to Chase that, although ornate, it was the result of the subdivision of a much larger room. He knew he was in a palace previously belonging to the ex-king. It had been converted into government offices using the overriding principles of efficiency and economy. The man shook his hand.

'Sir Henry, how kind of you to come. Welcome to the Democratic Republic of Haranistan. I trust you have been made comfortable while you waited and my apologies for the short delay.'

The delay had indeed been short, less than two minutes, yet the president still saw fit to apologise. This was a man whom Chase decided he could respect.

'Mr President, thank you for your invitation and indeed the hospitality of all your staff. I have been made to feel most welcome.'

'That is good. Please be seated, Sir Henry. Coffee?'

Chase thanked him, accepted the coffee and sat down. To his surprise the president poured it himself.

'Sir Henry, I asked for this conversation just between the two of us since there are delicate issues I consider we should get out of the way before we proceed with the main topic, which is the purchase of your two destroyers.'

Chase nodded but said nothing.

The president continued. 'To start with, there are the deaths of two of our citizens on UK territory and one UK citizen on Haranistan territory.' He watched for a reaction, before adding, 'You seem surprised, Sir Henry?'

'Yes, Mr President, I was only aware of one

death; that of Crown Prince Helini in a bomb blast last week. We are investigating that incident. We know who carried the bomb but we believe her to have been unaware of the contents of the briefcase and an innocent victim of the bomb maker. We have so far been unable to discover who that is. Who are the other two victims?'

'Let us start with the first of the other two victims. He was a Haranistani citizen who visited the UK intending to do business with a UK citizen, one Charles Mancini. He was murdered by Charles Mancini and is, I suspect, the second body your police discovered in your newly built service station on the M25 in Surrey.'

'You are very well informed, Mr President. Much better than me on this matter, but I will investigate and get back to you on the identity of that body.'

'All I ask of you, Sir Henry, is that you arrange for the return of the body for a State Funeral. That man is a hero of our republic. The other matters have already been resolved.'

'How do you mean, resolved, Mr President?'

'Moving on to the second victim, Charles Mancini. He was extradited to Haranistani soil, tried, found guilty of both theft and murder, and punished for both. He was executed by the previous regime, on the yacht used by ex-King Harani XLVII. His body, minus the head and left hand, were thrown overboard and I understand it was washed up in Norway. The head and hand were sent to his brother as a warning. I regret that, but was powerless to prevent it. Here are the papers relating to Charles Mancini's trial and execution. It would not be accepted as justice in the UK or indeed under the laws of the new Democratic Republic of Haranistan, but at the time it was a legal execution.'

'Again your knowledge has me at a disadvantage, Mr President. Please tell me how you know this?'

'Because I was there, Sir Henry. As a lowly official within the previous government. It was one of the things that stiffened my resolve to permanently change the government of Haranistan for the better.'

The president allowed his words to sink in before he continued.

'That leads me to the third death, that of ex-King Helini XLVII, whom you probably knew as Crown Prince Helini. It was he who deposed his father and became king, albeit for five minutes before we, the people, overthrew him in a coup d'état. It was he who ordered the bomb to be made and put in a left luggage locker at Waterloo. He intended to kill William Mancini and as many of his family as he could. He was not content with the execution of the murderer of his agent. He wanted to take revenge on the whole family and I could not allow that. I did not have time to inform your authorities, but I was able to divert the bomb to the ex-king. It was a necessary act of revolution, but I deeply regret the other deaths and injuries to innocent Haranistani citizens. I sincerely thank the British medical teams for the effort they have put in to the care of our citizens.'

The president hesitated before continuing, 'I should be forced to deny what I have just told you, should it ever become public knowledge, which it should not, because only you and I know it. That is unless Mike Chambers recognised my voice when I gave him the order, from the Crown Prince as he then was.'

For a third time the president allowed his words to sink in before continuing. He could see the shock on Chase's face. After a while he considered it right to continue.

'By our admission we have done damage to British citizens and property and although some of it was as a result of the murder of one of our citizens, it does not make it right. I am asking the UK to forgive these acts and recognise our new government. I am also asking it to return the body of our citizen, but my requests do not end there.'

The president drew breath.

'Your criminal justice system is holding an ancient artefact, the ERECOT, stolen from Haranistan by Brian Farquhar. We ask that you return it to us because, even though it does not have a high financial value, it is of great symbolic meaning to both Haranistan and its neighbour, the Republic of Ensharla. You also hold a copy of the ERECOT, sent by an anonymous source, which is of value because it contains a ruby. I know this because it came from Haranistan, with the express wish that it went to the family of Alice Adams. I was the one who arranged for it to be sent. We are happy for this to remain a gift to her family from the people of Haranistan on the understanding they are willing to repatriate the ERECOT stolen by Brian Farquhar.'

This time Chase did respond.

'Mr President, the request for the return of the remains of one of your citizens is a request the British government will be happy to grant, as indeed any civilised country would. All we will need to do is to somehow identify those remains. I will convey your request relating to the two ERECOTs to the family of Alice Adams and will strongly urge them to accept what is a generous offer. I suspect I might be pushing at an open door, because I'm told the family thinks it to be cursed.'

He hesitated, preparing to give less good news.

'As regards the recognition of your government by Britain, with its implied forgiveness for an act of terrorism to which you are not prepared to admit, this could be more difficult.'

'This does not surprise me, Sir Henry, so let me add what our government is prepared to do in return for recognition and one other thing I will come to in a minute. We will purchase from Britain, for the sum of eighty million Haranistani Crowns each, the two Type 42 destroyers you would like to sell to us. This price to include full training for our officers and crew on how to operate these ships effectively.'

'You drive a hard bargain, Mr President. You do realise we are asking ten million pounds each for these ships and that doesn't include training. Your offer is equivalent to eight million pound each at today's exchange rates.'

'Sir Henry, I think we both know you cannot sell your ships at ten million pounds to any buyer to whom you are prepared to sell. It is our intention to apply to join NATO, so with this deal these ships would remain at its disposal for vital protection work in this area.'

Chase began turning this offer over in his mind, soon realising he needed to know something else first.

'What was the other thing that you wanted?'

'It has come to our attention that the genuine ERECOT, stolen from the Golden Cyclops, has come into your possession following the payment of a reward for its safe return. We would ask that it is returned to Haranistan as a gesture of great kindness from the UK government following its recognition of our government and the sale of your ships to us.'

Chase was not prepared to let the chance of success slip from his grasp. He could argue that the training would come from UK servicemen already being paid for by his government and that it would be of benefit to NATO. He had paid personally for the reward for the safe return of the ERECOT specifically for this purpose.

'I would have to fix the exchange rate of your offer, ideally to eight million sterling each, or if you prefer, we could fix it against the dollar, euro or Swiss franc, but with the recent volatility of the Haranistani Crown we would have to insist on a price in one of those currencies. Also, we would need confirmation of Haranistan joining NATO. Otherwise, I think I can arrange what you are asking. Please give me a little time to sort things out at home.'

'I understand, Sir Henry. I can tell you that within the next few days I shall announce an event, which will be a state occasion, intended to lift the spirit of the nation after the trauma of the revolution and the state funeral of our hero, whose body the UK will return to us as soon as it obtains proof of identity and nationality. The event will be on September fifth and we would like to invite the heads of state of countries who have recognised our government. Can you arrange everything by then?'

'That will be my target, Mr President.'

'Thank you, Sir Henry. If you can, we have a deal. On the matter of identifying our citizen would the provision of dental records and the DNA of his brother be acceptable?'

'If it's taken by our agent or in the presence of one of our embassy staff and it's a match, of course, Mr President.'

'Fine, I shall arrange with your embassy to take a sample of my DNA for your test.'

'Your DNA, Mr President?'

'Yes, Sir Henry, the victim was not only a hero of our republic, he was also my brother, Ibrahim.'

95 – 18th May 2006, New Scotland Yard.

Peters sat in the video-conference suite at New Scotland Yard together with his sergeant. At the other end, in Oslo, were Sven Ffolkes and Commander Magnussen. He opened the proceedings.

'Gentlemen, we will soon be joined at this end by Professor Arnold Roberts, Dr Max Fleet and Dr Simon Blake of Empire College, but before we are, I should like to clear up some matters which are only of concern to us as law enforcement officers. Thanks to intelligence obtained from our Defence Minister's recent visit to Haranistan, we have been able to close our murder cases on Alice Adams, Lenny Clark, Charles Mancini and Crown Prince Helini of Haranistan. Each victim was killed by the next and the prince was killed by his own bomb, which he intended for William Mancini, but which was redirected back to him as part of the coup d'état that established the Democratic Republic of Haranistan. There was a fifth victim, Ibrahim Mohammed, a Haranistani national, killed by Charles Mancini. We will be returning his body very soon. I can add that Mike Chambers has confessed to abduction and is on remand awaiting trial. We are currently still considering charges against William Mancini, who is in custody. We certainly have enough to charge him with abduction and false imprisonment, but may not be able to do any more than that, which is a pity. However, this is now a matter exclusively within our hands so I do not need to bother our Norwegian colleagues with it. What I do want to do, when we are joined by the team from Empire College, is to try to resolve all the issues surrounding the ERECOT, or ERECOTs as it transpired, in case further criminal charges should be brought in relation to them. Are there any questions before I bring them in?'

There were no questions, so the Empire College team were called in and introduced before Peters handed over to Ffolkes.

'Gentlemen. To understand the parts these ERECOTs have played in the deaths of five people we must go back into the history of Haranistan from its creation following the uprising under Harani I, through the death and burial of Harani XVI and the oil rich kingdom of Harani XLVI, to the coup d'état that led to the formation of the Democratic Republic of Haranistan. We need also look beyond that, to what could happen in the future as a result.

'It is an historical fact that Haranistan was established in the second century AD, by an insurrection led by Harani Anshalari I. He was proclaimed leader of a democratic community, which had, over the generations, deteriorated into a despotic kingdom ruled by suppression and taxation of its people. In an attempt to trade on the respect Harani I was held in by his people, all his successors, who are from the same family, called themselves Harani. Latterly the lot of the people had been improved by the introduction of a civilian government, which significantly reduced the burden of taxation. However all government actions had to be approved by the king, who retained absolute rule until he was deposed by the recent coup.

'Legend built up around a cyclops who came from Thebes to help Harani's forces and who was instrumental in the winning of the battle against the Greeks. This legend is now deeply engrained in Haranistani folklore and culture. Even its flag includes a red-eyed cyclops and Cyclops Square has pride of place in the centre of the capital Haranibad. The cyclops is claimed to be buried beneath the square, but the government has not allowed independent excavation, so we do not know what is under there.

'In a gesture of great kindness to me before he was deposed, King Harani XLVI took me to the burial chamber of King Harani XVI, the location of which is secret, for the specific purpose of helping me to bring murderers to justice. From that access, I have agreed to reveal only those facts needed to assist in this purpose. The existence of the cyclops, and if it does exist, the location of its tomb, are not relevant to this case.

'By the time we reach 620 AD, the dynasty has become so wealthy it decides to copy the practices of the pharaohs by building magnificent tombs, full of gold, silver and jewels for the deceased kings to take into the next world. The finest example of this is the tomb of Harani XVI, built by his son and placed in a location which, for protection from treasure hunters, was known only to the Anshalari family. Legend is important because of the stories surrounding this tomb, which includes the existence of a golden statue of the Cyclops. In 1917, Sir Archibald Chase led an expedition seeking to discover the tomb. An expedition which ended in tragedy when a rock fall killed all but one of its members. Sir Archibald was rumoured to have found the tomb and triggered a trap causing the rock fall. The rumours also suggested the sole survivor, Brian Farquhar, had escaped with the ERECOT. Farquhar would never speak of it, claiming to have been too traumatised to recount the detail, but he did leave something resembling the ERECOT to his nephew, Alfie.

'Alfie asked his brother Freddie, a jeweller, to make a ruby engagement ring from it for his fiancée, Alice Adams. Freddie realised that the ERECOT contained, not a ruby, but what he thought to be glass and of no value. Being a good brother, he made a ring from rubies he had in stock and kept the ERECOT, but let Alfie believe he had used it. Unfortunately for poor Alice, the underworld thought her ring contained a genuine pigeon-blood ruby of immense value so Lenny Clark, a thief sent by Charles Mancini, stole it and murdered her in the process.

'When the king took me to the tomb, he showed me that it is indeed, as legend claims, full of treasures and guarded by a golden Cyclops, with a red eye made from a pigeon-blood ruby set into an ivory casing. Whether the statue is cursed or not, I cannot say, but I can tell you it is intact and a famous international jeweller has certified that the ruby in its eye is genuine, so I shall refer to this as the true eye or T-ERECOT. Exactly where the tomb is, I do not know, because I was taken there through a closed underground system.

'So what then is the significance of the eye discovered by Sir Archibald Chase and stolen by Farquhar? And why was it used as a booby trap to kill anybody who tried to take it? It is now clear to me this eye was not the T-ERECOT, but a copy of the eye which, for the purpose of this explanation, and for reasons I will explain later, I shall call the G-ERECOT.

'The rumour of a copy of the ERECOT has existed for many years, because of the belief that the T-ERECOT had been stolen in the Period of Darkness and that the Haranistani Royal Family had replaced it by a copy. The king told me the family encouraged this rumour as a means of protecting the genuine statue and T-ERECOT from would-be thieves. Since there was no theft, there was no copy made to replace the original, yet a belief that there was gained credibility. Even though it did not exist, the belief in this decoy eye is important so I will name it the D-ERECOT. The king even told the story to his son, Crown Prince Helini, swearing him to secrecy, but knowing that eventually his son would tell somebody, probably whilst drunk. Unfortunately for the king, his son was more discreet than he had hoped and when he did spill the beans it was to Professor Roberts, who guarded the secret jealously, until he felt compelled by these murders to reveal it to me. Prior to then, there was only the gossip in the bazaars, which nobody really believed, although they did help the king's cause a little.

'We must remember how rumour had it that the RECOT was fitted with a copy eye and the true eye was stolen and hidden somewhere, whereas we now know almost the reverse was true. We can conclude it was the G-ERECOT that was kept by Brian Farquhar, who thought he had discovered the T-ERECOT.

'This set me two puzzles.

'One: what was a copy doing in the ante-chamber of the tomb of Harani XVI, if indeed Sir Archibald had found the tomb?

'Two: why was it booby-trapped?

'There is a superficially obvious explanation that answers both questions. The copy was there to divert the attention of any potential thieves from the RECOT and then to kill them, with a rock fall, when they tried to steal it. This explanation, however, has two flaws.

'Firstly, why would any thieves expect to find an isolated eye when they were looking for the complete RECOT? They would expect the RECOT to be intact and would surely be suspicious of a single item?

'Secondly, a collapse of the antechamber would certainly block the tomb and might damage or even destroy the RECOT, other treasures and the tomb itself. Those who commissioned the tomb would not accept this risk. So we need to look for a different explanation, and for that the booby trap is the clue. Whoever set the trap didn't mind if the fall destroyed the RECOT and blocked the tomb. We must conclude it was the builders of the tomb who set this trap, because who else had the ability to construct it? It was certainly not ordered by the *designers* of the tomb, because their purpose was to preserve everything, but let's remember who actually *built* the tomb. They were African slaves. Did they put it there and set the trap, and if so to what purpose?

'To decide that, I sought the advice of Dr Blake. I first showed him the eye we recovered from your unnamed source. Our experts told us the eye was made using a small ruby enclosed in a modern ivory case made of two, machine-turned halves screwed together. This is the same design as the original, but the materials are different and the eye is smaller. The king's advisors told me the original has a pigeon-blood ruby of much greater quality encased in ancient ivory with a hand carved screwing mechanism. There is also another difference. This copy has black markings inscribed into the back of the iris, which the original does not. We already knew from its construction that the eye was modern and probably less than ten years old. So, using my classification, we know that it is neither the

T-ERECOT nor the G-ERECOT, but merely a modern fake, so I will call it an F-ERECOT. I say "an", because we know for a fact that more than one fake exists, although not all have genuine rubies. As a curio with a ruby, it had a value of a little more than the ruby itself, so I concluded there must be more to it for somebody to want to kill for it.

We took a very careful look at the hieroglyphics. As you all know by now, the code inside comprised Chinese numeric characters, which when translated to Arabic characters becomes: 313, 761, 221, 613, 13 and 25. Our objective was to determine what these numbers meant, so I went back to legend, which held that the eye would lead the holder to great treasure. But why, if this eye is a modern fake would it carry any information about treasure buried hundreds of years ago?

'This is a very good question and one which had me thinking for some time, until I realised that those who sought it, although they would probably know it was a modern fake, might believe it to be a faithful copy and pay highly for it because of where it could lead them.

'I worked on the principle that the code was intended to provide a location, so with six numbers, a map reference was an obvious bet. The use of numbers alone also meant the code was not language dependent. I thought of asking Inspector Peters to get GCHQ involved, but then remembered the second part to the legend, which states that possession the eye is not enough. To solve the code requires more information, presumably in the form of a decoder. I also remembered the Haranistanis had released some further information about the RECOT on their website, including an inscription on the base. This is, allegedly, a quote from the Cyclops, stating, in Greek, "To receive the rewards of life we must use our own resources and learn from the work of our enemies".

'At the time I thought it strange that such a specific, single piece of information had been released and wondered if it had been the work of a hacker. Or was it genuine and had an ulterior motive. I was able to confirm it *was* genuine when Haranistan issued its first sets of commemorative postage stamps and coins. Both a coin and a stamp included this quote.

'When I was in the tomb I checked the statue of the Cyclops and the eye has no inscription on it. None of the king's curators knew anything of an inscription, so they too thought it might be a hoax perpetrated by a hacker… until the stamps came out. So who was responsible for the issue of the stamps and coins of Haranistan? Whoever it was, was putting this information out there for his own purposes. So, if this information had any relevance, it had to be in relation to the modern F-ERECOTs. The enemy of Haranistan at the time of the Cyclops was Greece and the writing was in Greek, so I suspected I was looking for the work of a Greek to help me solve a number problem. I also believe the set of numbers should convert to a grid reference, which would mean the first and fourth each had to be less than 180, because they are degrees respectively from the Greenwich Meridian and the Equator. The others would be less than 60 because they are minutes and seconds. These figures do not fit those criteria, so we needed the help of a Greek mathematician to convert them to numbers that do.'

'Pythagoras?' Peters suggested.

'Pythagoras indeed and his most famous theorem in fact.'

'But how does his theorem help us?'

'Have you noticed all the figures are odd numbers? There is a method of generating the dimensions of the sides of right-angled triangles where the shortest side and the hypotenuse are both odd. It's one of those things I remember from my school days. The most famous is the 3-4-5 triangle, where the sum of the two longer sides, nine in this case, equals the square of the shortest side. The difference between the two longer sides is always one. This fact works for a whole series of right-angled triangles, with the next ones in the series being 5-12-13 and 7-24-25. The series goes on indefinitely. So what if our sequence gives, in each case, the length of the hypotenuse and we need to convert it to the equivalent shortest side? This would give us: 25, 39, 21, 35, 5 and 7. This does fit a map reference, for Myrtos in Crete.'

Peters interrupted. 'But why would the Haranistanis locate a tomb or whatever else in Greece? Even in a modern context, if a fake hoard of treasure had been placed at a location purporting to be where the real treasure of Harani XVI's tomb is, then a location in Greece makes no sense?'

'Indeed it does not, George, but let us not forget the other part of the non-existent advice, which is to use our own resources. Suppose we reverse the eastings and the northings in our code? This gives: 35, 5, 7, 25, 39, and 21. This *is* in Haranistan. Before you ask, there is a huge new town being created there by the Haranistani Government, which has contracted the Mancini Construction Company to build it. It is intended for the accommodation and entertainment of the miners who will work in the re-opened gemstone mines. All the details of the contracts were negotiated by Crown Prince Helini and are secret, but I would guess there is a clause or two relating to what happens should any treasure be found at the site. The company appears to be pouring a lot of money into the project for little reward at the moment.'

Peters interrupted again. 'I've heard about this contract. The company seems to be losing its shirt on it. Its estimated value has dipped to a tenth of what it was at its peak. There's a rumour that it will go into liquidation, bankrupting Mancini, because he owns it privately and is responsible for its debts, which are mounting by the day. I wouldn't mind being a fly on the wall when that contract ends and it comes to the payment for the building works and the distribution of any finds.'

'You and me both, George.'

George nodded, but then realised he had not received a complete explanation. The existence of the fake eyes explained the murders of Charles Mancini and Crown Prince Helini, but what of Alice Adams?

'Sven, you mentioned a booby-trapped G-ERECOT earlier, which survived the fall that killed Sir Archibald Chase and all but one of his team. It was the one the Mancini family thought Freddie Farquhar had made into a ring for Alice, but I discovered it was not. Freddie gave the G-

ERECOT to me when he gave me the documentation relating to the ring. It was made from a piece of polished obsidian encased in ivory, so even though it was very old it was of little value. Also I was told by Sir Henry Chase that Haranistan wanted it back, but was prepared to let Alice Adams' family keep a much more valuable copy in its place. He presented it as an altruistic gesture, but my suspicious police mind says there was more to it. Nonetheless, the family accepted the offer and the G-ERECOT has been returned to Haranistan. Why was it so important to Charles and William Mancini that they were prepared to kill for it? Did you get anywhere with it professor?'

Roberts picked up the explanation. '"Very old" hardly starts to describe it. We believe it dates back to the building of the tomb itself, in the seventh century. Since the red stone is a piece of obsidian of no value we worked on the theory it was the marks on the ivory case which were significant, so I turned to Dr Simon Blake, our expert in the symbols and language of the time. Simon?'

'Thank you, professor. I confess to being baffled by these markings at first, because they weren't like any of the other writing I had seen from seventh century Haranistan. They bore much closer relationships to those of the neighbouring African countries, so I worked on the assumption they were written by the slaves. This also explains why the eye was made with cheap materials, which would have been all that was available to them. What would be the most important thing slaves wanted to tell each other that they would not want their masters to know?'

'What they really thought of them?' Peters ventured.

'No, something much more important than that, which was how to escape from them. The Haranistanis thought the Herendits were impassable, but a few of the slaves knew the passages through them. So this is not an ancient treasure map as Mancini thought, but rather a seventh century escape map, which slaves memorised before they attempted to escape. They could not take the eye with them because doing so would deprive others of the opportunity to escape. If the Haranistani guards tried to take it in order to follow escaping slaves then the booby trap mechanism would kick in. I suspect the slaves told the guards it was one of their customs to place an eye over the entrance to deter unwanted visitors and they chose the eye of the Cyclops in honour of its achievements. The result was the G-, or Guide-ERECOT. An escape map hidden in plain sight.'

Roberts concluded the explanation.

'To summarise, there is the T-ERECOT, which still sits in the golden statue of the Cyclops, the G-ERECOT made by the African slaves and then an indeterminate number of modern fakes, F-ERECOTs, all with Chinese numbers on the irises which are supposed to lead to a second hoard of treasure located on the site of this new city. Yet we now know that this hoard never existed. So they are a con, which Mancini has believed and contracted with the Haranistani government in the hope of finding. So, who instigated this con?'

Peters explained. 'From what I have been told by Sir Henry Chase, which has to stay confidential for a while at least, it has to have been the Haranistani Government or Crown Prince Helini to be more precise. Not only did he execute Charles Mancini for the murder of one of his representatives, but he decided to ruin the whole family as well and then blow up William Mancini to finish the job. Charming man, no wonder the new regime decided to get rid of him.'

'Yes, but he must have conceived the con before he targeted Mancini. It was his representative who was trying to sell the fake in the first place whom Charles Mancini murdered. That's what made the whole thing personal.'

Ffolkes added.

'I'm sure you're right there, Sven. We would seem to have covered everything quite nicely, except for the fact that Sir Henry Chase paid a large reward for what the Haranistani Crown Jeweller claimed to be the true ERECOT. He lent it to me to look at. It has no hieroglyphics, and a genuine ruby in an old ivory case, which has already yellowed.' Roberts held up the piece just to prove his point.

Ffolkes did not believe what he was hearing.

'When did he buy… sorry pay the reward for, this? I ask because I saw the original, in the statue of the golden Cyclops when I visited the king on the day of the revolution?'

'It was on 8th May. A woman brought it to my office and the Haranistani Crown jeweller certified it.'

'If that is true then the new government has sold it for £100,000. It must be worth way more than that and if they needed the money then why not sell the whole statue. It would fetch millions at auction. I can't believe that.'

'I agree with Inspector Ffolkes. Sir Henry told me they had asked for it back as a gesture of good will. The president claimed that the eye had been stolen during the Period of Darkness and now was the chance to get it back. That's the old official line, but we now know it not to be true.' Roberts added.

'The crafty lot.' Ffolkes exclaimed, as the reason dawned on him. '*We* know that the story of the theft in the Period of Darkness is not true, but we are the only ones who do. Just imagine the capital they could make from the return of the ERECOT to its rightful place. I bet they intend to open the tomb to the public, particularly tourists, with stories of a lost and recovered ERECOT. The replacement copy, which I'll bet they've just made and sold to Sir Henry, will be displayed as the piece used for the last ninety years. It's the D-ERECOT being brought into existence from legend. It's a new income stream for Haranistan. Good luck to them if they did, but it means Sir Henry has been conned. Can you check on the authenticity of that ERECOT?'

'I could.' Roberts began, 'but I'm not sure I should. If I go public on this fake then we expose the new Haranistani government as a bunch of con artists, it gets offended and refuses to buy our ships, whereas if I... we, say nothing then everybody is happy. Sir Henry gets his sale and probably a promotion. Britain benefits from selling its ships. Haranistan gets its income stream and recognition of its government from Britain. We all win... oh, sorry, Commander,

Sven; I don't see anything in it for Norway.'

'I do.' The Commander responded. 'Will you ask Sir Henry to make it clear to the Haranistani government that we know what went on, but will all keep quiet about it on the condition that it makes no attempt to extradite the ex-king and leaves him to live in peace in Norway?'

'I will, Commander.'

96 – 20th May, 2006, Tottenham

Inspector Peters walked into the mortuary where he was greeted by Dr Fiona Edwards, the police pathologist who had been appointed to examine the remains found in the new M25 service station.

'George, you asked me to look at these bodies, which you think are related to the murder of Alice Adams. Well, you're right there. One of them, the man who was over two metres tall was Leonard Alfred Clark, as you had surmised. He was killed from a single shot to the back of the head from a point two-two calibre gun. I suspect it was a Beretta, but I will leave your experts to determine that from the bullet. The other was also killed by a single shot to the back of the head, but with a different gun. A point three-eight calibre to be precise. It made a much bigger mess. Blew half the poor man's head away.'

'Yes, we think Charlie Mancini killed them both.'

'Do you now, George?'

'Yes, Fi. Why do you have anything to suggest otherwise?'

'I might. Was he left handed?'

'Yes, and he was known to carry a thirty-eight Smith and Wesson.'

'Then I suspect he killed the second man, because the bullet was fired from the left side and level with the victim's head.'

'That would fit with what we have been told, which was that the victim was seated at the time. But what about Lenny Clark?

'Clark was killed with a different calibre bullet, fired upwards from the right side. I think Clark was standing at the time. If I'm right the person who killed him was much shorter and right handed.'

'How short, exactly?'

'About one metre, sixty, or five foot, two and a half to you, George. Why do you know somebody of that description who might have murdered him?'

'Five, two and uses a point 22 Beretta? I certainly do. I think Mr Mike Chambers has a lot more explaining to do. Well done, Fi. It would be great to put him away for life.'

97 – 6th July, 2006, Wimbledon

Maisie sat in the lounge of the safe house feeling very pleased. She had just returned from the Crown Court where her evidence had helped to convict Mike Chambers for her abduction. She picked up a copy of the newspaper to see the headline, 'Haranistan's President to marry.' Even though she had no love for the country in which she had been held against her will for over nine years and repeatedly raped by its Crown Prince, she felt compelled to read on.

In his first speech, made after the funeral of his brother, Ibrahim, killed by the head of an organised crime syndicate in the UK, the new President of the Democratic Republic of Haranistan, Feisal Mohammed, said it was time for Haranistanis to look forward and celebrate their newly found freedoms. Having previously announced the discontinuance of all existing public holidays, which were 'inextricably linked to the regime of the past', he declared three new public holidays, Independence Day on 1st May, Hero's Day, which would be July 5th, the day of his brother's funeral, and President's Day, which would be September 5th. These holidays would be for this and next year only, after which time public holidays would be determined by the new Parliament of Haranistan. The president said he had promised the

Haranistani people a day to celebrate and could now announce his intention to marry on President's Day. It would be a state occasion when heads of state of all countries that had recognised his government would be invited. When drawn on who the bride would be he simply referred to her as 'the future Mrs Mohammed'. Asked if she would be referred to as 'The First Lady' he said it was not for him, but for the new parliament, to decide.

The president went on to confirm that, at the request of the Norwegian government, which recognised his government today, he had granted pardons to ex-King Harani XLVI and his wife, ex-Queen Fatima, who would henceforth be known as Mr Harani Anshalari and Mrs Fatima Anshalari, free citizens of the Democratic Republic of Haranistan, with unfettered rights of residence in Haranistan. The pardons were granted in recognition of the work the ex-king had done for the rights of women. He also granted 'immunity from prosecution' to the ex-king's younger son, the former Prince Stephan, explaining that Prince Stephan was not being pardoned because a pardon would not be appropriate since he had not been found guilty of any crime. At this time he did not intend to pardon ex-King Harani XLVII, the former Crown Prince who was killed in a bomb blast at his London home on 8th May, this year, because the extent of his crimes had not yet been established and further investigation would be undertaken.

The far-ranging speech went on to thank the UK both for recognising his government and for returning the Eye of the Red-Eyed Cyclops of Thebes, the ERECOT as it has become known, which he described as a National Treasure of Haranistan. He said it would be reinstated in the golden statue of the Cyclops and the whole burial chamber would open to visitors as soon as effective security arrangements could be put in place. Haranistan has purchased two former Royal Navy Type 42 Destroyers, which would be renamed the Democratic Haranistani Republican Navy (DHRN) Ibrahim and DHRN Feisal.

'So Crown Prince High and Mighty is not being pardoned', she announced to herself with satisfaction, mentally adding, "I should like to contribute to that enquiry into his crimes. I might even get an Order of the Cyclops, if they still exist, for blowing him up, even though I didn't know I was doing it. He'd have happily seen me blown up." She was still daydreaming about this when Sergeant Phillips came in to the room followed by Anna Fey, whom she recognised instantly.

'You' she cried.

'Easy, Maisie, I only wanted to introduce you to our other guest in this safe house. We couldn't do so before you'd given evidence against Chambers, but now he's safely behind bars, there no reason why you two shouldn't meet... again?'

'You helped put Mike Chambers away?' Fey declared, 'In which case I forgive you for nearly getting all my ribs broken.'

'You... forgive me? It was you who was trying to take the ERECOT from me.'

She laughed, Fey laughed and then they both hugged each other.

'Ladies and Gentlemen, might I introduce you to the founder members of the "We hate Mike Chambers" club.' Fey said as she held her arm out to Phillips.

'Come and give us both a hug, my great big, wonderful hero.'

'King Kong, hero.' He responded as he hugged both girls.

'Oh stop going on about it. You were going to break all my ribs at the time if I remember correctly.' Fey replied.

Maisie looked dumbfounded.

'Shall we explain it all to Maisie over dinner? I'll only be ten minutes, which should be enough for you girls to catch up. Oh, by the way, Maisie, you have a guest, but she won't be arriving until later.'

98 – 6th July, 2006, Wimbledon

Fey started the conversation after Phillips had served the meals.

'Alright, Maisie, can you explain how you hid the ERECOT from me.'

'So you were trying to steal it. I thought somebody might, which is why I bought the gobstopper in the paper bag and played with it in front of you. You know, that cost me a dollar.'

'One dollar! I used to buy them for ten pence, when my mum would give me the money, that is. I didn't know they were so expensive these days. It would have been alright to steal it if I'd known it was worth that much. Hang on though, there wasn't even a gobstopper in your coat. You didn't take that during your *thorough* search of me did you, Danny Phillips?'

'Nope, no gobstopper. There was an empty paper bag though.'

'I palmed the gobstopper when I put the bag back into my coat. My life has been a little dull over the last eight years, so I've been practising magic from a book I found in the har…, the apartment where I was staying.'

'I can say that you fooled me, Maisie, and I'm a professional, so well done you.'

Phillips gave her a very sharp look.

'Sorry, Maisie, I *was* a professional.

Sergeant Phillips here is helping me end my naughty ways.'

'My turn for a question now.' Maisie declared. 'Why King Kong and threatening to break all your ribs? It seems a somewhat harsh method, of stopping you from pickpocketing I assume?'

Fey told her the story of her capture and rescue.

'Christ, if I'd known you were going to go through all that, I'd have given you the damned thing. I think I might also have called you something worse, Sergeant Phillips.'

'That's a kind thought, luv, but as I explained, his search was thorough, so he'd have found it, even if you had given it to me. What is it about men and our private areas, they do seem to be obsessed with them. As if we would hide anything in them? Where were you hiding it, anyway?' Maisie blushed, but did not answer. Fey suddenly understood.

'Oh, so you *were* hiding it there. Wasn't it uncomfortable?'

'Not when it was covered in sealing wax, no. Anyway, it wouldn't have mattered because I was told to hide it there; by a man of course. To have disobeyed would have meant being killed. So painful or not, that's where it was going. It's not that bad; don't knock it until you've tried it.'

'I think I'll pass on that one.'

Maisie had noticed how Fey and Phillips appeared to be getting on very well.

'My turn for a question again. Anna, you called this guy King Kong, he strips you, gives you an intimate search and threatens to break all your ribs, yet you're still talking to him and if I'm not mistaken are getting on very well with him. What changed?'

'To be fair, both of us were in fear of our lives at the time and he did save mine. Then I told him I liked my ribs, and my face for that matter, the way they were and he said so did he. It started from there really. And of course there's nothing about me he doesn't know, both in terms of my history as well as what I look like.'

They smiled at each other and hugged.

'I am going to be Mrs Danny Phillips, fashion model, reformed pickpocket and advisor to the police on how pickpockets work. It wouldn't do to have a copper's wife up before the beak would it? I'm allowed to continue modelling, but now he wants me to keep my clothes on. Anyway, my turn again. What happened to this ERECOT you guarded so carefully?'

'I wish I knew, but it turned out I was carrying a golf ball.'

'A golf ball?' Fey responded before

breaking out laughing.

'Yes, a bleeding golf ball, alright. It didn't half piss off my police interviewer I can tell you. He threated to throw the book at me, because he thought I was hiding it.'

By this time Maisie was also laughing, with both girls close to tears.

'He should have got Sergeant Phillips here to search you. He'd have found it.'

At that point all three were laughing. None of them had heard a woman come in.

'I think I can answer that question for you.'

They all looked round. Maisie was the first to speak.

'Carol Anderson, how the hell did you get here?'

'Oh, Maisie, this is your visitor, but it seems you already know each other.' Phillips said, feeling concerned at his lapse in security that had let her come in unseen.

'We certainly do and have done for nearly ten years. Carol, how are you?'

She got up to hug Anderson.

'I'm fine, and to answer your other question I got here in his yacht and with a great deal of luck. I thought he was going to kill me, but he let me go and gave me a nice apartment, as well, but that's not important for now. It's good to see you and I owe you an explanation about the ERECOT. I kept it and gave you a golf ball covered in sealing wax instead.'

'I discovered that.' Maisie replied sardonically, as both girls broke down laughing again. Anderson looked perplexed, but continued.

'I handed the ERECOT to Sir Henry Chase in exchange for a reward of £100,000 for providing, "information leading to the recovery of the ERECOT, stolen from Haranistan during the Period of Darkness", or between 1916 and 1919 to anybody else.'

'What, the one that's claimed to be the genuine ERECOT? The one the UK has just sent back to Haranistan?'

'Yes, that one. Made by our crown jewellers in the last six months and certified by the very same crown jeweller as the genuine ERECOT, stolen nearly ninety years ago. Yes, that one, which our president will display in an exhibition case as the one that was in the Golden Cyclops before it was recently replaced by the original. It's a good story isn't it?'

'Sure is, and you made a hundred grand into the bargain. Nice one, Carol.'

'Not me, Maisie, that money will be used to help rehabilitate the poor UK girls abducted by our friend whom you kindly despatched to meet his maker, albeit in many parts. Anyway we needn't bore these good people with our matters, I've come to take you to the apartment he gave me. We plan to use it as a halfway house for the girls he abducted.'

'We?'

'Yes, the new president has agreed that this piece of Haranistani property can be used to help these girls. You are one of them, so you're welcome to come to stay for as long as you need.'

Maisie turned to Phillips, who replied.

'Maisie you are safe now Chambers is inside. Anna's evidence will take care of Mancini for a while, but he's not a threat to you anyway. You did him a favour by taking the bomb meant for him, back to Helini. He'd probably have given you a bung by way of thanks, but he's gone bankrupt and all his assets have been frozen. That's thanks to your Crown Prince, so he wasn't all bad. Anyway we are not going to charge you with anything and you are a British citizen with right of residence here, so you are free to go.'

'You can give him a hug and a kiss if you like, Maisie, but anything more than that and I'll scratch your eyes out.'

'That seems fair enough, Anna. Now come here my protector, so I can say thank you.'

She hugged and kissed him, then did the

same to Fey, before leaving with Anderson.

99 – 12th July, 2006 Notting Hill, London

Maisie and Anderson were both sitting in their dressing gowns drinking coffee. Anderson was the first to speak.

'Have you thought what you're going to do with your new found freedom, Maisie?'

'What, after I've dyed my hair black, had it frizzed up, got all my piercings redone and put all the studs back?'

Anderson looked shocked.

'No, just kidding, Carol. I think that life's behind me. A sixteen year-old punk maybe, but at twenty-six, it wouldn't work. I've not given it that much thought, actually.'

'Would you go back to Haranistan?'

'What? To the hell-hole where they threatened to kill me half the time and the other half when I was bored stiff. Why in heaven's name would I want to do that?'

'It's not the place it was, Maisie. The new president is working wonders. You probably don't know it, but Haranistan is running out of oil so he's got to find ways of generating foreign exchange to make up for it, otherwise the people will starve. That's the one bit of good our ex-master started, which the president is bringing to fruition. Haranistan will open its doors to tourists. Cruise ships, holiday packages, sports events, you name it, we're looking at it.'

'We? You seem to know a lot about this, Carol. What is it you're not telling me?'

'The new president wants me, and you, to be part of it. Would you like to meet him and talk to him about it?'

'Me, meet the president of Haranistan? When?'

'In about ten minutes?'

'But I'm not dressed'

'You'd better hurry then. Western clothes will do and nothing see-through.'

100 – 12th July, 2006 Notting Hill, London

'Maisie, this is President Feisal Mohammed of the Democratic Republic of Haranistan.'

Maisie curtsied.

'Mr President.'

'Please call me, Feisal and I'm very pleased to meet you at last, Maisie. Carol has told me so much about you.'

'I'm sorry, Feisal, I didn't even realise Carol knew you. I'm pleased to meet you as well. What is it you think I can do for you?'

'Before I start telling you that, can I tell you something about the Crown Prince?' Maisie could feel the anger building up inside her. Mohammed spotted it, so continued quickly.

'I know he was an evil man and what he did to you, and to me for that matter, was unforgivable, but he was not all bad.'

'But he had girls killed. He would have had me killed. How can I forgive him that?'

'You can't and you shouldn't, but we wouldn't have let him kill you or any of the girls.'

'But he did. Carol showed me the video.'

'Staged, Maisie.' Anderson told her as she hugged her. 'We staged it to frighten you into submission because that was better than him telling us to kill you. We took away the girls he wanted killed and hid them. They didn't have the life you had, although they are free now. You can meet the girl who acted the part if you like. She's got a place at RADA. She may be famous one day.'

'And we will look after the other girls using this flat and the £100,000 that Carol earned for our fake ERECOT.' Mohammed added.

'But that was you and Carol risking your lives. What did *he* do?' Maisie protested, almost in tears.

'He was the one who found out Haranistan was running out of oil. He realised the population would starve unless we did something about it. The old king didn't have a clue. The old king wasn't evil, which is why I authorised his escape from Haranistan even though some of my more zealous revolutionaries wanted him executed. That's one of the reasons I pardoned him. He was just blind, but the Crown Prince started something and I will finish it. Despite that, the Crown Prince *was* evil, so he had to die. He was irresponsible with my brother's life and my family paid the price for his stupidity. That is why I told Chambers to redirect the bomb to him.'

'*You* ordered it. That means you were prepared to let *me* die.'

'No, Maisie, never. We are not those kind

of people. Do you remember the man to whom you handed the briefcase? The man who refused to let you in, but snatched the briefcase from you. He was one of us. He risked his life to ensure the bomb got to the Crown Prince, and ensure you were not hurt.'

'My god. What happened to him?'

'He was hurt by the blast, but survived and will make a full recovery, I'm very pleased to say.'

'Can I see him? Can I thank him?'

'Yes you can, but not for a while. I want to keep contact to a minimum while the British police investigate. We have gained a valuable friend in Britain and I cannot afford to lose them. Will you do this for Haranistan, if not for me?'

Maisie was in tears.

'I'll do it willingly, for the people of Haranistan and for you, but most of all for Carol, because she says you're worth it. I just pray she's right.'

Anderson hugged her tighter.

'Thank you, Maisie. He is, I assure you.'

'Maisie, you can do even more for the Haranistani people if you wish. Whatever you decide, you will be welcome in Haranistan and you can have dual Haranistani-British nationality as well. Heaven knows you've earned it. Would you come back to help us to set up and run our tourist industry. Much as we might not be proud of it, our royal ancestry, with harems and the like, is part of our history and tourists will want to know about it. You know about it first-hand. It may seem voyeuristic, ghoulish even, but tourist money will prevent our people from starving. Don't answer now, think about it and let Carol explain more about it to you. You owe Haranistan nothing, in fact Haranistan owes you for what the Crown Prince did to you, but we ask for your help now and we will not be ungrateful. You would have a good life with us.'

Maisie was crying on Anderson's shoulder when he left.

'You poor girl, we've laid too much on you, haven't we?' She let Maisie cry herself out.

101 – 12th July, 2006 Notting Hill, London

'Are you feeling better now?'

'Yes, thank you, Carol. It's just that it was a lot to take in. I had no idea you and he were taking so many risks while I was lazing about. It doesn't seem fair.'

'It was fair. It wasn't your battle. Let's talk about something much nicer, shall we?'

'Yes please.'

'I'm getting married, will you be my maid of honour?'

'Married? That's great news, and a surprise. Of course I will. You've worked fast. You've only been back in England for a couple of months.'

'I not marrying an Englishman, Maisie. I'm marrying a Haranistani, in Haranistan.'

'What?'

'Yes, and we can have a lift on his Excellency's yacht. It's being returned to Haranistan to become a tourist attraction and it's being escorted by our two new destroyers. They're going to practise close protection.'

'Sounds fun. All those matelots protecting us. Since you've been spoken for, they'll all be paying attention to me.'

'Down, Maisie, did I teach you nothing in those ten years?'

'Yes, survival and boredom. I thank you for the former, so I can enjoy the ability to avoid the latter in the future.'

'I can't argue with that. So we're on then?'

'Yes, we're on. When's the wedding?'

'September 5th.'

'But that's the new national holiday; President's Day. So you're getting married on the same day the president is getting married. Won't it be a bit crowded?'

'I hope so Maisie, I've always wanted a big wedding.'

'But they'll all be at the president's wedding. Hang on you're not…'

'Yes, Maisie, I'm marrying Feisal.'

Printed in Great Britain
by Amazon

57294186R00244